SPRING COMES TO EMMERDALE

Based on the hugely popular soap opera, this saga explores the lives of Emmerdale's much-loved families during the Great War and beyond.

Can the nation's favourite village keep calm and carry on? World War I rages on and the families of Emmerdale are trying their best to move on from tragedy, while the effects of war still resonate throughout the village of Beckindale. Though grief and loss permeate, life carries on in The Woolpack pub and on Emmerdale Farm. Maggie Sugden, Annie King and the other inhabitants of the village are also discovering more independence, the chance to make their own happiness – and even opening themselves up to finding love.

SPRING COMES TO EMMERDALE

SPRING COMES TO EMMERDALE

by

Pamela Bell

Magna Large Print Books
Gargrave, North Yorkshire,
BD23 3SE, England.

British Library Cataloguing in Publication Data.

A catalogue record of this book is
available from the British Library

ISBN   978-0-7505-4746-8

First published in Great Britain in 2019 by Trapeze,
an imprint of The Orion Publishing Group Ltd.

Published in Large Print 2019 by arrangement with
The Orion Publishing Group Ltd.

Magna Large Print is an imprint of Library Magna Books Ltd.

Printed and bound in Great Britain by
T.J. (International) Ltd., Cornwall, PL28 8RW

My thanks go to Alasdair Gordon for his help with the manuscript, Linton Chiswick for the storylines and Ollie Tait, Alice Lee and Izzy Charman at Lambent Productions for their part in unearthing stories that inform the novel and the ITV factual series, *Emmerdale 1918*.

Summer 1918

Chapter One

Dot climbed down from the cart and nodded her thanks to young Fred Airey when he handed her down her bag. She had been lucky to see him at the station in Ilkley. She'd grown so used to trams and trolleybuses in Bradford that she'd forgotten that the only way to get to Beckindale was to hitch a ride on a cart. Or to walk, of course, and Dot hadn't fancied that.

It had been strange coming back along the narrow country lanes. Swaying on the wagon seat next to Fred, Dot had stared at the fells as if she had never seen them before. Had the hillsides always been that vibrant a green? The limestone tops that bleached? Cow parsley and buttercups frothed along the roadside and the blackthorn blossom still lay like a thick milky white tablecloth over the hedgerows. Dot remembered wandering along the lanes with her brother, Olly, in spring and eating the sweet new blackthorn leaves. Bread and butter, they had used to call them.

Olly had been reported missing, presumed dead, a year ago. They had no idea what had happened to him. He was just ... gone. He had been nineteen.

Dot stood for a moment, her bag at her feet and her hands pressed to the small of her back, while the silence hummed in her ears. It was so *quiet*. Had Beckindale always been this still? How had

13

she stood it? Used now to the clattering and drilling and hammering and hubbub of the munitions factory, Dot had forgotten what the countryside was like.

As her ears tuned in, she realised it wasn't entirely silent; she could hear hammering from the wheelwright's. A baby was crying somewhere. A dog barked and a voice was raised to shush it. From a distance came the faint bleating of sheep on the fells and a woodpigeon burbled from a rooftop.

She was a long way from Bradford. The air there was dirty and dark, the streets were crowded and noisy with the rattle of motor vehicles, but Dot loved it. Working as a munitionette might be dangerous but the other girls were always up for a laugh, and when they had finished their long, back-breaking days, they went to the pub and bought their own drinks and smoked their own cigarettes. The men didn't like it, of course, but Dot and her friends were doing their bit for the war effort and why shouldn't they enjoy their free time?

Dot hoped the war would end soon, of course, but sometimes she wondered what life would be like afterwards. The men would all want their jobs back, and she had no intention of going back to being a servant. She'd worked at Emmerdale Farm before the war, and although Maggie Sugden wasn't as bad as she had thought at first, Dot didn't want to go back to that. Cooking and cleaning and washing and ironing, and nothing to do in the evening but go to bed and then get up the next day and do it all over again. And all for a

14

pittance. No, thank you. Dot wanted more than that.

But first there was the war to be won.

As if they didn't all have enough to deal with, now the flu was running out of control. The trickle of cases had turned into a flood and now the sound of a cough made everyone uneasy. Agatha Tucker had gone home one night and the next day they'd heard that she had died, just like that, and she wasn't the only one. Dot had heard rumours that the factories would close to stop the flu spreading any further, but that was ridiculous. They had to keep producing ammunition for the troops, didn't they? A few people had taken to wearing masks, and some of the girls were refusing to go to the pub after work, but as Dot said to her friend Ellen, there were so many ways to die at the moment, they might as well die happy.

Now the flu had even reached Beckindale. Her mother had sent a frantic message to say that her father was seriously ill and when Dot had asked the factory manager for leave, he had nodded. 'You might as well go to the country while all this flu's going round,' he'd said. 'Breathe some fresh air, eh?'

Well, it was certainly fresh, Dot thought. The fresh smell of cut grass and warm earth laced with a strong smell of manure. She had forgotten that, along with the quietness.

Bending to pick up her bag, Dot set off down the familiar street towards the cottage where she had grown up, but when she came to the Woolpack, she stopped and stared at the blackened ruin until the sound of her own name made her turn.

15

'*Dot?* Dot Colton? Is that you?'

Janet Airey and Betty Porter were coming out of the village shop and waving to attract her attention. Janet was tall and angular while Betty was short and round. They were both carrying baskets and both were, in Dot's opinion, the biggest gossips in Beckindale. The news of her return would be round the village in no time.

'Janet, Betty.' She nodded at them. 'How do?'

'Mustn't grumble,' said Janet. 'The summer's good for my joints, that's something.' She eyed Dot critically. 'You've changed.'

'Have I?'

'You've cut your hair.' Janet's voice was almost accusing.

'We have to be careful of our hair in the munitions factory and cover it with caps,' Dot explained, touching the ends of her bob. 'It's much easier to manage like this.'

'I don't know,' said Janet, shaking her head. 'You young girls will do anything nowadays. Cutting your hair, wearing trousers, shortening your skirts,' she added with a pointed look at Dot's ankles, 'and who knows what else.'

'And smoking and drinking,' Betty put in. 'Where's it all going to end, that's what I want to know.'

'It'd be nice to think it would end with us getting the vote,' said Dot, but Janet and Betty looked at her as if she had sprouted an extra head so she changed the subject quickly. 'What happened to t'Woolpack?'

'Didn't your ma tell you? It burned down, it did, and Ava Bainbridge in it. Terrible shock, it

16

was. When was that, Betty?'

'Winter 1915, it were,' said Betty. 'I remember because that was the year we lost Alfred.'

'And nobody's done it up?' Dot's eyes went back to the pub. The stone walls were blackened but still standing, while the roof timbers had caved in and through the empty windows and doorway she could see a charred mess where the bar had once been. It was so different from the jolly pubs she had known in Bradford, which were always packed with people talking and laughing and doing their level best to forget about the war for an hour or two.

'Who's going to take it on with this wretched war on?' said Betty. 'Percy Bainbridge moved away with his children after the fire. Didn't have the heart for it any more, I suppose. He used to lease it from old Jack Micklethwaite over Ilkley way. That right, Janet?'

'Aye, but Jack doesn't care about the Woolpack now either. He had four sons and every single one of them 'as died in France now.' Janet shook her head. 'Nobody's got the heart to think about it, specially not with this flu on top of everything else.'

'It looks sad,' said Dot.

'Aye, well, my Dick misses it that's for sure,' said Janet. 'But we don't have anyone with the energy to rebuild it, even if they could afford to buy it off Jack.' She gestured at the pub. 'It's a crying shame about the Woolpack. The place is a mess, but there's nowt to be done about it. All we've got in the village now are old men, young boys and invalids.'

17

'And women,' said Dot.

There was a disapproving silence. Betty and Janet exchanged glances. 'Women can't run pubs,' said Betty after a moment.

'Why not? We're doing all sorts of jobs that only men did before.'

'Not in Beckindale,' said Janet firmly.

And *that* was why she would be heading back to the city the first chance she had, thought Dot as she said a wry goodbye to Janet and Betty and walked on.

'Oh, Dot, thank goodness you're home!' Agnes Colton almost fell on Dot when she opened the door to her.

Dot was shocked to see the change in her mother. Agnes had once been a brisk, practical woman, sturdily built, but now she was thin and tearful and trembling with fatigue.

'Your poor pa,' she kept saying. 'Your poor, poor pa. I don't know what to do.'

Dot could hear him coughing upstairs. 'I'll go and look at him,' she said, though she didn't know what she could do either. What did she know of nursing? She could pack a shell with explosives but that was no use to her now.

If she had been shocked by the state of her mother, she was aghast at how ill her father looked. He lay grey-faced and sweating in bed, racked by a terrible gurgling cough. As Dot watched in horror, he leant over the side of the bed and retched into a bowl that held bloody sputum.

'Pa ... oh, Pa...' She went over to hold the bowl for him and as the coughing fit eased, she helped him back onto his pillows.

He opened red-rimmed eyes to focus on her face with an effort. 'Bess?'

Dot swallowed. Her older sister had always been his favourite. She had died of pleurisy seven years earlier.

'It's Dot,' she said. Alarmed by his struggles to say more, she put a hand on his shoulder. 'Don't try to talk, Pa,' she said, but he was determined to get the words out.

'Your ma ... must ... look after ... her, Bess,' he managed.

She didn't bother to correct him this time. 'I will.'

'Promise...' he gasped.

'I promise,' she said, shaken.

Downstairs, she found her mother sitting numbly at the kitchen table, wringing her hands. Somehow the sight of her sturdy, brisk mother so undone was worse than seeing her father so sick.

'Have you called the doctor?' she asked and Agnes looked at her with dull eyes.

'We can't afford the doctor.'

'I've got some money, Ma. Let me send for him.'

But the doctor, when he came, shook his head. 'There's nothing I can do for him. I'm sorry.'

That was nonsense, Dot decided instantly. Of *course* there was something to be done. This was her *father.* She couldn't let him die like this. Scowling ferociously, she took on the flu as a personal enemy and refused to admit defeat. All night, she ran up and down the stairs, refreshing bowls of water and wringing out cloths as she tried to wipe the sweat from her father's face and cool his fever as his body arched in pain and delirium.

It was easier to do that than to remember the woody smell that clung to his clothes, the pipe that had always been clenched between his teeth. A cooper, Bill Colton had been a quiet, un-demonstrative man, but Dot would never forget the time he had lifted her onto his shoulders and carried her out through the deep snow to show her the moon rising over the fells like a bright silver penny. Once, when she had fallen and badly grazed her knees, he had carved her a little wooden mouse and her delight in the unexpected toy had quite eclipsed the stinging in her legs.

Dot pushed the memories aside and concen-trated on saving her father. She held his head over the bowl as he coughed and coughed and coughed, and she wiped the blood from his mouth. She sponged his body and tried to spoon broth into him to give him strength, only for him to be sick all over her. Grimly she cleared up the bloody mess, and went back to trying to make him comfortable while he tossed and thrashed and cried out in pain and desperation as his lungs filled in spite of everything, and he drowned in his own blood.

And in the end, the doctor was right. There was nothing Dot could do for her father. He died that night, his distraught wife weeping by his side and when she heard those awful, gurgling breaths stop at last, Dot let the cloth slip bleakly back into the bowl, too exhausted to comfort her mother.

The Coltons weren't a family much given to gestures of affection but their life had always been a decent one. The cottage in the heart of Beckindale had three bedrooms, a kitchen and a parlour and, behind the house, a vegetable plot with rows of cabbages and leeks and her father's prizewinning marrows.

This was the home Dot had left to go and work in Bradford. In the morning, when Bill Colton had been laid out in the parlour, and Agnes had been persuaded to lie down for a while, Dot sat at the kitchen table and looked guiltily around her.

She should have come home earlier, she thought. Her parents had always been such no-nonsense people, she had assumed they would deal with the reports that their son was missing as stoically as they had dealt with their elder daughter's death. She hadn't realised how the loss of Olly would devastate them, but she could see it now in the neglected cottage, once kept pin clean by her mother, and the overgrown vegetable garden which had been her father's pride and joy. It was as if they had both stopped caring when that telegram had arrived.

When would it all end? Dot wondered bleakly. Her parents were the last people she would have expected to give up, but after four years of war, the flu epidemic was crushing the last flickers of spirit out of everyone and it was all too easy to give in to despair.

It was left to Dot to arrange a funeral for her father. Mr Haywood, the vicar, spoke in sonorous terms about God's purpose, but Dot wasn't really listening. Her mother had started coughing that morning, and Dot had stripped the sheets and made up the bed so Agnes could lie where her

21

husband had just died. Mary Ann Teale had offered to sit with her mother while Dot was at church to see her father buried.

Maggie Sugden came to the funeral. 'It's good to see you again, Dot,' she said after the service. 'I wish it hadn't been under these circumstances.'

Maggie was looking pale and tired. 'You don't look so good,' Dot told her, and Maggie smiled faintly.

'Blunt as ever!'

'Sorry,' muttered Dot. She had always been one for plain speaking and she forgot sometimes that honesty wasn't always the best policy.

'It's all right,' said Maggie. 'You're right, I'm not looking my best. We've had flu at Emmerdale Farm too. One of our land girls had to go home she was so ill, and I caught it too, though not so badly. And then Jacob nearly died. It was a difficult time.'

'Jacob?'

'My little boy.' Maggie shook her head. 'It must be a good three years since you left, Dot. A lot has changed since then.'

'I'd like to hear your news, but I need to get back. Ma's not well.'

'Of course.' Maggie touched Dot's arm. 'Come and see me before you go back, Dot. I've missed you.'

Agnes Colton was in bed for a week. She was not nearly as ill as her husband had been and she was soon out of danger, but the illness left her even weaker and more lethargic than before, and her once bright eyes now swam with tears.

'How will I manage without your pa?' she asked Dot constantly.

Dot was coaxing her to drink some broth she had made. 'I'll look after you,' she said, but Agnes wasn't reassured. Her eyes filled. 'But for how long?'

Dot suppressed a sigh, remembering the promise she had made to her father. 'As long as you need me,' she said.

Mary Ann Teale popped in most days from next door. 'I'll make a brew, will I?' she always said as she bustled around the kitchen, putting the kettle on the range, as at home here as in her own house.

Dot sat wearily at table one morning and looked around the kitchen. Once, it had been spotless, but now everything seemed faintly grubby and there were crumbs on the floor that she hadn't had time to sweep up. 'Mary Ann,' she asked, 'how long has Ma been ... like this?'

Mary Ann didn't pretend to misunderstand. 'Since she heard about Olly. It broke her heart it did.' She sighed. 'There's a lot of hearts been broken since the war started.'

Dot felt guilty that her own heart wasn't broken. Oh, she had grieved when she had heard about her brother, of course she had, but she had kept living, just like everyone else had to do. Was that wrong?

'You're looking peaky, Dot,' Mary Ann told her. 'You've been shut in here too long. You go and get some air, and I'll sit with your ma.'

Too tired to argue, Dot obeyed. Her mother had been so ill that Dot had barely been outside all week, and now she blinked at the sunlight as she stepped outside. It was a beautiful summer day, and it felt good to get out – but where was there to go? The village didn't even have a pub now – not that she would have ever been allowed to go there. Dot thought wistfully of life in Bradford. It was tough, yes, but they were never short of somewhere to go or something to do. Sometimes she and her friends went to a music hall or to the picture palace. Dot had seen Charlie Chaplin in *A Dog's Life* – what a hoot that had been! – and had been thrilled by *Tarzan of the Apes*. And there was always the pub.

In Beckindale there was ... nothing.

Well, there was no use moaning, Dot told herself briskly. She would just have to get on with it.

She did feel better for being out, and she wandered a while before realising that her feet were taking her to the bridge, the way she had walked so often when she worked for Maggie Sugden. She would go to Emmerdale Farm.

Chapter Two

Maggie was collecting eggs in her apron when Dot arrived. The collie at her side – surely that couldn't be timid Fly? – barked once, sharply, to warn of Dot's approach and Maggie looked up with a smile. 'I'm so glad you came,' she said. 'I was sorry not to have a chance to talk to you properly at your father's funeral. Let me just get

24

rid of these and we'll have a cup of tea.'

Following Maggie inside, Dot saw a pretty young girl at the range where Dot herself had so often stood. 'Do you remember Molly Pickles?' Maggie asked as she put the eggs in a bowl. 'Frank's sister.'

Dot wouldn't have recognised little Molly, but she remembered Frank all right. He'd been the farm lad when she had worked at Emmerdale Farm, a big, slow boy, a bit daft but harmless.

'Is Frank...?'

Maggie shook her head and Dot sighed. How many more had died in this wretched war? 'I'm sorry,' she said to Molly, who nodded and ducked her head.

'Shall I put t'kettle on, Mrs Sugden?'

'Yes, please, Molly. It's such a nice day, we'll have it outside.' Maggie turned to Dot. 'I'm afraid there are a lot of changes since you were last in Beckindale.'

Dot nodded. 'I heard George bought it too.'

'That's right. But there are some nice changes too.' Maggie rested her hand on the head of a small child who was staring suspiciously at Dot, his finger in his mouth.

'This is Jacob.'

Dot eyed him warily. She never had much to do with children and didn't know what to say to them. 'How do, Jacob?' she tried, and his look of suspicion deepened. 'How old are you?'

'He's two and a half,' Maggie answered for him. She gestured behind Dot. 'And you remember Joe, of course,' she added in an even voice.

'*Joe?*' Dot echoed in surprise and turned.

The sunlight through the open kitchen door threw a bright patch on the flagstones, but the light at the end of the room was mercifully dim. Still it was enough for Dot to catch her breath in shock at the sight of the man sitting by the fireplace, where a small fire burned in spite of the warmth of the day.

She remembered Maggie's husband as a vicious bully, a square, stocky man she had avoided as much as possible. It had been a relief to all when he had gone to war.

Joe was unrecognisable now. Half his face had been blown off and the reconstructed skin was puckered and shiny and pulled hideously out of shape. His left eye was sunken to little more than a slit and what was left of his nose had been squashed into a grotesque lump.

Swallowing down her instinctive grimace, Dot managed an unsteady smile. 'Hello, Joe.'

Joe didn't respond. Apparently oblivious to the presence of a stranger, he was sitting in his chair, rocking a little, clenching and unclenching his hands, as he stared blankly at the empty chair on the other side of the fire.

Maggie had seen her shock. 'I'm sorry,' she said, pouring tea out of the pot into two cups. 'I thought someone would have told you.'

'No.' Dot was more shaken than she would have expected. Not that she cared for Joe, but nobody deserved that. She had seen plenty of soldiers with terrible injuries in Bradford, but nothing like Joe's. 'I haven't really had a chance to catch up on the news.'

'Come and sit in the sun.' Maggie gave her a

cup and saucer and Dot was glad to follow her outside to sit on the bench by the kitchen door. Even then, her hand wasn't quite steady as she drank her tea.

'What happened to him?'

'He was blown up by a shell,' Maggie said. 'When I got the telegram, I thought it would say that he was dead. I hoped for it, to be honest. You remember what he was like.'

Dot nodded as she set her cup carefully back on its saucer. 'Aye, I do.'

'But the message was just that he'd been injured and that he was being sent to a hospital in Sheffield. I didn't know how bad it was until he was transferred to Miffield Hall. It's a hospital now.'

'Yes, I'd heard that.' Dot hesitated. 'It must have been a shock when you saw him.'

'It was.' Holding her cup and saucer in her lap with one hand, Maggie stroked the collie who rested its head against her knee. 'I wasn't even sure that it *was* Joe, but they told me there was no mistake. After a few weeks, the doctors said there was nothing more that they could do, so they sent him home, and how could I refuse? I'm his wife, this is his farm.'

'How do you manage when he's ... like that?'

'It's easier than when he was Joe.' Maggie smiled faintly. 'He's very quiet. He just sits there like that. Sometimes he gets distressed, and he doesn't like sudden or loud noises, but when he starts to whimper, I just soothe him the way I would Jacob. It's like having another child.'

'Does he know who you are?'

'I don't think so. He understands what I'm

27

saying. He responds to simple instructions: *get dressed, come to the table, drink this, be careful, it's hot* ... that kind of thing.'

Dot made a face. 'What about, I don't know, going to the privy?'

'He can do that by himself, thank goodness, and he sleeps in the cupboard bed under the stairs. He can even dress himself although I have to help him with buttons and laces.' For the first time, revulsion crossed Maggie's face. 'I hate it, but what can I do? I'm torn between disgust and pity and remembering how much I loathed him.'

'I'm sorry,' said Dot after a moment. 'It must be difficult. And what about the little lad?' She nodded down at Jacob who was squatting in the dust with a puppy that was still at the stage of tripping over its own feet. 'It must be scary for him, in't it?'

'He's too young to have known Joe any other way. He just takes Joe's deformities for granted. He calls him Pa and crawls over him sometimes, and Joe just sits there. Jacob thinks that's normal,' said Maggie. 'Perhaps it's better that way. He's like Laddie here.' She nudged the puppy with her foot and smiled as it pounced on her shoe with mock growls. 'Laddie likes Joe, but Fly won't go near him.'

'I wondered if that were Fly,' Dot said leaning round Maggie to look again at the dog. It was hard to credit that the glossy, contented collie leaning so trustfully against Maggie was the thin, cowering bitch that had once been the target of Joe's beatings and kickings. 'She's changed a bit.'

Maggie rested her hand on Fly's head and Fly

closed her eyes blissfully. 'I can't recognise Joe, but she can. She can smell him.'

It was a crying shame he hadn't been killed outright, Dot reflected. Joe had been a vicious bully, God knows, but this was worse than no life at all, and harder for Maggie too.

'Does he ever speak?'

'Not yet. The doctors say that's quite common with head trauma.' Maggie sipped her tea. 'Part of me wants him to stay like this. I worry that if he gets better, he'll start to remember and then...' She lifted her shoulders. 'I'm afraid of what might happen then, but what can I do?'

'Nowt,' said Dot, understanding. What could any of them do but play the hand they'd been dealt. 'What about t'farm? How are you managing?'

'I had someone to help me for a couple of years. Hugo.' Maggie's face softened as she said his name.

Something in one of her mother's letters was ringing a bell in Dot's head. 'Hang on, was he the conchie?'

'He was a Quaker,' said Maggie. 'His beliefs wouldn't allow him to kill anyone, so he chose to come and help produce food for the country instead. Oh, everyone was up in arms, of course,' she said, clearly reading Dot's disapproving expression without difficulty. 'Nobody would have anything to do with me for a while because I was employing Hugo and they all thought he should have been off fighting and killing, but what was I supposed to do? All the farmers despised me for trying to run a farm by myself – they still do – and

29

I couldn't get an able bodied man to come and work for me. Tom Skilbeck wanted me to give up, hand over my stock and let him grow his crops on my fields. I wasn't going to let him do that. This'll be Jacob's farm one day, and I was prepared to do whatever was needed to keep Tom Skilbeck's hands off it, even if it meant giving shelter to a conscientious objector.'

Much as she disapproved of the idea of anyone wheedling their way out of fighting, Dot couldn't help admiring Maggie. She had never cared what anyone else had thought.

'As it turned out, Hugo helped me turn this farm around,' Maggie went on. 'Of course, the village didn't like it and made sure I knew it, but when the Woolpack was on fire, Hugo was the one who ran in to save a child.'

'I saw the Woolpack had burned down,' said Dot. 'It's sad seeing it like that.'

'The fire was terrifying. Nobody who saw Hugo run in there ever thought he was a coward again,' said Maggie. 'He's one of the bravest and best men I know,' she added quietly. She looked directly at Dot. 'I love him, and he loves me.' Incredibly, a smile trembled on her lips at the memory. 'He told me the night before he went away.'

Dot's jaw dropped. She might admire Maggie for the way she stood up for herself, but she was still shocked at her honesty.

'Oh, we never did anything about it,' Maggie said. 'Hugo's a good man. It would have been adultery. We were just dear friends, but when Joe was sent home, Hugo decided it would be wrong if he stayed, feeling as we did for each other. I begged him not to go,' she said, 'but he went to France as a stretcher carrier. I don't know if he's still alive or not,' she added sadly. 'I'm not sure if I will ever know.'

'And the farm?' Dot had worked at Emmerdale Farm long enough to know that no matter what was happening, the cows had to be milked, the sheep fed and sheared, the fields ploughed, the crops sown and harvested.

'Now I've got three girls from the Women's Land Army. Tom Skilbeck disapproves of them almost as much as he did of Hugo. He doesn't think it's fitting for women to do the hard physical labour on a farm, but they've been wonderful. One of them, Grace, has become a real friend. Jacob loves her, don't you, Jacob?' she said as her small son scrambled to his feet, alert at the sound of a favourite word.

'Gace!' he shouted.

'Grace'll be back soon,' Maggie reassured him. 'I don't think she'll be staying much longer,' she added in an undertone to Dot. 'Sam Pearson is very smitten. He's always hanging around here on any excuse. Last week he brought us Laddie here.'

Fly looked on disdainfully as Laddie recognised his name and scrabbled at Dot's skirts for attention. Dot put down a hand so that he could lick it excitedly.

Dot remembered Sam Pearson from school. He was a couple of years older than her, a quiet, steady boy, but she had always liked him. So he was sniffing around after one of the Women's Land Army, was he? Good luck to him, she thought, with only a tiny pang. She had long ago accepted that as far as men were concerned, she was a pal, and not the kind of girl they fell in love with or handed over puppies as an excuse to see her.

'Last I heard Sam was in Mesopotamia,' she said. 'I'm glad he made it out all right.'

'He was in a bad way for a while, but he's come through, thank goodness.' Maggie bent down to put her cup and saucer on the ground. 'Anyway, what about you, Dot? Are you heading back to Bradford?'

'I wish I could,' Dot sighed. 'But I promised Pa I would look after Ma. I never thought she'd need looking after – you remember what she was like? – but she's different now.'

Maggie nodded her understanding. 'Four years of war and now the flu... It feels like the end of the world. We're all so tired,' she sighed. 'Sometimes it seems as if the suffering is never going to end. I can understand why she has just given up.' Her eyes rested on her small son. 'If it hadn't been for Jacob, I think I might have given up too.'

Dot drank her tea thoughtfully. Maggie was such a strong person, it was shocking to hear her even talking about giving up. Was there something wrong with her that she didn't feel that way?

'I'll have to find work,' Dot said.

'What will you do? There'll be lots of people who would leap at employing a decent cook – the vicar's wife, for one. You could have your pick of jobs.'

Dot grimaced. 'I don't want to go into service again. Not wanting to give offence,' she added, and Maggie smiled.

'None taken. I don't blame you,' she said. She thought for a bit. 'What about the hospital in Mifield Hall? They might need help in the kitchen and you're the best cook I know.'

'That's a good idea. I'll ask.'

Dot sipped her tea, watching a pair of house martins darting busily in and out of their nest under the stable eaves. 'Can I tell you something awful?'

'What?'

'This war ... it's horrible but there's a bit of me that doesn't want it to end.'

Maggie's brows lifted and Dot struggled to explain herself. 'Before, if you were a woman, you didn't have much choice about what you did. You went into service and hoped to get married so you could look after a house of your own. But because of the war, we've been able to try new jobs and be independent. I don't want to lose that.' She glanced at Maggie. 'I used to think suffragettes were barmy, but now I wish I had listened more to what they were saying.'

'What would you do if you could do anything you wanted?' Maggie asked after a moment.

'I'd like a job in Bradford. Not in munitions, but something else. Something so I could earn my own money and live on my own. Be independent and not have to do what someone else told me to do. Is that too much to ask for?'

'No,' said Maggie, thoughtfully. 'No, I don't think it is.'

Chapter Three

He called Rose his 'Angel'.

It had been ten days since William Petty had been brought by ambulance to the auxiliary hospital at Miffield Hall. He was terribly injured on one side. His left arm had been blown off by a shell and his leg was so mangled that they eventually had to amputate it. Rose had helped to dress the quivering stump. It wasn't the first amputation she had assisted at – she had grown used to dealing with grotesque injuries that only four years ago would have made her faint away – but her stomach had still heaved.

William was secretly her favourite patient. Many of the soldiers invalided from the front were astonishingly cheerful and stoical about their injuries – just glad to be back in Blighty, they said – but William had a glint in his eyes that reminded her of Mick. He was young – her age perhaps – with a funny, monkey face and terrible teeth, but he had a way about him that was hard to resist.

The first time he'd opened his eyes and seen her, he had gaped. 'Gawd, I've gone to heaven and met an angel!'

'No angel,' Rose had said, shaking her head and thinking of the secrets she kept. 'I'm just a VAD.'

But William insisted on calling her his angel. 'Have you got a sweetheart, Angel?' he would ask as Rose eased off the stiff, stained wads of gauze where his arm had been. Her bottom lip was caught between her teeth as she concentrated on being as gentle as she could.

'I do,' she said.

'Throw the lucky blighter over and marry me instead.'

Rose smiled, knowing the banter distracted him from the pain of the dressing being changed. 'If he doesn't come home soon, I may do that.'

'What–' He broke off with a gasp.

'Sorry.'

'What's his name?' William persisted in a voice thready with pain.

'Mick.' Rose didn't feel like lying or prevaricating when William was lying there, his one good hand clenched in the sheet, his face white. Besides, she had so few chances to talk about Mick, it was good to be able to say his name out loud. 'Mick Dingle.'

'Mick,' William repeated hazily. 'Lucky bugger.' He sucked in another breath as Rose started on cleaning the stump of the arm which had been blown off above the elbow. 'He serving?'

Rose nodded. 'He's in France, or was last time I heard.' She hadn't heard from Mick for over a week. The post was pretty good, so when you didn't hear, of course you worried. And if something *did* happen to him, the news wouldn't come to her. It would go to his brother Levi.

'An officer, is he? A lady like you, course he is,' William answered his own question and then grinned. 'He won't like it when you throw him over for me.'

35

'He won't,' Rose agreed, breathing through her mouth as she cleaned the awful wound. It had been patched up hastily in the field hospital before they sent William home, and it was starting to heal, but the smell of torn flesh, dried blood and stale iodine was still foul.

'If we can keep that leg clean, he'll have a fighting chance,' she had heard the doctor say after examining William.

'So, why aren't you engaged?' he demanded. 'If I were Mick, I'd have put a ring on your finger straight away.'

'I haven't told my parents about him yet,' Rose confessed. 'Mick's not an officer and they wouldn't approve.'

'And there was me thinking you'd be marrying a real toff. Maybe I'm in with a chance after all! Course, there might be a problem with me mam,' he went on. 'She's a terror, she is. She'd have to approve of you first.'

Rose couldn't help laughing. 'I bet she wouldn't think anyone was good enough for you.'

'What's your Mick doing out there?'

He had survived the terrible battle of the Somme that had killed his brother, Nat, but Rose didn't think William wanted to hear about that. 'He seems to be driving those new tanks now.'

'Them great big machines?' William looked impressed. 'They're monsters, they are.'

'I shouldn't have told you that I've got a sweetheart,' Rose said, glancing over her shoulder. 'I don't want Matron to know either.'

'Don't you worry, Angel,' he had said. 'Your secret's safe with me.'

He had begged her to tell the doctors not to take off his leg. 'I can manage with one arm or one leg that side, but what'll I do without both? I won't be able to use crutches even. What girl'll have me now?'

But the terrible odour of gangrene was unmistakable and when the bandages had been removed to reveal the slimy, tell-tale green wound, there had been no choice. Even then William had given Rose a cheery thumbs up as he was wheeled away to the operating theatre.

That had been two days ago. A haemorrhage the first day had been stopped but now he was burning up with fever and the normally stern Sister Dawkins had told Rose to sit with him. 'He doesn't have much longer, Haywood. The infection has taken hold and we can't shift it now.'

So Rose was sitting in a screened off cubicle, holding William's hand as he drifted in and out of consciousness. She should have gone off duty an hour ago, but she couldn't bear to leave him.

How much longer would this wretched war go on? For three and a half years, men had been fighting and dying in the Flanders mud. For the past two, she had been a VAD here, making beds, emptying bed-pans and giving bed baths. She helped with dressings and sometimes even assisted at operations, but most of the time she dusted lockers, swept floors and straightened the ward. She scrubbed the blood and discharge from the bed-mackintoshes that protected the mattresses and polished wheelchairs. The hours were long and the work exhausting but at least Rose felt that she was doing *something*.

Except at times like these, with William's hand limp in hers, something wasn't enough. What good was she really doing? Rose asked herself wearily.

A gramophone at the end of the ward was playing 'When Irish eyes are smiling' *again*. Rose had liked listening to the record at first. It reminded her of Mick, but it had been played so often to keep the men in their beds entertained that she had stopped hearing it most of the time. Now, though, the scratchy sound mingled with a whole array of different coughs, sometimes barking, sometimes phlegmy or dry, and the muttering and mumbling and occasional groan or restless crackling of the bed-mackintosh beneath the sheet as a patient tried to get comfortable. Rose could hear the murmur of nurses' voices, the squeak of their shoes on the linoleum floors, and somewhere in the distance, a telephone ringing.

The noise scraped at her nerves and made her head ache. She was easing the pins that kept her cap in place and her blonde hair covered when she saw William's eyes flutter open.

'You still here, Angel?' he managed.

'Yes, I'm here.'

'I'm cold.'

'Shall I get you another blanket?'

'No.' His hand twitched feebly in hers. 'Don't leave me,' he whispered.

Rose had started to rise but at that she sat back on the chair. It felt as if there was a hand clamped viciously around her throat. 'Don't worry, I won't leave you, William.'

He lapsed into unconsciousness again for a

while but then seemed to wake with a shudder. 'I want my mam,' he said clearly, but his eyes were unfocused as they turned to Rose. 'Is that you, Mam?'

Rose swallowed. 'Yes, it's me, love. I'm here.' She squeezed his hand. 'You've had enough, William,' she said, her voice cracking. 'You can go now.'

Something that might have been a smile twitched at his lips and he sighed. Rose waited for his next breath, but it never came, and his fingers grew cold in hers before she made herself accept that he was dead. Very gently, she drew her hand over his eyes to close them.

She should get up and let Sister know. The orderlies would need to lay out the body and the paperwork would have to be filled in. Someone would write to his mother, and none of that could happen until she stood up. But Rose couldn't move. A wave of exhaustion rolled over her and she dropped her head to the bed to rest her forehead on the blanket next to William's still hand.

When Sister Dawkins put her head around the screen, Rose lifted her head as if it was a terrible weight. 'I don't think I can do this any longer,' she said.

Sister Dawkins's angular face warmed with compassion. 'You're tired,' she said. 'We all are. Go home, Haywood. Get some sleep. Come back tomorrow and we'll do it all again.'

Wearily, Rose made her way down the grand staircase to the entrance hall. It smelt of disinfectant and there were bare patches on the walls where portraits of long-dead Verneys had once hung. In the past two years, she had become used to Miffield Hall being a hospital. It was only at odd times, like now, when the memory of how it had been before the war snuck up on her un- awares, and the house seemed to shimmer. She could see the butler opening the front door, could see herself being shown into the drawing room, now a ward, and taking tea with Lady Verney.

Once she had played croquet with Ralph on the lawn where a row of huts now stood. In the orchard behind the Hall she had met Mick for the first time, but even that seemed impossibly distant now. Remembering gave her a vertiginous feeling, as if she were peering over an abyss into another world where she was young and innocent and carefree. A world where no one had sus- pected that a terrible war was looming and that everything would change.

Only three and a half years ago, Rose reminded herself as she paused on the front steps, blinking at the golden light. It was all wrong that it should be such a beautiful summer evening when Wil- liam Petty had died, and there was so much ugli- ness and grief in the world. As if the war were not bad enough, the epidemic of flu was still raging. Rose had heard that thousands were dying in the cities. Even in Beckindale, her father had been conducting funerals on an almost daily basis for weeks now.

'Haywood!' A voice broke into Rose's thoughts and she turned to see one of her fellow VADs, Sybil Edwards, waving an envelope from a pile she held in her hand. 'Letter for you,' she said. 'Thought it might cheer you up. I heard about Petty. Rotten luck.'

Sybil was one of the few people who knew about Mick. One of the best things about working at the hospital was being able to receive and send letters without having to meet Mick's brother, Levi.

And without having to go through Hannah Rigg at the Post Office. If Hannah knew who Rose was writing to, everyone would know, and so far no word had got back to her parents. She would be twenty-one later that year, and she wouldn't need her father's permission to marry Mick then. She didn't want to hurt her parents, but at long last she would be able to make her own decisions.

Not that any decisions could be made until this wretched war was over and Mick was safely home anyway.

Rose took the letter, her heart lifting as always at the sight of Mick's untidy scrawl. 'Thanks, Edwards.'

'Any time. I wish Peter wrote as often as your Mick.'

'He doesn't say much.' Rose put the letter in her pocket to read at home.

'They never do,' said Sybil. 'But at least you know they're thinking of you.'

And that they were alive. Or had been when they wrote. The young women both knew that a telegram or letter could come at any time with news that the men they loved had been killed or injured or were missing.

Except that Rose wouldn't get the letter. She would have to hear the news about Mick from Levi, and the thought made her shudder.

When Levi first came to Beckindale, she had been friendly for Mick's sake, knowing how

41

much he cared for his brother. For a while Levi had acted as intermediary for their letters but he had always made Rose uncomfortable. There was something unnerving about the way he devoured her with his eyes, about the intensity of his expression and the way he always stood just a little too close. His manner was an unpleasant mixture of ingratiating complacency and banked aggression, and she would be happy if she never saw him again, but what could she do? They both had to live in Beckindale.

Rose avoided him as much as she could but there was no getting away from Levi. He was Mick's next-of-kin and until she and Mick were married, she depended on him for news of the man she loved so desperately and missed so much.

Chapter Four

Oh, she had to stop fretting about Levi, Rose told herself as she set off down the avenue towards the lane. There was so much else to worry about at the moment. Both her brothers were 'somewhere in France', which was all they were ever allowed to say in their letters home.

John had been invalided home for a while with trench fever, but to her father's dismay had spent most of the time sitting with his batman, Robert Carr, who was suffering terribly with shell shock. Once a bright, lively boy who had delivered the papers from his bicycle, Robert was now a trembling wraith, cared for by his elderly mother. John had spent long hours with Robert, reading poetry to him and guiding his shaking hand to his mouth as he helped him eat.

When he came back to the vicarage, John's face was set and he refused to talk about his life in France. Rose didn't blame him. She never talked about what she saw at the hospital either. She wouldn't tell her parents about William Petty. Her father in particular hated her working at the hospital and was always trying to persuade her to give it up.

Rose's younger brother, Arthur, was much less complicated. He had joined up on his eighteenth birthday earlier that year. Rose could still remember his boisterous pride as he announced that he had enlisted and the way the colour had drained from her father's face.

Arthur's smile had faltered as the silence stretched. 'I thought you'd be pleased,' he said, aggrieved.

'I am pleased. I'm proud of you, my boy,' Charles Haywood said painfully after a moment. 'Very proud. But there's no need to be hasty. You are only eighteen today. I know Colonel Barker on the Military Service Tribunal, and if we explained–'

'Explained what?' Arthur interrupted. 'I'm not looking for an exemption, Father! Far from it! I want to serve my country, just like you said we all should. It's a matter of honour, you said. We're fighting for God and the Empire. You were happy when John joined up,' he added accusingly.

'I was, yes, but that was in 1914...' Charles was floundering. 'We had no idea that the war would go on so long or the cost would be so high.'

'All the more reason for me to go and do my bit now,' said Arthur. 'I want to take my turn at pushing back the Hun. I won the shooting medal at school last year,' he reminded them all. 'I've already trained as an officer. I'm fit. I'm not going to be one of those snivelling cowards that weasel around looking for excuses not to go and fight. I *want* to get out there and be part of it all.'

There had been no news from Arthur for a while, Rose thought, turning into the lane that led back to the river and Beckindale beyond. She imagined him bouncing around the trenches like an overgrown puppy, treating everything as a game, boasting about scrapping with Jerry, and throwing rugby balls around.

And then there was Mick. 'Don't worry,' he always wrote in his letters but how could she not worry? He had been in France since 1915. He had survived the Somme where his beloved older brother had been killed. He had dodged exploding shells and had been shot at. Three times he had been evacuated to a field hospital, and three times he had been sent back to the front line. He wrote cheerily of the scars he now wore. 'Matron says I'm indistructibel,' he had written after the last time. Rose still smiled and winced at the memory.

Recently, he had been transferred to work on tanks and it was clear to Rose that he loved it, spending hours tinkering with their engines. She told herself that it must be safer than in the trenches, surely, but he too had been silent for a while and it had been a huge relief when Edwards handed over his letter.

Standing in the middle of the lane, Rose pulled the letter out of her pocket. She couldn't wait until she got home to read it.

Mick's letter was as short and badly spelt as ever. *My darling Rose,* he started, as he always did. *Well, just a few lines from me. You must have been wondring why I hadn't written for a while it is not that I haven't been thinking of you but I have been back in hospitil again. I had a touch of the Spanish flu, it was not too bad and Matron soon kicked me out again. I would sooner have all the shrapnal picked out of my side again than have the flu, I was sick as a dog. Now I am back with my tanks and very glad to be here and not in a ward coffing. I am one of the lucky ones. Some of the men have had it very bad. I hope it is not in Beckindale and that you are safe and thinking of me as I think all the time of you, dear. The war can't last for ever, there are roomers it will be over soon and I will turn up in Beckindale like a bad penny and then what?*

That was the question, thought Rose as she read to the end and refolded the letter. Then what? She loved to get Mick's letters and to know that he still thought of her, but it wasn't the same as having him in front of her. Sometimes she was afraid that she was forgetting him and she panicked, convinced that she could no longer picture those dancing blue eyes and that curling mouth. But then she closed her eyes and summoned his image and remembered his warmth and his humour and the way the sight of him always made her feel as if a great smile was un-furling deep inside her and spreading to her lips.

She would never be able to explain that to her parents. For them, Mick would always be Irish and working class. Her father in particular, would never recognise Mick as a suitable husband for his precious daughter. He would be appalled at Mick's letter.

Rose loved her charismatic papa deeply, and hated the thought of disappointing him. But she loved Mick too. She couldn't imagine being happy without them both in her life, but how would she ever get her father to approve of Mick?

And what was the point of worrying about that either, when this war dragged on and on?

The sound of a motor car approaching made Rose move hastily to the side of the road, and as she lifted a hand to cover her nose and mouth against the dust churned up by the tyres, Mick's letter fluttered to the ground.

She was bending to pick it up when the car lurched to a stop beside her and with a sinking heart she recognised the driver.

'Levi!'

'Hello, Rose.' She hated the way he said her name, as if he were rolling it around his mouth, licking it, *tasting* it. Pushing a pair of goggles up onto his forehead, Levi hopped out of the car. He patted the bonnet proudly. 'What do you think?'

'You've bought a car,' she said stupidly.

'A Vauxhall. The latest model,' he assured her.

'Mick would like it,' Rose said without think-ing, and Levi's brows snapped together.

'Mick would never be able to afford a car like

this,' he snapped.

But he would be a better driver, Rose thought. Mick was the mechanical Dingle. Levi had been good with horses. After his brothers had shot him in the leg to spare him the danger of fighting at the front, Levi had found a home and a job with Will Hutton, the blacksmith, but over the past couple of years he had spent less and less time with horses and more time engaged in underhand deals. Ostracised by the villagers as a coward, Levi had turned to the bad.

Mick didn't understand how warped Levi had become. Rose knew that he still thought of his brother as a gentle boy to be protected.

'I didn't think you liked cars,' she said after a moment.

'They're practical. Besides, I spend so much time doing business in Bradford, a motor makes more sense than a pony and trap and a train. It's easier on my leg too.' An edge to his voice told Rose that he was thinking of the limp his brothers had caused. 'I'm a businessman now, and I can afford it,' he added complacently.

'Isn't petrol rationed?'

Levi smirked and tapped his nose. 'That depends on who you know, Rose.'

Thinking of William Petty, Rose found herself hating Levi at that moment. While William had been fighting for his country, Levi was making money from the war. He seemed adept at avoiding the law, but was widely suspected of profiteering from the black market. He had arrived in Beckindale a penniless Irish recruit, invalided out of the army before he could serve. That wasn't his fault, Rose could acknowledge, but he should have found other ways to support the war effort instead of simply making money. Who would have thought three years ago that Levi Dingle, of all people, would be in a position to buy a motor car?

Levi stepped closer, almost treading on Mick's letter. Before Rose could protest, he had bent to pick it up, his face creasing with irritation as he recognised his brother's scrawl.

'I see Mick is still writing to you.'

'Yes.' Rose looked up and down the road in the hope of rescue, but on this summer evening all was quiet. The fells across the dale rose hazily in the warmth and the air smelt dry with pollen and hay dust. Butterflies fluttered aimlessly over the tired hedgerows and she could see a buzzard circling over its prey hidden amongst the golden stubble in the field beyond. It reminded her of Levi, constantly watching and waiting with ferocious concentration for his moment.

'He's had the flu,' she said. 'But he's back on the front line now. He says he's one of the lucky ones.'

'Of course he is,' said Levi unpleasantly. 'Mick's always lucky. He's got more lives than a cat, that man. How many men who went over the top at the Somme died? Thousands! But not Mick! Oh, no, *he* survives. Everyone dropping like flies in a flu epidemic, but Mick gets better.'

'You should be glad.' Rose was shaken by the vitriol in Levi's voice. 'I'd have thought you'd be grateful your brother was lucky.'

'It's not fair!' Levi's expression was petulant as he frowned down at the letter in his hand. 'Why is it always Mick who gets all the luck? Will Hutton got flu and *he* died.'

'I was sorry to hear that,' said Rose carefully. It was almost as if Levi was put out that his brother had survived.

Will Hutton, the village blacksmith for many years had succumbed to flu only the previous week. A taciturn man who had lost his only son in the first year of the war, Will had given Levi a job and a roof over his head when he first came to Beckindale. Levi had repaid him by making the smithy a cover for his secretive business deals and, so Rose had heard, had spent the last days of Will's life in Bradford.

A shadow crossed Levi's face. 'I'll miss him,' he said. 'Will was the only person – apart from you, of course – who ever gave me a chance in this village,' he said bitterly.

'Will you take over the forge?' Rose asked, anxious to get him away from the subject of Mick.

'I don't think so.' Levi glanced complacently down at his new suit. 'I have too many other businesses to run.'

He had thickened out over the past three years and was more solid and imposing than he had been when he first arrived in Beckindale. He still limped, of course, but they had all grown inured to horrific injuries these days and a limp was barely worthy of mention. With his dark hair and blue eyes, Levi should have been an attractive young man but there was something repellent about him, Rose always thought. It was something to do with his lightning changes of mood, with the intensity of that pale gaze and his habit of running his tongue over his teeth.

It was stupid to be afraid of him, but she was.

She looked away. 'The village will miss having a blacksmith.'

'I'm not going to keep it on just because the village want a smithy,' said Levi sharply. 'When has the village ever done anything for me? Besides,' he went on with a smug look at the gleaming lines of his car, 'motors are the future.'

That was what Mick had always said too. Rose knew better than to remind Levi of that.

'I must get on,' she said. 'Could I have my letter?' she added, carefully casual, and Levi looked down at the letter as if he had forgotten that he held it.

He lifted it mockingly out of her reach. 'Come for a spin,' he said.

Rose clenched her teeth. 'Thank you, but I'm very tired,' she said, thinking of William Petty. 'I've had a long day.'

'Then I'll drive you home,' he said instantly. 'I haven't seen you for ages,' he went on. 'Anyone would think you'd been avoiding me! After all I've done for you too.' He laughed as if that could only be a joke.

Rose's answering smile was stiff. 'I've been busy.'

'You're always busy,' he pouted. 'Come on, get in, and you can have your precious letter.'

Rose's feet were aching and she could feel the stones in the hot track through the thin soles of her shoes but the last thing she wanted was to get in the car with Levi. Why wouldn't he take the hint and leave her alone?

'I've got a bit of a headache, Levi,' she said shortly. 'I would really rather have the air. Now, please could I have my letter?'

In response, Levi unfolded the letter and read it. *My darling Rose,* he read out sneeringly. 'Oh, dear, Mick's not much of a speller, is he? Imagine what your dear papa would think if he saw this letter!'

The fact that the same thought had crossed her own mind only made Rose angrier. 'Give it to me,' she said, snatching at the letter but Levi held it tauntingly out of her reach.

'Ah, ah! Not until you ask nicely!'

Rose clenched her fists. 'Please may I have my letter back,' she said through gritted teeth.

'Oh, come, you can be nicer than that, Rose,' he said. 'Think how nice you are to *darling* Mick, and he can't give you a fraction of what I can. I've got a house, a car, a successful business. What has Mick got? Nothing!'

'Levi, I love Mick,' Rose said carefully. 'You know that. I don't love you.'

His eyes flashed. 'Don't say that!'

'It's true.'

'I'd do anything for you,' he cried. 'You *know* what I've done for you, Rose!'

A chill crept down Rose's spine. She was very much afraid that she did know.

'But you don't even *try* to love me,' Levi complained. 'You're not even nice to me.'

'I am nice to you,' she said wearily.

'No, Rose, you're not.' He shifted so that she was wedged between him and the car. All at once he was too close and Rose stiffened. 'Let's not quarrel,' he said, his voice thickening. 'Let's kiss and make up. One kiss, just one, and I'll give you your letter.'

'No!' She put out her hands to ward him off, but he grabbed her wrists and twisted them viciously, bringing tears of pain to her eyes.

'I'm sick of hearing no from you, Rose.' His expression chilled dangerously, and she tried desperately to turn her head away as he pinned her against the car and brought his wet lips down on hers.

Chapter Five

'No!' Rose cried out, wrenching her mouth from Levi's in disgust.

She struggled to free herself, kicking him and wriggling, but he was bigger and stronger than she had realised. Her nurse's cap slid off her hair and into the dust. 'Let me go!' she shouted, beating at him with her fists.

'Sorry to interrupt.' A cool voice broke through Levi's grunted attempts to stop Rose and startled, he straightened.

Dot Colton was standing there, in a neat jacket and hat, her expression pleasant but implacable.

'What do you want?' Levi snarled.

'I was wondering if Miss Haywood would like some company?'

'Go to hell!' Levi swore, and made a grab for Rose who had taken advantage of his distraction to snatch the letter and push past him, wiping her mouth with the back of her hand. She evaded him, her eyes brimming with tears of rage and revulsion.

'I was only thinking of going as far as Beckindale,' Dot said. She turned to Rose. 'Would you like to accompany me, Miss Haywood? It's a nice evening for a walk.'

'No!' said Levi, just as Rose said, 'Yes ... that ... that would be nice,' in a trembling voice.

'Rose–' Levi began but she turned her head away. Oh, how she longed to tell him to go away and never come near her again, but he was Mick's brother. There was no way she would be able to avoid Levi once Mick came home and it would destroy Mick if she told him how his much-loved brother had behaved.

'Let's just forget it,' she said coldly.

'Don't let us keep you,' Dot added.

Glowering at Dot, Levi had little choice but to get back in the car and drive off with a squeal of tyres.

There was silence as the two young women waited for the dust to settle after him.

'Charming,' said Dot at last. She glanced at Rose. 'You all right?'

'Yes.' Rose let out a shaky breath as she refolded the letter and pushed it back into its envelope with unsteady hands. 'Yes, yes, thank you,' she said, putting it in her pocket.

'Did he hurt you?'

Rose rubbed her wrists. 'No, not really. I don't know what he would have done if you hadn't come along.'

Dot bent to pick up Rose's cap and knocked it against her leg to dislodge the worst of the dust. 'There's summat wrong with that Levi Dingle,' she said frankly. 'He's not right around the eyes.'

'I know. I wish he'd leave me alone but...' Rose trailed off, not wanting to explain the bonds that tied her to Levi.

'Aye, that's the worst of living in a village,' Dot said, handing the cap back to Rose. 'It's better in t'city. You can avoid anyone you don't want to see.'

'Unfortunately I can't leave Beckindale at the moment.' Rose sighed, thinking of Mick. If only the war would end and he would come back. Perhaps they could go away then? Everyone said the war would be over soon.

'You and me neither,' said Dot. They fell into step along the narrow lane.

'You used to work at Emmerdale Farm, didn't you?' Rose asked after a while, trying to distract herself from the memory of Levi's hot, wet mouth on hers. She shuddered at the thought of it.

'Aye. I went off to the munitions factory in Bradford for a while, but my ma was took bad in the flu and I'll need to stay here for a while. I'm working in the kitchen at t'hospital now,' she added, jerking her head back in the direction of Miffield Hall. 'I heard you was a VAD there. What does t'vicar say about that?'

'He hates it,' said Rose with the glimmer of a smile. She wasn't surprised that Dot knew who she was. Everybody in Beckindale knew everybody else.

54

Dot was a slight, brown-haired girl, unremarkable looking apart from a pair of sharp eyes and a stubborn set to her chin. She had a brisk, capable air about her and her hair was cut into a fashionable bob.

Before the war, the vicar's daughter and a farm servant would never have talked so easily to each other as they walked down the hill and over the bridge. Rose listened admiringly as Dot told her about her work in the munitions factory and her determination not to go back into service.

'I want to be me own mistress,' she said. 'Mebbe it's just a dream, but I'm not giving up yet.'

'Independence is a good dream,' said Rose, and found herself telling Dot in return about Mick. 'That's why I can't cut Levi completely.'

'Tricky,' Dot agreed. 'Mebbe we can walk to and from hospital together,' she suggested. 'Least that way you'd have company if Levi comes after you again.'

'I'd like that,' Rose replied, smiling. They had reached the end of the lane that led up to the church and the vicarage beyond. Rose held out her hand. 'I'm going this way. Thank you so much, Dot.'

Dot shrugged off her gratitude and gave her hand a brisk shake. 'It were nowt.'

The vicarage was very quiet when Rose let herself in. She stood in the hall listening to the grandfather clock ticking. She could smell beeswax and dried lavender, and it felt like sanctuary. Levi couldn't reach her in here, she reminded

55

herself, rubbing her lips once more to rid herself of the memory of that disgusting kiss. How could it feel so different to when Mick kissed her?

Dropping her crumpled cap onto the hall table, she peered into the mirror and patted her hair into shape, but something in the quality of the silence made her pause. Perhaps her parents were in the garden?

'Mama?' she said. Usually she could hear them talking, or the kettle whistling in the kitchen, *something*, but now there was just the stolid ticking of the clock.

'Papa?' Filled with a sudden foreboding, she opened the drawing room door. Her parents were sitting opposite each other in silence.

'Mama?' Rose said again, and when Edith looked up, Rose's heart almost failed at the lost expression in her mother's eyes. 'What is it?'

Too late she saw the telegram her mother held in her lap. 'No,' she said quietly.

Rose didn't want to take the telegram Edith held out to her without speaking. She felt like putting her hands behind her back, but she took it without opening it. 'John?' she whispered fearfully. Her elder brother had signed up on the day war was declared, and for nearly four long years they had dreaded this moment.

But her mother was shaking her head. She swallowed and moistened her lips. 'Arthur,' she said.

'Arthur?' Rose repeated blankly. It had never occurred to her to be worried about her younger brother. Arthur was so boisterous, so confident, irritating at times but indisputably alive. *Arthur* couldn't be dead.

'There must be some mistake,' she said, staring down at the telegram. After his training, Arthur had set off for France in tearing spirits, but he had only been there a matter of weeks.

But there was his name written clearly: 2/Lt Arthur Haywood.

Abruptly, Rose's knees buckled and she groped for the nearest chair, all thoughts of Levi wiped from her mind.

'Arthur,' she whispered.

She had never loved her younger brother the way she loved John, who was quiet and sensitive and who had tolerated her following him around as a little girl. Arthur, in contrast, was like a friendly puppy: a little thoughtless, a little clumsy, but well-meaning. The thought of him being dead made her mind spin hopelessly. It didn't seem possible.

There was a heavy silence.

'How...?' Rose broke it at last, but her voice faltered and she couldn't continue.

'It doesn't say.'

'Don't they usually tell you what happened?'

'What does it matter? He's dead. *Dead.*' Rose had never heard her mother sound like that before.

Charles Haywood moistened his lips. 'We must believe he did his duty.' His voice was thin and cracked but even as it wavered, Edith was on her feet.

'Duty?' she spat. 'What comfort is duty? This is your fault, Charles!'

'Mama,' Rose tried to put in, shaken, but Edith

would not be stopped.

'*You* filled his head with all that nonsense about honour and glory from the moment war broke out. *You* told them war was a glorious thing. You stood up in your pulpit and encouraged all those young men to go and fight – and for what? A few yards of mud!'

Rose was horrified at the bitterness in her mother's voice. It was as if a bandage had been ripped off a wound to reveal a gaping sore beneath.

She stumbled to her feet, not sure if she should comfort her mother or her father more, but Edith took the decision out of her hands, throwing out her arms to keep Rose at a distance. Rose had the impression that her mother was afraid to be touched in case she would shatter into a million pieces. Backing away, Edith turned and ran out of the room.

Her throat tight, Rose turned to her devastated father.

'Papa ... she's just upset.'

'No, Rose, she's right,' he said dully. 'It *is* my fault. I was wrong. I thought the war was an honourable cause worth fighting for, but it isn't. It's a vile, stinking mess and too many young men have died for it. And now my son is dead.' He raised trembling hands to cover his face and for the first time in her life, Rose saw her father weep. 'Arthur is dead, and it is all my fault.'

Winter 1918

Chapter Six

Outside, the mist hung low over the hills and the apple trees in the orchard at Miffield Hall dripped in the murky light. Dot was on her way back from the vegetable garden when she heard the peal of church bells and she paused.

So it was true. The war was over.

Rumours had been growing over the past few weeks. She had been unbuttoning her coat in the hospital kitchen that morning when young Bob, who washed the dishes, had burst in. 'Have you heard?' An armistice had been signed at five that morning, he'd told them excitedly. Hostilities would cease at eleven o'clock, and that would be it. The war was won.

She should be happy, Dot knew. She could hear cheering from the wards as the word spread and windows were opened to let in the sound of the bells that were being rung as a signal of peace at last. During all those long years of war she had imagined this moment and how relieved and thankful she would be, and she *was* relieved, of course she was, but standing there in the vegetable garden with her arms full of cabbages, Dot felt weary more than anything else. Weary and worn down by it all.

The war might be over, but there were still terribly injured men lying in the hospital beds. The flu, which they had thought had peaked, had returned with a vengeance, and in an even more virulent form. This time it was the young and fit who were suffering more than the children and elderly who had died in such numbers earlier in the year. How much more could they all endure? Dot wondered.

'Dot! Dot!' Bob was beckoning her excitedly from the kitchen. 'Can you hear the bells? Come and celebrate!'

It didn't feel like a great victory. It felt as if sheer exhaustion had dragged the war to a close, and what was there to celebrate in that? But Dot didn't want to be a killjoy. She carried the cabbages inside and smiled and kissed and was hugged by the terrifying Matron of all people.

That evening she walked back to Beckindale through the mizzle with Rose Haywood. The air smelt of damp leaves and wet earth tinged with rotting fruit. 'Quite a day,' said Rose, but she was thoughtful rather than elated.

'Aye, one to remember.' Dot paused. 'I just thought I'd feel more excited when it came to it.'

'I did too.' Rose hugged her nursing cloak around her against the chill. 'I suppose for a long time I imagined that when the war did end everything would go back to the way it was before, but of course that's never going to happen. Nothing's going to be the same. And it's hard to feel ecstatically happy when Arthur is still dead.'

'You heard any more about what happened to him?'

'No, it's strange. My father has written several times but keeps coming up against a brick wall.'

'He could be missing,' Dot suggested but Rose wasn't convinced.

'Surely they'd say if that was the case?'

'You'd think so,' said Dot. 'You must be glad to know your Mick made it through, though?'

'Yes,' said Rose after the tiniest of hesitations. 'Yes, of course I am.'

Dot looked at her. 'You don't sound very sure.'

'It's just that...' Rose sighed, clearly struggling to find the words to explain herself. 'I've been dreaming of this moment for years and there's part of me that is just so relieved that he's all right. But there's another part of me that's already starting to think, what will it be like when he's here all the time?'

'He came back on leave, didn't he?'

'He did, but it wasn't as perfect as I hoped it would be,' Rose confessed. 'I do really love Mick, but I was working and we couldn't meet openly so it was hard to find time to be together. When we did, it was like he was pretending to be himself. I can't really explain it,' she said. 'We'd been such good friends before, and suddenly it was like we were standing on opposite sides of a river trying to talk to each other. He couldn't tell me what it was like in France and I couldn't explain what I felt when I was changing a dressing or holding a soldier's hand as he died.'

'It's not easy for any of us,' said Dot. 'No one else knows what was it was like in t'factories either and I've given up trying to explain. Only someone else who was there will get it.'

'I suppose we're all in the same boat.'

'I reckon so.' They were quiet for a while, the

mist clinging to their faces and the sound of their footsteps loud in the dark night. Somewhere an owl hooted.

'I'm sure you and your Mick will be all right once you get used to each other again,' Dot broke the silence at last. 'You going to tell your parents soon?'

'Not yet. They're too upset about Arthur, at the moment.' Rose's pretty face was sad. 'The news has really broken my mother. John was always her favourite. I think she spent so much time dreading losing him that she wasn't prepared for it to be Arthur, somehow. As for Papa ... I just don't think he could take another shock at the moment.'

'Would it be so bad?'

Rose gave a mirthless laugh. 'His precious daughter marrying an Irish soldier without any means to support himself? He'll be horrified! He's got such rigid ideas, but I love him and I don't want to upset him. I'll just have to wait for the right moment.'

'There never seems to be the right moment to do the things you really want to do,' said Dot a little gloomily. 'Ma hasn't been well enough for me to tell her I want to go back to Bradford, and now the war's over, I don't suppose we'll be able to keep working. The men'll all be wanting their jobs back.'

'Let's hope there's no call for any more munitions ever again,' said Rose.

Dot didn't answer immediately. She was thinking of the job she had enjoyed so much. Well, not the job perhaps, but the independence and the sense of purpose and the companionship. The munitions factory had given her all of that. But Rose was right. Of course she was.

'Amen to that,' she said with a sigh.

They stopped for a moment on the bridge. Beckindale lay calmly in the dark, a few windows warmed with lamplight but no streetlights, no bands, no excited crowds.

'The girls in Bradford will be dancing in the street, tonight,' Dot said. 'They'll be laughing and singing and kissing any man they can get their hands on. Doesn't look like owt's happening in Beckindale, does it? I tell you what, Rose, this village needs the Woolpack up and running again,' she went on, warming to her theme. 'At least then we could all meet there at times like this. What have we got now? The church! Not to speak disrespectful of your pa,' she added quickly.

'He wouldn't let me within a mile of a pub,' said Rose enviously.

'Why not? Women can go into pubs in the city. There's no reason the Woolpack shouldn't be friendly and welcoming and safe, a nice place to sit and have a chat without feeling like trollops.'

Rose looked amused by her vehemence. 'You should do it, Dot.'

'Aye, when I meet a millionaire, mebbe I will.' Dot shoved her hands into the pockets of her coat. 'I'm not holding my breath, mind.' She had to admit that she found the idea tempting. If only she had the money, she could make something of the Woolpack, she knew she could.

It turned out that Beckindale wasn't as lacking in celebratory spirit as Dot had thought. There

65

was to be a service of thanksgiving at the church that Sunday, but afterwards the entire village was to gather for a party in the village hall.

Mary Ann told Dot all about it when she got home. 'Janet and Maggie have arranged it between them,' she said, hauling herself up from the chair where she had been sitting with Dot's mother. 'We'll all take a dish or what we can for the table and Maggie's got Tom Skilbeck to pay for two barrels of beer – though how she got that old skinflint to part with his brass I don't know!'

'I could bring a pie or two,' Dot offered, cheering up at the prospect of a party.

'You do that, lass. You always did have a hand for pastry.'

Dot inspected the pantry as soon as Mary Ann had gone. Normally her mother spent the summer preserving and bottling, but since Bill Colton's death in June, she had shown little interest in cooking or anything else. Dot came back from the hospital every day and cooked a meal for her, but she had no time to do anything else. Now the shelves were empty of jams and pickles. There were no jars of preserved fruit or vegetables and no hams hung from the kitchen ceiling as they had done before the war.

But she had eggs from the hens that scratched around the back door and there were still a few apples clinging to the gnarled tree at the bottom of the garden. Dot used their ration for some flour and Maggie Sugden gave her some butter so that she could make some apple pies. At Maggie's request she made a pile of havercakes, too, with some oats. 'Because nobody makes them like you,' Maggie said.

That Sunday, Dot encouraged her mother to get up and dressed in time for church. They sat together on the hard pew and listened to the vicar, who was a whole lot more subdued than he had been in 1914, Dot thought, remembering his fiery sermons. Mrs Haywood's face was set, and there were plenty of tears shed over those who had been lost, but Janet Airey was determined to get everyone in the right spirit. She chivvied them all along as they filed out of church.

'Come on, now,' she told them briskly. 'We've seen too many long faces over the last four years. We've all been through this war together, so let's celebrate the end of it together too. Let's have a party!'

And Janet was right, Dot thought, standing in the crowded hall. It was good for them to all be together. She felt more cheerful as she saw the effort everyone had made to provide something for the tables: cakes and pies and ham and home-baked bread and cheese. Petty squabbles had been put aside for the day. Beckindale might not have been bombed, and perhaps rationing hadn't hit them as hard as some, but they had suffered too during the war. They had sent their young men to fight without question, and the young women had gone to tackle jobs they'd never done before. Those left behind had endured loss and grief, and the flu was still ravaging families. Only the previous day Walter Dinsdale had died.

But on that Sunday, those who had survived refused to be sad. Looking around, Dot saw that only a few faces were missing. Joe Sugden wasn't there, which was no loss, she thought frankly to herself. He had been a mean bugger before the war, and though it was hard not to feel sorry for his disfigurement, the eerily blank stare would put a damper on the proceedings. Dot didn't know how Maggie stood it.

Robert Carr had stayed away too. He was another one with shellshock, reduced to a trembling wreck and unable to cope with the shrieks of the children or sudden laughter. But otherwise, everybody was there, even that slimy Levi Dingle, staring greedily at Rose from across the room. Maggie had come with her small son and two girls from the Women's Land Army. Dot saw Betty Porter and Janet Airey teasing Maggie about some cake she had made and was surprised at how well Maggie took it. She didn't think she had ever seen Maggie laughing with the other women. Once upon a time she'd have been too proud to take their ribbing.

Someone had put up bunting and with Tom Skilbeck's barrels of beer the party soon warmed up. They sat at long tables, passing food up and down, and afterwards the women cleared away the tables and the two Toms – Tom Teale and Tom Harker – got out their fiddles. Clarence Terry had an accordion and one of the Pickles boys a tin whistle, and at the last minute, Sam Pearson limped up to join them, another fiddle in his hand.

Dot loved to dance and she refused to be a wallflower. She had long accepted that she wasn't pretty and that even if there had been a lot of young men around she wouldn't be inundated with partners, so she had learnt to do the asking. She danced with old men and young boys, with Mary Ann and her mother, and with one-legged Jim Airey on his crutch, which was tricky but it made them both laugh.

Perhaps it wasn't so bad here after all, Dot thought. When the little band took a break, she found herself standing next to Maggie and one of the land girls who Maggie introduced as Grace. She was tiny, slender and very pretty, with a cloud of dark hair and huge pansy-coloured eyes. She was from Leeds, she said, and Dot couldn't understand what she was doing in Beckindale.

'Don't you miss the city?'

'No,' said Grace.

'Not at all? I do,' Dot said with a sigh. 'I miss being able to jump on a bus or a tram, and go out. And what about the pictures? There must be a picture palace in Leeds, in't there?'

Grace wrinkled her nose. 'There is, yes, but I like it here.'

'But it's so *boring!*' Dot objected.

'I don't think so,' said Grace, and her eyes slid to Sam Pearson who was coming towards them with his slow smile.

'How do, Dot?' he said easily.

Sam was a few years older than her, a quiet lad, but easy to like. There was nothing fancy about Sam – what you saw was what you got – and he did nothing in a hurry, but he was no fool either, though judging by the way he was looking at Grace, he was ready to make a fool of himself over her. No prizes for guessing why Grace found the country so appealing, Dot thought.

69

What was it about those fragile, nervous types that men fell for every time? she wondered. They never seemed interested in a capable lass who didn't need fussing over.

Not that she would want to marry Sam and spend the rest of her life in the country making butter and cheese and bringing up bairns, Dot reminded herself. In fact, she didn't want to marry anyone.

And that was just as well, she thought, looking around the village hall and seeing how few young men there were. There were lanky lads, still too young to have been called up, and older men, but the men of Dot's generation were mostly dead or injured. Their ghosts were ranged around the edges of the hall: George Kirby who had kissed her once behind the barn at Emmerdale Farm, Frank Pickles and Bert Clark, Alfred Porter ... the sad list went on and on.

No, Dot wouldn't be setting her heart on a wedding. She had quite a different plan in mind, one that meant shaking the dust of Beckindale from her feet the moment her mother was well enough to be left, and heading back to the city.

Chapter Seven

Icicles hung from the guttering and the snow that had fallen the night before was packed now into a slippery white coating over the farmyard cobbles. When Sam Pearson knocked at the door, his breath hung in a cloud in the rigid air.

'Chilly out,' he said with characteristic understatement.

Grace was winding her scarf around her neck. 'Are you sure you won't come too?' she asked Maggie, who shook her head.

'Jacob's asleep. I can't leave him on his own with Joe.'

'I don't mind staying,' Grace began, but Maggie shooed her towards the door where Sam was stamping the traces of snow from his boots.

'Off you go,' she said. 'You'll like the Christmas Eve service, and it'll be special this year now that we're at peace again.'

She watched as Grace took Sam's arm and set off across the farmyard, laughing as their feet skidded on the ice. She was glad that their romance seemed to be working out. Sam moved slowly, but Maggie had no doubt he would get what he wanted in the end. She would miss Grace, though, when she married Sam. The other two land girls had gone home soon after the Armistice, but Grace had said she'd like to stay on. Between war and flu, she had no family left, and besides, she liked it at Emmerdale Farm.

Grace might look fragile but she liked to milk the cows and had turned into a dab hand in the dairy. Maggie didn't know what she would do without her. The Women's Land Army was being disbanded as the men came home to take up their old jobs, but how many able-bodied men were there going to be, even if she could afford to pay them? There was no sign that Joe would be in any state to help on the farm any time soon.

She was hoping that now the war was over, young Ned Pickles would be able to avoid conscription. If he came to take Frank's place, Maggie thought she could manage.

Giving the fire a poke, Maggie sat down in her chair opposite Joe. He was sitting with his hands on his knees, as blank-faced as ever, and she had to close her mind to the memory of Hugo sitting there, waiting for her that other Christmas Eve, looking up with a smile as she brushed the snow from her hat at the door. Getting up to help her off with her coat, to push a warming glass of punch into her hand. Urging her towards the fire to get warm. Making her feel safe and cared for. Making her feel loved.

Maggie's heart clenched at the memory. She couldn't bear to look at the chair opposite. Hugo was gone, and in his place sat Joe, a lump of flesh, a millstone from the past. Why couldn't he have died in that explosion? It would have been so much better for him than this half-life. So much better for her too. Why lie to herself about that?

If Joe had died, Hugo would still be there. They could have been married by now. They would have been talking, making plans for the future, perhaps. If there had been a silence, it had been a companionable one, warmed with a smile when they glanced over to catch each other's eyes. That silence had been so different to the spongy silence now, where Joe's contribution was his harsh, uneven breathing.

With a sigh, Maggie picked up her knitting. She was putting the last touches to a hat to give Jacob the next morning. Missing Hugo was a constant,

72

dull thudding inside her. Sometimes it quietened to acceptance, barely more than a tremor deep in her bones, but at other times like now, the thud became a painful roar, slamming against her ribs and booming in her ears. Where was Hugo now? What was he doing? Did he think of her as she thought of him? Was he even alive?

Would she ever see him again? And if not, how would she bear it?

The Armistice had been signed in November, but it was taking a long time to demobilise the troops. Rose Haywood hadn't seen Mick Dingle yet, though it seemed her brother John was on his way home. Hugo had been carrying stretchers rather than fighting but presumably he had to wait his turn to get home like all the other men.

She might never know.

She was so very tired, Maggie realised. Tired of keeping her head up, tired of doing the right thing. It had been foolish of her to think that the end of the war would mean that all their troubles would be over. Once the party in the village hall had finished, life was just as hard as it had been before. Food was still rationed, soldiers were still suffering, families were still grieving.

And now the Spanish flu again. Just when they thought they had seen the last case, it swept savagely back. Maggie had heard that it was rampant once more in the cities. In a bitter twist to the Armistice celebrations, the hugging and the kissing in the streets had spread the flu with devastating efficiency while the men returning from the trenches had taken it with them along the roads and railway lines that led them home.

The flu had made it to Bradford and to Ilkley, and now back to Beckindale. Joan Carr had died of it only the week before, and who would look after poor Robert now?

Maggie's hands had fallen still as she was overwhelmed by a sense of hopelessness, but when a soft 'whoomp' from a collapsing log startled her out of her thoughts, she pulled herself together. Things were not all bad, she reminded herself, settling another piece of wood on the fire. Tomorrow would be Christmas Day and for the first year Jacob would be old enough to understand and enjoy the excitement. She had some nuts to put in his stocking, with a little wooden sheep that Sam had carved, some pieces of toffee, and this hat, if she got it finished in time. She would take him to church in the morning, and they would have a fine dinner afterwards. She had a prime piece of beef resting in the larder and Molly had made a plum pudding with a silver sixpence hidden inside. Jacob would love looking for that.

Glad to be thinking more positively, Maggie picked up her knitting once more. She let her mind drift back to the year she had set off through the snow to the Christmas Eve party in the village hall, and had ended up helping to deliver Polly Warcup's twins on the way. Margaret and Rose were three today and a rare handful for Polly. Maggie smiled at the thought of them. Little minxes! Jacob had been born a month later, and when the three of them got together, there was no stopping them.

None of them would remember the war, Maggie reassured herself. That was a good thing.

Her hands moved automatically. It was very quiet in the kitchen, with just the sound of the clicking needles and the occasional crackle and spit from the fire. She hadn't bothered with a paraffin lamp and the room was dark, lit only by the warm, wavering firelight that threw shifting shadows over everything. When Maggie glanced up, even Joe's lumpen figure seemed to be moving as the flames leapt and guttered.

Her gaze passed over him and then went back. It wasn't a trick of the light, she realised. He was shaking.

'Joe?'

Putting her knitting aside, she got up. 'Joe?' she said again. As she bent over him, she could see that he was shuddering convulsively.

She laid a hand on his forehead and it was so hot she almost snatched it away. 'You're burning up,' she said. 'Come on, let's get you to bed.'

It was difficult to know how much he heard or understood, but he let Maggie urge him to his feet and he leant heavily on her as she led him across to the cupboard bed. Fortunately it wasn't far.

Head lolling, Joe slumped onto the edge of the bed while Maggie grimly unfastened his braces and started to undo the buttons on his shirt. She hated touching him still, but it had to be done. His skin was hot and damp as she peeled off his shirt. He seemed to be barely aware of her as he shivered and put an unsteady hand to his head as if it was hurting.

Maggie set her jaw and undid his belt. 'Lie back now,' she said, her voice strained, and he collapsed obediently onto the pillow so that she could drag his trousers down and pull them off.

In spite of his illness, he was still a weight and Maggie was breathing heavily by the time Joe lay helplessly on the bed before her in his long johns and vest. It was impossible not to remember a time when she had been the helpless one, when he hadn't even bothered to take off his trousers before forcing himself down on her. Her throat closed at the memory of his savage thrusting, his suffocating hand over her mouth and the blows that had left her head ringing.

Almost reluctantly, Maggie drew the sheet and blanket over her husband and stood looking down at him, his shirt and trousers in her hand. Jacob had been ill like this in the summer. It had started like this with a fever and shivering, and wailing at the pain in his head.

Joe had the flu.

Her son had nearly died, and he had not been an invalid like Joe, his system weakened already by a terrible injury. The flu might have better success with Joe.

He might die.

The thought slipped into Maggie's head and shimmered there, impossible to dislodge, impossible to unthink.

She was all alone with him, and he was ill and too weak to defend himself. This was the man who had shot her beloved dog, Toby, who had beaten and kicked Fly. He had lashed out at Maggie herself, had taken his fists and his boots to her and raped her right there on the kitchen floor. Perhaps he didn't remember now, but he was a brutal, vicious man. He didn't deserve her pity.

Maggie's eyes flickered to the pillow that had fallen to the floor when Joe struggled onto the bed. Slowly, she bent to pick it up, then looked from it to Joe as he lay unconscious. How hard would it be? It might even be a kindness to put a stop to his wretched existence.

When she realised what she was thinking, Maggie sucked in a startled breath and threw the pillow back onto the ground. What would Hugo say if he knew what she had let herself consider for even a moment?

Call herself a Christian woman? Ashamed, Maggie folded Joe's clothes with hands that were not quite steady. Of course she couldn't help Joe to die. What had she been thinking? She had to care for him the same way she would care for a sick animal.

She would do her best, she resolved. She would try to save Joe.

But he might die anyway.

Maggie pressed her fingertips to her forehead, trying to remember what she had done for Jacob when he had been ill. She had been so terrified of losing him then that it was all a blur.

She found a cloth and wrung it out in cool water so that she could sponge Joe's face and try and cool the fever. There was no terror this time. Jacob had had the flu and so had she, so she had no fear of them catching it again. But she couldn't let Grace back in. When they had been ill in the summer, Grace had been living with the other land girls in the rooms above the stable. She would have to go back there, or better still, go to Pearson Farm with Sam.

But when Grace came back, glowing, after the Christmas service and, Maggie strongly suspected, some dallying on the road with Sam, she flatly refused to leave Maggie alone.

'You can't possibly manage on your own,' she said.

'It's too dangerous for you to stay, Grace,' Maggie tried. 'I can't risk you getting sick too.'

'I've been living here with Joe anyway, so it's too late to worry about that,' Grace pointed out. 'Besides, it's Christmas tomorrow, so Molly won't be coming. Someone has to milk the cows and feed the sheep and do the cooking and keep an eye on Jacob.'

Maggie looked pleadingly at Sam. 'Sam, you try and talk sense into her.'

'Can't be done.' He looked fondly at Grace. 'She's nearly as stubborn as you, Maggie. I reckon I'll save my breath, but I'll come up tomorrow and give you a hand with the stock.'

'There,' said Grace. 'That's settled.'

Maggie had to admit that she was glad of their help over the next few days. Sam spent nearly as much time at Emmerdale Farm as he did at his own. He managed all the heavy work, mucking out the stables and barn, lugging hay to the sheep and loading the milk churns on to the cart, while Grace dealt with the milking and drove the churns to the station. They even managed to cook Christmas dinner between them and Jacob was thrilled with his toy sheep and his toffee, although his hat remained on Maggie's knitting needles.

Maggie dozed in the chair next to Joe's bed the

first night as he shivered and sweated. By the morning he had developed the tell-tale cough that got steadily worse. Maggie sponged him down, gave him sips of water to drink and held the bowl as he coughed up bloody sputum again and again, and not once did she allow herself to flinch.

Her expression was impassive, but inside she couldn't stop her thoughts running in a frantic circle: will he die? Will he die? That dreadful cough, the sweating and thrashing around as he gasped for breath. How could he possibly survive?

On the third day, Joe was so ill that Maggie began to allow herself to hope, to imagine, as she held Joe's head and he vomited up blood. Emmerdale Farm would be safe for Jacob. Without Joe to care for, she would have more time for farming.

More importantly, she could try and find Hugo. Everything in Maggie leapt at the thought. How would she do that? Oh, there must be a way! She could write to the Red Cross, to the Quakers. *Someone* must know where he was! And then he could come home for good. There would be no impediment to them marrying if she were a widow. No one would blame her. Everyone in Beckindale knew the man Joe had been, and they had seen how terribly injured he was. It was amazing that he had survived this long at all. She would not be expected to grieve.

Maggie wiped the bloody mucus from Joe's ruined mouth and let herself imagine the next Christmas, when Hugo would be back, and how a great weight of loneliness and despair would have rolled off her back and let her stand tall again.

By the fourth day, Maggie told herself that it

couldn't be long. She sat by Joe's bed and listened to his tortured breathing. It got slower and slower, each rasping breath punctuated by an echoing silence and each time Maggie would tense and lean forward, wondering if it had stopped at last, only for Joe to suck in another shuddering gulp of air.

How could he still be breathing? He was unconscious, or as far as Maggie could tell, and his lungs were choked, but still they kept working. Each laborious breath was followed by another, and another, and then another still, until Joe opened his one good eye and it seemed to be clearer than before.

That was when Maggie sat wearily back in her chair and accepted that Joe was not going to die at all, not then.

He would survive and she would not be writing to the Red Cross. She wouldn't try and find Hugo. She would keep on doing what needed to be done at Emmerdale Farm while the future stretched bleakly ahead of her and the hateful, hopeless burden settled back comfortably into place on her shoulders.

Chapter Eight

Rose hesitated at the end of the path and looked at the summer house across the clearing. Frost glittered on its roof and rimed every twig on the trees behind it. Her stomach was jittery with nerves and she pressed her fist against her heart to quiet its hammering. In only a few yards, a few seconds, she would see Mick again at last.

She had waited and waited for the day he would be demobilised and able to come home, and now that it was here, she was paralysed with uncertainty. What if she didn't recognise him? In a panic, she realised that she couldn't picture his face properly and for one cowardly moment she wanted to turn and run away.

Instead she took a deep breath and walked across the clearing, her boots crunching on the frosty grass. She wouldn't let herself pause at the bottom of the steps but walked straight up into the summerhouse.

And there he was, waiting for her.

Of *course* she recognised him, Rose thought in a rush of relief. There was no way she could have forgotten those blue eyes, fanned with laughter lines, or the creases bracketing a mouth that seemed permanently twitching with a smile. But he looked different too, bigger in his army great-coat. Taller, thinner, paler.

Whenever Rose had imagined this moment when she would be reunited with Mick after the long years of war, she had pictured them rushing into each other's arms. Sometimes she thought Mick would swing her exuberantly round, at others she was sure they would share a deep, pas-sionate kiss. She'd never imagined that they would just stand and look at each other uncertainly.

Rose felt as if she were trembling on the edge of a dizzying drop, as if the past four years had been a dream and she was about to wake up to reality.

Mick's eyes were moving over her face wonderingly. What was he seeing? Rose wondered. The spoilt, rather silly girl who had fallen in love with him four years ago, or the young woman she had grown into?

'Miss Haywood.' Mick broke the silence at last, the formality an old joke between them.

'Corporal Dingle,' she said a little shakily. She gave a gasp of laughter. 'Oh, isn't this ridiculous? I'm shy!'

'Me too,' he said and she shook her head.

'Don't tell me that you have ever been shy, Mick Dingle.'

'All right, not shy,' he amended, 'but overwhelmed.' He came closer to Rose. 'Overwhelmed to realise that you're actually here, that I survived.' His voice was deep, his eyes serious for once. 'I thought of you every day in the trenches, *acushla*. When there was nothing but mud and rain and blood and filth and men dying and feet rotting and guns firing and shells screaming towards us, you were like this idea of heaven,' he said. 'You were everything that was clean and sweet and innocent and so beautiful, and now I'm back at last and you're not an idea at all, and it's overwhelming to remember that you're *real*.'

Rose reached out and took his hands. 'Yes, I'm real,' she said as his fingers closed around hers. 'I've been worrying about the same thing, whether I just have an idea of you in my head that's not the real you at all.'

'I'm just the same,' said Mick. 'A bit thinner, to be sure, and a bit battered, but otherwise the same.'

82

'No.' She shook her head. 'You're not the same, Mick. You've seen terrible things over the past four years, and endured terrible conditions. How could you possibly be unchanged by that? I'm not the same either,' she told him. 'I'm not the ninny I was when I met you.'

'You were never a ninny,' he protested.

'A ninny,' she said firmly. 'I was spoilt and selfish and *silly*, but I'm not now. I've spent three years on the wards and I've seen things so awful I could never even have imagined them before, sights that I will never forget, just like you. Those memories are part of us now and we're both different because of them.'

Mick was still holding her hands. 'Are you trying to tell me you don't love me any more, Rose?'

'No,' she said instantly. 'Oh, no, Mick, not that. I just think we need to get to know each other again.'

'You're right,' he said. He paused and cocked a brow at her with a return to his cheeky manner. 'Does that mean I don't get to kiss you?'

Reassured by the familiar glint in his eyes, Rose relaxed. 'I think it would help if you did, don't you?'

'Definitely,' said Mick so emphatically that she laughed and put on an innocent look.

'The thing is, I'm not sure I remember how to do it.'

'It's like riding a bicycle, *acushla*,' he reassured her. 'You never really forget. You'll pick it up again, I promise. Here,' he went on, letting go of her fingers to cup her face between his palms, 'I'll show you.' His warm gaze moved over her face as if memorising her. 'So, first, I tell how beautiful you are, to sweeten you up a bit. I tell you that you have the prettiest brown eyes that I've ever seen.'

'I *think* it's coming back to me,' said Rose, teasing. 'Is this the bit where I put my arms around your waist?'

'No, not yet. We have to get rid of your hat first, fetching as it is.'

'Not my hat!'

'I'm afraid so. It's just going to get in the way.'

In spite of her token protest, Rose was already lifting her hands to unpin the hat, and Mick tossed it onto the bench that ran around the edge of the summer house.

'Whenever you're ready,' he invited her and she slid her arms around him. But the greatcoat was too bulky and Rose drew back to unbutton it carefully before slipping her hands underneath. She could feel a tweed waistcoat and a coat and beneath that the warmth of his hard body.

'A bit tighter,' Mick advised. She pressed obediently closer and he pretended to consider. 'Yes, that's much better,' he said. 'Now, where was I?'

'You were admiring my eyes.' Rose was enjoying herself. Mick had always been able to make everything fun and yet exciting too. He was so different to the frighteningly intense Levi. Mick made her smile, he made her feel desirable and she trusted him absolutely.

'Ah, yes.' He grazed her cheek with his knuckle, lingering at the curve of her jaw. 'The prettiest eyes and the softest skin, and hair like sunshine,' he went on, winding a strand around his finger.

84

'Altogether you're the most perfect thing I've ever seen, and that's a fact. But that's not why I want to kiss you, Rose.'

'It isn't?'

'No, I want to kiss you because you're brave and you're strong and you're loyal. Because of that naughty glint in those eyes. Because when you smile at me the way you're smiling now, my heart's so full, it hurts.'

The teasing note faded from his voice and their smiles evaporated at the same moment, both recognising that the joke was over and that something deeper and more intense had taken its place. It was Rose who lifted her arms and put them around his neck.

'Kiss me, Mick,' she said.

His mouth came down on hers, and the touch and taste of him was so piercingly sweet that Rose gasped and pressed closer. His lips were so warm, so sure, so unlike Levi's hot, wet, angry kiss. Abandoning herself to the swirling pleasure of it, she pulled Mick closer and kissed him back. This was what she had remembered, but the reality was so much better than memory. He had washed before he came out and she could smell the soap on his skin. She tangled her fingers in the wiriness of his clean hair and pressed against him, aware of the insistent thud of desire, and frustrated by the layers of clothes between them.

When Mick raised his head at last, she murmured a protest and felt his frame shake with soft laughter. 'We need to stop while we still can, *acushla*,' he told her and rested his cheek against her hair, his breathing ragged. 'Didn't I tell you that you'd get the hang of it again?'

'You did and you were right.'

They sat close together on the hard bench, their hands entwined, and Rose sighed.

'This is better,' she said. 'I don't feel shy any more. I hated that. This is better than when you came back on leave too. I'd looked forward to it so much but it felt awkward, as if we were both pretending to be in love. We never seemed to have enough time to talk properly and it was almost as though you couldn't wait to go back.'

Mick made a face. 'It was a strange time. Like you, I couldn't wait to get here and see you, but when I was here, everything felt so distant. I couldn't get the trenches out of my head, and I didn't want to tell you about it. I wanted to keep you separate from all of that. It felt as if I would have been staining you with my memories.'

'I understand that better now. I didn't tell my parents about what I did at the hospital for the same reason.'

'You're right,' Mick said after a moment. 'We should get to know each other again, Rose. Things are different now. When the war was on, it was difficult to think too far ahead, but now I need to get a job. I can't ask you to marry me until I can support a wife.'

'We should wait anyway,' she said. 'I can't talk to my parents at the moment. They're still so upset about Arthur. I wrote to you about that, didn't I?'

'You did,' he said after hesitation so brief that Rose decided that she must have imagined it. 'I'm sorry. Poor lad, he was so young.'

'My parents can't rest until we find out what

happened. We've been writing letters but can't get anywhere.'

'I would leave it, Rose. There's nothing can bring him back.'

'I just think it would be easier if we knew what happened.'

'Sometimes it's easier not to know.'

She shifted round to look at him. 'What do you mean?'

'Just ... if you knew he'd died trying to stop his entrails falling into the mud, or knowing that both of his legs had been blown off, that would be a picture you'd have in your mind for ever. Better to think it was a clean shot and that he died instantly.'

'I suppose so,' Rose said doubtfully.

'Anyway,' Mick went on, 'we should be looking forward not back. So, do you want to hear my plan?'

'You've got a plan already?'

'I've only been thinking about it for four years,' he told her. 'I want to start a garage.' His voice warmed with enthusiasm. 'I learnt a bit about petrol engines in the Army and motors are going to be the future. Not just motor cars, but tractors and other machines to make farm work so much easier.'

'I see,' said Rose, trying not to let doubt creep into her voice. She couldn't see her father being impressed by a garage. 'Will that be expensive to set up?'

'I'll need to persuade someone to invest, yes.' Mick's eagerness faded at the harsh realities of finance and Rose hesitated.

'Will Levi help you? He's got a car now.'

'I know, and a beauty it is, too. Where did he earn enough to buy a Vauxhall, Rose?'

'He seems to have fingers in a lot of pies,' she said cautiously.

'So it seems. He's been building a house too.' Mick frowned down at his shoes. 'I'm pleased for him, sure. He's done well.' But he didn't sound certain.

Rose said nothing. She didn't want to be the one to tell him that Levi had made his profits on the black market, or that his own brother had tried to turn her against him, but Mick was bound to pick up on Levi's unpopularity sooner or later.

'I don't think all of Levi's deals are entirely above board,' she said after a minute and Mick's frown deepened as he glanced at her.

'That's what I was afraid of. I want everything above board, so I've written to my cousin, Jonah. He's a man with money to invest and a taste for risk. I'm thinking my garage will be just the ticket for him.'

'I didn't know you had a cousin,' said Rose, and Mick looked at her in disbelief.

'We're Irish,' he said. 'Of course we've got cousins! Now, Jonah, he's one of the rich Dingles,' he went on, settling unthinkingly into storytelling mode.

Rose loved to listen to him like this. His lilting Irish voice span tales out of nothing, and she would be spellbound, only to find at the end that there was no great denouement. The rambling was just Mick taking the pleasure of telling a story.

So she shifted until she was sideways on and made herself comfortable. 'The rich Dingles,' she prompted him. 'You never told me there were any of those. I thought you'd all come straight from the bog?'

'Well now, sadly our side of the family ended up in the bogs but my da's older brother was called Amos. He was a canny one, by all accounts, and he could see no future for himself in Ballybeg. So he took himself off to Dublin when he was just a lad of fifteen. He got a job with some English landowner, and the next the family heard, he was organising the cattle boats for him and making a tidy profit on the side.'

'Cattle boats?'

'Seven sailings a day there used to be, sending cattle to England. My da always said Amos could sniff out money, and he made plenty of it, enough to set himself up in business and get married. We never saw the new Mrs Dingle in Ballybeg of course, but we heard she was very grand and fashionable. They had two boys, Adam and Jonah. We never saw them in Ballybeg either but we heard all about them. Adam was the golden boy. He was clever and handsome and charming and a brilliant sportsman and good and kind, and his parents thought the sun rose and set by him, my da said.'

'And Jonah?'

'Ah, Jonah was a different story. He took himself off to Australia and what did he do there but find a great big lump of gold!'

'No!'

'Yes,' Mick insisted, pleased with Rose's reaction to his story. 'Of course, none of us knew any of this. We just heard that Jonah had gone overseas and never been heard of since. But I had a spell behind the lines in France driving a truck and one day we were sent out to bring back a couple of airmen and whatever we could salvage from their plane. The pilot turned out to be a Captain Dingle so of course I commented on the name and he was none other than Cousin Jonah.'

'And he really found gold?' Rose was fascinated.

'That's what he said. He sold the gold and was on a fair way to squandering his money on going as fast as he could on motorcycles and motor cars and aeroplanes when the war intervened and he joined the Flying Corps. It's usually reserved for posh boys who've been to the right schools, but I suppose knowing how to fly made it worth pretending that he wasn't a rough Irishman at heart.'

'He survived the war then?'

'He did,' said Mick. 'Unlike a lot of pilots. He's got more lives than a cat, that one,' he said, unconsciously echoing what Levi had said about him. 'He was pretty banged up after a crash not long after we picked him up, and I heard that they put him on training new pilots, though I hope he didn't train them to take the same risks that he did. Nat always used to call me reckless,' Mick went on, 'but I'm a staid fellow compared to Jonah Dingle.'

'But is he reckless enough to invest in your garage?' said Rose.

'He might be. He told me to get in touch after the war, so I did. I sent him a letter today, in fact.

I got the impression that he's easily bored, so he might be off for the Dominions again soon and I don't want to waste months while my letter chases him around the world.

'So all's not lost yet,' Mick told her. 'We've just got to put our faith in Jonah.'

Chapter Nine

Maggie wound her woollen scarf more firmly around her neck as she closed the door quickly behind her to keep the heat in the kitchen. It was bitterly cold in the farmyard. A few flakes of snow were drifting through the late afternoon gloom in a desultory manner and she squinted at the sky. A blizzard was the last thing she needed right then, but the clouds didn't have that heavy, swollen look that presaged deep snow.

Still, she was glad that she had brought the sheep off the hill well before winter had really started to bite. She had learnt her lesson well three years ago when she had lost her way in a blizzard. If it hadn't been for Hugo, she might have died up on the fell, and her unborn baby with her.

But she couldn't let herself think of Hugo, not now when her bitterness over Joe's survival was so raw. Maggie knew that it was wrong to regret that he hadn't died, but she couldn't help herself. She wanted to shake her fist at God. So many good men had lost their lives in the war; why had Joe been saved? It wasn't fair.

His death had been so close. Maggie had been able to feel it. For those few moments when Joe had struggled to suck in enough air, Death had bent over the bed with her, had reached out to pluck him down to whatever hell was reserved for men who beat women and children and dogs. But at the last second, it seemed, it had drawn back. Joe's lungs had trembled on the edge of giving up. Maggie had waited and waited for the silence that had never come. The silence that would have meant that he had stopped breathing and that everything had changed.

The difference between drawing a breath and not, that was all it had been.

It was her fault, Maggie knew that. She had let herself hope that things would be different, and now her disappointment was all the more acute because after all the dreaming and the imagining and the hoping, nothing at all had changed. Joe was still trapped in a ruined and useless body, and she was still trapped with a husband she could never love, a husband she would forever associate with fear and humiliation and who couldn't even contribute to work on the farm.

Joe, in fact, seemed better now that he was recovering. It was hard to put her finger on it, as he had still said nothing, but Maggie sensed that he was somehow more present. She was aware, too, of his one eye watching her now. His expression was clouded but not as vacant as it had once been and he had stopped rocking back and forwards in the way he had done before. That morning she had caught him looking at his hands as if wondering what they were for.

Please let him not remember, Maggie prayed as she opened the barn door and whistled for the dogs. If Joe must live, let him not become the man he was before. Let him not remember what pain and humiliation those hands could inflict. If he did that, if he lifted a finger to Jacob, she would regret that she had let that pillow drop.

Fly had jumped up instantly from her bed in the straw, snarling at Laddie who gambolled around her, excited at the prospect of activity. At eight months, Laddie was a gangly adolescent, one collie ear cocked, the other turned comically down. He was still playful and in need of being put in his place by Fly but Maggie thought that he was shaping up nicely as a sheepdog.

Hauling a bale of hay onto her back, she trudged out to the field, the dogs alert at her side. She was very tired after the broken nights nursing Joe, but she had refused Sam Pearson's offer to feed the sheep again. Sooner or later, they had to get back to normal.

Because nothing had changed.

With a sigh of relief, Maggie dumped the hay onto the ground and stretched out her back with a grimace. When the sheep came running she banged her gloved hands together for warmth and counted the sheep as they jostled for hay. One was missing and, calling Laddie to heel, she set off around the field in search of it. It was Fly who found it first, giving a sharp bark at the sight of the sheep hidden in a dip behind a tussocky outcrop. It was stuck on its back and unable to get up. Grunting with effort, Maggie hauled it over and up and the sheep ran off to join the others at the hay without a backward look.

'A thank you would be nice,' Maggie shouted after it, then sighed. What was it coming to when she was reduced to talking to sheep? She had barely slept for four days thanks to Joe, and tiredness was catching up with her. 'Come on, dogs, let's go back,' she said.

It was almost dark by the time she got back. She had left a paraffin lamp hanging in the barn and a thin band of light sliced across the farmyard. Maggie noticed it with a frown. She must have left the barn door ajar. It was unlikely that the cows would take themselves anywhere but still, it wasn't like her to be careless. She really must be tired.

Fly had started to bark but her tail was wagging too. Laddie did the same, a little uncertainly as if he didn't know why he was barking but was willing to copy Fly. Puzzled, Maggie walked slowly towards the barn, her heart beginning to thud against her ribs. At the door, Fly pushed past her into the barn, her whole body wriggling with pleasure and then, half hidden in the shadows, a man in a greatcoat rose from the hay bale, bending to pat the dogs that were fussing around him before he looked up with a smile.

'Hello, Maggie.'

Maggie stood as if frozen, her hand on the barn door while shock and joy rocked giddily through her. 'Hugo?' she whispered, afraid that her tired brain might be playing tricks on her. 'Is it really you?'

He nodded.

For a moment she could only stand there, staring at him, then she let go of the door and walked towards him unsteadily. 'Oh my dear one,' she said and her voice cracked. 'I am so glad to see you. I have missed you so.'

'And I have missed you.'

Hugo held out his arms and she went into them. They were both bundled into heavy coats and swathed in scarves, but Maggie didn't care. She could feel the glorious solidity of his body. It was enough to know that he was there, that she could hold him, and when she lifted her face with a trembling smile, it seemed the most natural thing in the world to kiss there in the wobbly light of the lamp.

The cows shuffled their hooves on the straw and blew out ruminative breaths, and the air smelt of hay. Careless of the cold, Maggie and Hugo sat close together on a bale and held hands. Maggie had stripped off her gloves, needing to feel the warmth of his flesh.

'I shouldn't have come,' Hugo said. 'I wasn't going to. I told myself that it would be a mistake and that I should let you get on with your life. I know that's what I should do and I will,' he said, softening the blow by putting his arm around her, 'I couldn't do it without seeing you once more. I've seen so many terrible things over past year and a half,' he told Maggie. 'I needed to see you and remind myself about what matters. I wanted to tell you that the thought of you is all that has kept me going since I left.'

'Hugo, I've been so lonely without you,' Maggie said. 'I have friends, of course, but it's not the same. You are the only one who truly understands me.'

'You have Jacob,' he reminded her. 'How is he?'

'He's a terror,' she said with a faint smile.

'And Joe?'

She looked away, her smile fading. 'Joe is here, too. He is alive, but not fully alive. It is as if he is stuck halfway between life and death. It is horrible.'

'I'm sorry,' said Hugo quietly.

'For him or for me?'

'For both of you.'

'I wanted him to die,' Maggie said, low and ashamed. 'I thought he would. He caught the flu and he was so sick and God help me, I hoped that he would die, but he didn't. He's survived,' she said bitterly. 'If he hadn't, you could have stayed. We could have wed and you could have been a father to Jacob and we could have been happy...' Her voice broke and Hugo pulled her close.

'Hush now,' he said. 'I cannot wish death on another man. I could not have that on my conscience.'

'The worst thing is that he's not even Joe any more. I can't hate him the way I did. He's just ... blank. He's not angry or sad or happy or bored or ... or *anything*. He's just *there*. It's just so unfair.'

'Oh, Maggie.' Hugo rocked her quietly as she wept.

She pulled herself away at last, dashing the tears angrily from her checks, hating her own weakness. 'I don't want to waste time crying,' she sniffed, and forced a wobbly smile. 'Tell me how you are, Hugo. I've wanted to know so often.'

'I'm sad,' he said honestly.

96

'Was it very bad?'

'As bad as it could be. It was hell out there. We'd be staggering and slipping through the mud with a stretcher, stumbling over arms and legs, picking up men blown to pieces, and trying to get them back to safety without being blown to pieces ourselves. Sometimes we'd get out to a trench or a manhole and you could tell that there would be nothing the medics could do to save them. We had to–'

Hugo broke off with a cough but waved away Maggie's worried look. 'I'm fine,' he said. 'Just a tickle in my throat.' He patted his throat. 'We had to leave them there,' he went on. 'We'd give a hypodermic of morphine and leave them there to die. It was sickening,' he said, the muscles in his face twitching with remembered horror. 'All of it. Piles of amputated limbs, horribly mutilated bodies, boys face down in that bloody mud, bullets in their backs.' He stopped abruptly. 'I'm sorry, you don't want to hear all this.'

No, but perhaps he needed to tell it, Maggie thought.

'You sound bitter,' she said sadly.

'Not bitter, just tired. My God, Maggie, those men were brave! We'd get them to the field tent and they might still be cracking a joke. When we put them in ambulances they'd all be wearing the Blighty smile that meant they'd be going home.' Hugo dragged a hand over his face and coughed again. 'The world cannot go on like this, Maggie. We have to change. We *must*. We can't go through anything like this again.'

'We need peace,' Maggie agreed. 'But at least

you are safe,' she said. 'How did you get here?'

'I managed to get on a boat three days ago. I went to London, got a train, and Tom Teale gave me lift from the station to the end of the lane.'

'You must be tired.'

He lifted her hand to his lips. 'I just wanted to get here.'

'Are you hungry?'

'Yes,' he said with a grin.

She should take him into the warm kitchen and give him something to eat, but Maggie didn't want him to see Joe. Jacob would be all over him, and Grace would be there … the truth was that she didn't want to share him.

As he so often did, Hugo seemed to know what she was thinking. 'Could you bring me some bread and cheese, do you think? I'll be fine in my old room above the stable. Believe me, I've slept in worse conditions!'

Reluctantly, Maggie disentangled herself from him. 'I suppose I'd better get back before Grace starts to worry. I'll get you some more blankets and something to eat,' she said. 'And when Jacob's in bed, I'll come over and we can be alone.'

She had made a stew earlier, eking out the little meat they had with turnips and cabbage. They would all be glad when Molly was back in the kitchen. Maggie had told her to stay home while there was flu in the house, but she would send a message for her to come back the next day and they could have some decent food again.

In the meantime, they would have to make do with Maggie's uninspired meals. She had never been much of a cook and Grace didn't seem to know one end of a saucepan from another either. So it wasn't much of a meal, but it was hot, and perhaps it would be better than Hugo was used to. It would have to do.

She poured a good-sized helping into a bowl and took it over to the stable with a hunk of bread, a piece of doughy fruit pie and a bottle of beer. Hugo had made himself comfortable with the blankets she had taken over earlier and he sat cross-legged on the bed to eat while Maggie sat close, not wanting to miss a moment with him.

When he had finished, she took the bowl and plate back to the kitchen. She ate with Grace and Jacob and then she put Jacob to bed, and all the time she was fizzing with the knowledge that Hugo was really there. She told Grace the truth, and asked her to listen out for Jacob, and Grace had nodded unhesitatingly. If she was shocked by Maggie's intention to commit adultery, she said nothing.

'I'll listen out for Jacob,' she said. 'Stay with Hugo as long as you want.'

As she passed the cupboard bed, Maggie bent to check on Joe, who was sleeping restlessly. It was clear that the flu had left him exhausted, and he had yet to get out of bed.

Picking up the extra blanket she had left over the back of a chair, Maggie looked at Grace. 'I'm going to the stable,' she said, smoothing the blanket over her arm. 'Don't wait up.'

The snow was falling more thickly as Maggie made her way to stable. She could hear Hugo cough again as she climbed the rough steps. He was sitting on top of the bed, leaning against the

99

wall, his stockinged feet crossed. He looked better, she thought. The food had done him good.

They smiled at each other and Maggie felt her heart swell. Hugo held out a hand and she took it. She let him draw her down beside him and they turned to each other, continuing a wordless conversation with their eyes. His fingers were featherlight, tracing the lines of her face as if committing them to his memory, and Maggie tugged his shirt free so that she could slide her hand beneath to explore his flank. His skin was warm and his muscles flexed in response to her touch.

'Are you sure?' he asked softly and she raised herself up to kiss him. This might be the one and only night they spent together. After missing Hugo so desperately and for so long, he was here at last. It was no time for doubts or hesitation.

'I'm sure,' she said.

Chapter Ten

Later, they lay close together under the blankets, talking quietly. Maggie rested her head on Hugo's chest, listening to the steady beat of his heart while her hands smoothed lovingly over his warm flesh. His care for her had been a revelation. She had only ever known Joe intimately, and at the best of times he had been brutish and rough. At the worst ... well, she wouldn't think of that now, not when the dark dazzle of passion shimmered still in her veins.

Another cough shook his frame and she stirred as he murmured an apology.

'What now?' she asked.

Hugo's arm tightened around her. 'Now I have to go.'

'Go where?'

'Australia? South Africa? I don't trust myself to stay away if I'm in the same country as you.'

'Will you write and tell me where you are?' she asked. 'Then I could let you know if … if Joe…' She trailed off, unable to put it into words, and Hugo laid a finger across her lips.

'Don't say it, Maggie. I cannot wish a man's life away. What we have done is wrong.'

'Adultery?'

He sighed. 'It's an ugly word.'

'It doesn't feel ugly,' said Maggie. She pushed herself up so that she could gaze down into his eyes. 'It feels right.' She took his face between her hands so that he couldn't look away. 'I want you to know that I will never, ever regret this,' she said. 'Promise me that you won't either.'

'Oh, Maggie … how could I?' he said, tugging her down for a soft kiss. 'I'll remember this night for the rest of my life. I'll never be sorry that we were able to love each other this way, I can promise you that. But I want you to promise me something too.'

'What?'

'I want you to be happy without me. Promise me you'll look forward, that you won't resent Joe or Jacob or the farm. You belong at Emmerdale Farm. Promise you won't waste your life wishing that you could be somewhere else.'

101

Maggie let out a long sigh, imagining the years without Hugo stretching out before her. Her eyes stung with tears. 'I'm not sure I can promise that. I can promise to try.'

They made love once more, and then Maggie made herself get up. She sat on the edge of the bed as she buttoned her blouse. 'Do you have to go tomorrow?'

'The longer I stay, the harder it's going to be to say goodbye,' Hugo said, his last word lost in a bout of coughing.

'I don't like the sound of that cough,' said Maggie, lacing her boots.

'I'll be fine, Maggie.' He swung his legs out of bed and pulled on his trousers so that he could say goodnight.

When Maggie was dressed she put her arms around him and hid her face in his warm chest. 'I don't want to leave you,' she said, and her voice cracked with sadness at the nearness of their passing.

'I know, my darling.'

'You won't leave me without saying goodbye?'

'Of course I won't.'

'Promise?'

'I promise.'

Drawing away from him, Maggie mustered a smile. 'I'll bring you some breakfast before you go then.'

Her body was still humming with remembered pleasure as she let herself into the quiet farm-house. The snow had cleared to leave a clear sky and in the starlight she could make out the dark humps of furniture. She tiptoed around the table towards the stairs only to freeze as she caught a faint gleam from the cupboard bed, and her heart lurched into her throat where it lodged, fluttering like a trapped bird.

Joe was lying on his side, his eyes wide open. He made no sound and it was impossible to tell whether he had seen her, if he wondered where she had been, or what she had been doing. The old Joe would have been waiting for her, drunk and roaring. He would have taken his fists to her and beaten her bloody. But this Joe just lay there, looking but not seeing.

And she was trapped with him, afraid always that the old Joe would stir without warning.

Be happy without me. Maggie was seized by a sudden fury. How could Hugo ask that of her? How could she possibly be happy without him? Her throat was tight with longing for him. How was she going to bear it?

She slept badly, only dropping into a restless slumber early in the small hours and waking with a dull sense of foreboding the next morning when she heard the click of the latch and careful footsteps on the wooden stairs. Grace was going out to do the milking.

Maggie got up and dressed and went to light the range. Joe was still asleep, lying with his face to the wall.

Hugo was going today. Last night had been a dream, and this morning she had to face reality.

She made porridge and tea and having checked that Jacob was still sound asleep too, she carried a tray of breakfast over to the stable. Yesterday's

103

snow had vanished, leaving the air raw and rigid.

Blossom, the horse, greeted her with a whicker as Maggie opened the door and pushed it back into place with her hip, but Maggie barely heard her over the ominous sound of coughing overhead. This was no tickle in the throat. It was a deep, gurgling cough and what felt like a ball of ice solidified in her stomach.

'Hugo?' She hurried up the rough steps and shoved the tray onto the chest so that she could drop to her knees next to the bed where Hugo lay huddled under the blankets, racked by that terrible cough.

'Hugo!'

'Sorry...' he gasped between coughs. His eyes were red-rimmed, his face a ghastly grey. '...should ... go.'

'You can't go anywhere! You're sick.'

A spasm of coughing had Hugo struggling for breath and the handkerchief he pressed to his mouth came away stained with blood. Maggie fought down panic. Yes, it was the flu, but Joe had just had the flu, and he had got better, she reminded herself. Hugo would get better too.

Running back out to the farmyard, she saw Grace carrying the milk cans to the dairy. Trying to stop her voice wobbling up and down, she asked Grace to look after Jacob and Joe while she nursed Hugo, and some of her fear evaporated at Grace's calm response. 'You go back to him. I'll bring you over some cloths and water.'

'You mustn't come near, Grace!'

'I'll leave them at the bottom of the steps for you. Don't worry about Jacob. He'll be fine with me, and Sam will come and feed the sheep.'

She had wanted longer with Hugo, but not like this. Maggie stayed at Hugo's side all day and all night. She bathed his face and body, trying to get the fever down, and she held his head as he coughed blood wretchedly into a basin, but there was little else that she could do. Only the night before he had held her in his arms, and now he barely knew who she was.

'No,' she kept saying out loud. 'No, this isn't fair.'

He'll get better, Maggie told herself desperately. Joe had recovered, and look how near to death he had been. She wouldn't lose hope, not now that Hugo had come back to her.

She made bargains with God. If Hugo got better, she vowed, she would let him go to Australia. She wouldn't try to contact him. She wouldn't wish Joe dead in his place. She would do anything, she told God, if he would just let Hugo live.

And for a time it seemed that God was listening. Hugo's cough eased a little and his eyes cleared. He blinked up at Maggie as she bent anxiously over him.

'You're here,' he murmured and then, 'Are you real?'

'Yes, I'm here,' she said through her tears. 'I'm real. You've been ill, Hugo, but you're going to be fine now.'

She laid her hand on his forehead but it was still hot. Biting her lip, she wiped a cool cloth over his face. 'Better?'

'Head ... hurts.'

'I know. Try not to talk.'

Hugo ignored her. 'Sit up,' he muttered, struggling to raise himself. Maggie gave up arguing and helped him up against the pillows, encouraged by his strength.

'Do you think you could manage some broth?'

'Little.'

She perched on the side of the bed, giving him spoonfuls of soup as hope surged through her. Hugo wouldn't be drinking soup if he wasn't getting better, would he? Surely the danger had now passed. Her shoulders relaxed slightly. The broth would give him strength and he would sleep. He would recover.

And then ... Maggie wouldn't let herself think about what would happen then. She could only think about Hugo getting well.

She smiled tenderly at him, only to see his eyes roll back in his head. Without warning, he was seized by a paroxysm of coughing and threw up a ghastly mixture of soup and blood that splashed over her hands and apron and the bed.

The bowl of soup fell to the floor with a crack as Maggie jumped to her feet and rubbed his back frantically, trying to ease his lungs, but blood kept bubbling out of Hugo's mouth.

'No, no, no!' she cried, sobbing his name. 'No, you can't die! Not now! You're getting *better!*'

Desperately, she sat beside him, trying to stem the blood that was choking his lungs, and listening to his agonised breathing as she had listened to Joe's, willing him to keep drawing in the air, one breath at a time.

'One more,' she urged him as his chest trembled

with effort. 'Come on, Hugo, you can do it. One more breath and it will get easier.' A gasp, a gurgle and he sucked in a thread of air. 'Yes, that's it,' she said through her tears. 'Now another one.'

Another choking sound came from Hugo's throat, but this time the breath Maggie waited for didn't come.

'Come *on*, Hugo, *breathe!*' she shouted at him, slamming her fist on the mattress. 'Breathe!'

Hugo's chest stayed obstinately still, ominously silent. In a frenzy, Maggie pushed down on his ribs, trying to make his lungs work, but it just sent more blood oozing out of the corner of his mouth.

Still his chest would not lift, still no breath came. No breath ever would.

Hugo was dead.

'*No!*' she screamed, beating at his body in despair. 'No, no, no!'

Collapsing onto her knees beside the bed, Maggie rested her head in the bloody mess on the sheets and wept in raging despair at the unfairness of a world in which Hugo could die while Joe Sugden lived still.

She never knew how long she stayed huddled by Hugo's body but at some point Rose Haywood was there, laying a gentle hand on her shoulder.

'Leave him now, Maggie,' she said as she helped Maggie clamber stiffly to her feet. 'You need to rest.'

Maggie looked at her blankly. 'Rose,' she said, as if realising who was there for the first time. 'What are you doing here?'

'Grace sent for me. She thought I might be able

to do something to help Hugo.' Rose glanced sadly at the bed. 'I'm so sorry, Maggie. I know how much you loved him.'

Maggie could feel herself crumbling from the inside out. It was a terrifying feeling, as if all the strength she had ever had was dissolving and as her face began to crumple, she buried it in her hands.

'I can't bear it,' she said brokenly. 'I can't, Rose, I just can't...'

'Come,' said Rose. 'I'll make you some tea.'

'Hugo...' Maggie dropped her hands and made herself look at the body lying so horribly still on the bed.

'I'll take care of him for you,' Rose promised, taking Maggie by the elbow and steering her towards the door. 'You're exhausted. You need to sleep.'

In the kitchen, Maggie let Rose close her hands around a mug of sweet tea and stand over her until she drank it. Numbly, she let Grace untie the bloody apron and undress her and when Grace told her to get into bed, she did. She lay stiffly under the sheet, imagining Rose clearing up the terrible mess in the stable, laying out Hugo's body, until exhaustion hit her like a hammer and she dropped into merciful oblivion.

But when she woke the next morning, Hugo was still dead. He had gone, and taken all hope with him.

Chapter Eleven

Rose huddled into her coat as she stood by the grave. Maggie had chosen a pretty spot in the shade of a holly oak on a rise above the beck and looking down the dale. Or it would be pretty in spring at least. Right now, on this damp winter day, it was cold and bleak and Rose was not the only one shivering. She shifted her feet surreptitiously.

Rose was shocked by what grief had done to Maggie. It wasn't so much her thinness as the dullness in her eyes, the hopelessness that bowed her shoulders and sagged in her face. Rose had seen Maggie grieve for her father and for Ralph Verney, her first love, but this time it was different. However bad things were, Maggie had always kept her chin up and her back straight but now it was as if all the strings that had held her erect had been cut. Rose was worried about her.

Maggie was making no secret of her love for Hugo. She called out Tom Teale to make a coffin and announced that Hugo would be buried at the farm. Rose's father had tried to make noises about a funeral in the church, but Maggie had just shaken her head.

'Hugo was a Quaker,' she said. 'He didn't go to church and he wouldn't want to be buried in the churchyard. He loved the land, and this is where he's going to be.'

As vicar, Rose's papa had disapproved strongly, but felt that he was duty-bound to attend. It was surprising, in fact, how many people had turned out for the funeral of a conscientious objector. Rose looked around and saw to her dismay that Mick had come, too. They hadn't had many opportunities to meet and perhaps he thought there would a chance to talk today, but how could she talk to him when both her parents were here? And what was *Levi* doing here? Rose stood between her parents and tried not to look at either of them.

Sam Pearson had volunteered to dig the grave and now he and Tom Teale were lowering the plain coffin into the hole.

Charles Haywood spoke to Maggie. 'Would you like me to say a prayer, my dear?'

'No,' Maggie said starkly. She drew a breath, perhaps realising how brusque she had sounded, and added after a moment, 'Thank you, vicar, but no. Hugo told me that Quaker services don't have prayers. He said that when his wife and baby son died, he sat with the Friends in silence until someone at the meeting was moved to speak. So I think we should do the same.'

There was some shuffling as nobody quite knew what to do, but Maggie kept silent, her head bent in grief, so they all did the same. Rose found herself pitying Maggie. She knew how deep her friend's feelings for Hugo had gone, and now Maggie was trapped with Joe Sugden, who was more dead than alive.

What if it were Mick who had died? Rose asked herself. Losing him would take away all her joy, all hope for future at a stroke. She stole a glance at him, standing on the other side of the grave, and saw him watching her. She would have to find a way to talk to her parents soon, but it was hard to broach the subject. Her father's beliefs about the way the world was had taken so many blows since the start of the war and now it felt as if class distinctions were the only certainties he could hold onto.

'People thought Hugo was a coward,' Maggie broke the silence after a while, and Rose hurriedly brought her attention back to the funeral. 'But he was the bravest man I have ever known. He lived according to his beliefs and he never wavered. He was wise and he was strong and he was kind. He was a dear friend and I loved him.'

She stared around as if daring anyone to disapprove and bent to pick up a handful of dirt. Tossing it into the grave, she listened to it spattering on top of the coffin before stepping back and relapsing into silence.

It stretched out while they all stood a little uncertainly, then Janet Airey stepped forward. 'I was one of them that called him a coward,' she admitted, 'but then I saw him run into a burning building to save a child. Maggie's right. He weren't no coward. He had courage of his own kind.'

There was another silence and then Sam Pearson touched Maggie's arm. 'Why don't you go in out of the cold, Maggie? I'll finish up here.'

Maggie nodded stiffly. With one last look at the coffin, she held out a hand to Jacob who had been watching with huge, solemn eyes, and the two of them started walking back to the farmhouse where Grace Armitage had arranged for Molly to lay out a funeral tea earlier.

After a moment, the other mourners followed. Rose tried to stick with her parents, but Levi was obviously intent on speaking to her and she didn't want them to overhear anything he might say. Pretending to have a problem with her shoe, she fell back.

'What are you doing here, Levi?' she asked sharply when he lingered nearby. 'You're not a friend of Maggie's.'

'I came because I knew you'd be here,' he said. 'I haven't had a chance to talk to you properly since that day we kissed.'

'*We* didn't kiss,' Rose hissed at him. 'You kissed me and I didn't like it.'

'You won't even talk to me now,' Levi complained as if she hadn't spoken. 'You've been avoiding me, Rose. You know you have. I used to see you all the time,' he said, exaggerating, 'but you won't even stop for a chat now. When I think of what I did for you too!'

Rose stilled. 'What do you mean?'

'You know what I mean, Rose. Ava Bainbridge was going to tell your father about you and Mick, wasn't she?' Levi put on a mocking falsetto, '"Oh Levi, what shall I do? Oh Levi, please can you get my letter back for me? Oh Levi, please make sure my father doesn't find out." And I made sure he didn't, didn't I? *Didn't I?*' he repeated savagely when Rose said nothing.

'I didn't ask you to set fire to the Woolpack,' she said in a low voice.

'But who would believe that? You were the only

one who had anything to gain from Ava's death. The letter disappeared, didn't it? If you tell anyone it was me, I'll tell them you begged me to do it. You've known the truth all this time, Rose, and not said anything. What would your precious parents say about that? Or the hospital? Think they'd still let you be a nurse if they knew what you'd done?'

No, they wouldn't. Even the hint of a suspicion of such a terrible thing would lead to her dismissal, Rose was sure. Arrangements were being made to close the hospital and move all the patients out so that Lord and Lady Miffield could take up residence in Miffield Hall again, so she would not be able to continue anyway, but even so, Rose couldn't bear to think of her nursing career ending on such a note.

She knew what it was like in a village. Once the rumour started, people would whisper behind their hands. They would tell each other there was no smoke without fire or say that they'd always thought there was something funny about the vicar's daughter. Rose could practically hear Mary Ann Teale or Betty Porter clicking their tongues and shaking their heads.

And when the rumour reached her parents, as it inevitably would, it would be even worse. They might believe that she hadn't asked Levi to burn down the Woolpack, but it would mean telling them that she had been keeping a secret from them for three years, and that she loved a man who was unlikely to ever meet with their approval.

'What do you want from me?' she asked Levi

dully, and he smiled and ran his tongue around his teeth.

'Just a little of your time, Rose, that's all. I want you to come and see my new house. I hope you'll like it. Why don't you come and I'll show you round? Half an hour: is that too much to ask?'

'Can Mick come, too?'

'No!' He frowned. 'I want you all to myself.'

'You're not going to try and kiss me again, are you?'

'I just want to be with you, Rose. Why can't you understand that?'

Why couldn't Levi understand that she didn't want to be with him? Rose thought wildly, but she replied, 'If I come and see your house, will that be it?'

'When can you come?' Levi's face lit up. 'Now?'

Rose glanced at the funeral party walking towards the farmhouse. 'No, of course not now!' Mick was looking over his shoulder at them.

'Tomorrow, then?'

'Soon,' was all Rose could bring herself to say. 'We'd better catch the others up.'

It was a relief to hurry after the others and to get away from him, but she was too unnerved to find Mick or her parents, especially her father, who loathed Levi and would want to know what she had been talking to him about.

Luckily she spied Dot, who was contemplating the spread of cakes and sandwiches in the parlour.

'Did you make all these cakes, Dot?'

'I thought I'd give Molly a hand,' said Dot. 'Maggie's no cook, and in no state to think about

114

cakes, neither, but you've got to give death a send-off, that's what Ma always used to say.'

'How is your mother?'

Dot made a face. 'She's getting better but she's still not herself.' Her eyes rested on Agnes Colton who was standing with Betty Porter and Mary Ann Teale, their heads close together over cups of tea. 'This is the first time she's been out for weeks. It was Mary Ann's idea. She said everybody always likes a funeral.'

'She looks like she's enjoying herself,' Rose commented.

'Aye, well, she'll be catching up with all the gossip from Betty – and there's Janet Airey, going over. She looks like she's got a little morsel for them, don't you think?' said Dot with a cynical look. 'They should have employed Janet on the front line. She'd have got the news up and down the trenches faster than you can say "Over the top, lads".'

Rose couldn't help laughing. 'I'm terrified of her,' she confessed.

'Oh, Janet's bark is worse than her bite. She'll stick her nose in where it's not wanted, but she's got a kind heart.'

Would she be kind enough to understand how Rose could possibly have let herself get embroiled with Levi Dingle, though?

Dot was eyeing the crowd. 'It's a pretty good turnout for a conchie,' she said. 'Look, even Clarence Terry's here. Probably just for the free tea and cake, the old skinflint,' she added indulgently. 'And there's Sam Pearson, making eyes at that Grace Armitage. Might as well hang out a sign to say they're sweet on each other.'

Rose followed Dot's gaze. Sam and Grace weren't touching at all, but something in the way they leant towards each other, the way their eyes met, made it obvious that they might as well have been the only people in the room. As Betty Porter tried to squeeze past on her way to the tea table, Sam put his hand on Grace's back to move her out of the way. It was just a small gesture, but there was an intimacy about it that Rose envied. Would she and Mick ever be able to stand together in public like that?

'I see all the Pickles are here, too,' Dot was saying. 'Course, Maggie were always very fond of Frank,' she went on. 'Killed in France, he was, she told me.'

'I remember,' said Rose, glad to contribute something to the conversation. 'He was under-age when he joined up. It was Ava Bainbridge who prodded him into enlisting and when Maggie heard that he'd been killed, she stormed into the Woolpack and went for Ava.'

'*Did* she?'

'They had to pull Ava and Maggie apart.'

Rose was beginning to wish she hadn't mentioned Ava. It brought back too many bad memories, especially with Levi in the room. She could hear him somewhere, laughing too loudly, sounding much more Irish than he usually did. When she risked a glance round, she could see him slinging an arm around Mick as he complained about the lack of whisky and announcing how the Irish managed their wakes much better.

'Isn't that right, brother?' he said, clapping

Mick on the back. Mick himself looked torn between feeling that Levi was acting inappropriately and pleasure at Levi's affection.

Rose sighed. A tension headache was nagging behind her eyes and she forced her attention back to Dot, who was saying that she didn't blame Maggie.

'I never liked that Ava. She were a nasty piece of work. And they should never have taken Frank. It must have been obvious that he were a daft lummock. No harm to him, but more than a few slates loose in his roof,' she said. 'Ned's nearly as big as him now, and a lot sharper by the look of him.'

'Yes, he's a nice boy,' said Rose, wincing inwardly at the sound of Levi's voice behind her.

'I'm surprised to see Polly Warcup here, though,' Dot went on. 'I wouldn't have thought she and Maggie had much in common.'

Rose was in the middle of telling Dot how she and Maggie had helped deliver Polly's twin girls, when her parents joined them. Rose suspected they were trying to get as far away from Levi as possible. Her father's lip was visibly curling.

Edith Haywood accepted with a smile of thanks as Dot offered to refill her cup of tea. 'How are you, Dot?'

'Fair to middlin',' said Dot in her brisk way. 'I'm sorry the hospital is closing. I mean, I'm glad there's no need for it any more, but I'll be out of a job.'

'I'm going to miss working there, too,' Rose agreed, very aware of Mick lurking, waiting to speak to her. She turned her shoulder deliberately

117

on him.

'Dot made all these cakes,' she told her mother. 'They're absolutely delicious.'

Edith nodded. She looked at Dot. 'If you're looking for a job, I don't suppose you'd consider coming to work at the vicarage?'

'It's nice of you to think of me, Mrs Haywood, but I don't want to go into service again. I'm hoping to go back to Bradford as soon as my mother's well enough.'

'Oh.' Edith looked down into her cup of tea, clearly thinking. 'What about if you came in to prepare some meals for as long as you're here? You wouldn't have to serve them. The maid or I could put them in the oven and cook the vegetables. We'd pay you well for that.'

Rose felt her father stiffen, while Dot put her head on one side to consider the matter. She looked like a little sparrow, with bright eyes and a deceptively dowdy plumage.

'That's an idea,' she agreed. 'I could mebbe pick up similar work in other kitchens too, just making pastry or cakes and odds and sods.' She smiled at Edith. 'I'll come and see you tomorrow, shall I? We can work out the details then.'

'That would be wonderful.'

As Dot moved off, Charles Haywood swelled with annoyance. 'Edith, what do you mean by making an arrangement without consulting me? *We'd pay you well*, indeed!'

'If you want decent meals again, Charles, you'll have to pay for them!'

Leaving her parents to the argument that seemed to be brewing, Rose stepped away only to

118

run into Mick, jolting her tea into her saucer.

'Oh, I'm sorry, I was in your way,' said Mick, and then, in an undertone, 'I thought I was never going to get a chance to speak to you!'

Uncomfortably aware of her father's eyes on her, Rose made sure her back was turned to him. 'Be careful,' she muttered, her headache tightening to a drilling pain behind her eyes. 'I don't want my parents to suspect anything. Papa's already disgusted by Levi's behaviour.'

'What do you mean?'

'Levi did everything he could to make Papa disapprove of you. That's why he was hanging round your neck and calling you brother in a loud voice.'

'He was a bit loud, I know, but he was only being affectionate.'

'He was doing it deliberately,' snapped Rose, her eyes bright with temper. 'He wants my father to disapprove of you as well as of him.'

'Ah, Rose, don't say that.' Mick put out a hand but she stepped sharply back.

'Don't!' she said, and the next moment her father was looming beside them.

'Is this fellow bothering you, Rose?' he demanded, glowering at Mick.

'No,' said Rose quickly. 'It's nothing, Papa. Nothing at all.'

Spring 1919

Chapter Twelve

'Rose, dear, why are you so restless today?' Edith Haywood looked up from her sewing as Rose threw down the book she had been trying to read.

I'm restless *every* day, Rose wanted to snap, but she didn't want to upset her mother, who was just beginning to lose the shattered look that she had worn ever since the news of Arthur's death had arrived.

'I don't know what to do with myself now-adays,' she said instead. The hospital had closed a month earlier and Rose was missing her life as a VAD even more than she had thought she would. Her father was delighted to have her at home again, but her days stretched emptily now and she was rarely alone. It was harder to slip away to meet Mick. His cousin, Jonah, had agreed to invest in the garage which Mick had now opened in the old smithy and their hurried meetings were often scratchy and unsatisfactory.

And they all wondered why Rose was restless.

'We're invited to take tea with Violet Verney at Miffield Hall this afternoon,' her mother offered, as if that could be considered a treat.

Rose didn't want to drink tea and listen to Lady Miffield complaining about how hard it was to restore the Hall after its use as a hospital. How could she sit in a room where she had watched men suffer and die and pretend to care about curtains and carpets and holes in the wall?

The telltale creak of the gate made her jump up, glad of the distraction. 'That must be the post. I'll go and see if there are any letters.'

'Perhaps there will be a letter for your father from the Army,' Edith said hopefully.

'I'll go and see.'

Rose was beginning to think that there was something the Army didn't want to tell them. Why else would they prevaricate in response to her father's anguished letters? Whenever she mentioned it to Mick, he got cross and told her that they should all drop the matter but how could they? Arthur had died for his country; didn't they deserve to know what had happened to him?

Whenever Rose remembered how good-humoured Mick had been when she first met him, a knot twisted in her belly. Nowadays it was rare to see the teasing glint in his eyes or the smile she loved so much tugging at the corners of his mouth.

It was partly her fault, Rose knew that. Mick didn't understand why she was reluctant to distress her bereaved parents by telling them the truth about him. He thought she should just come out with it, and how could Rose explain how devastated they would be, particularly her beloved papa, who had had so many of his illusions shattered by the war and its aftermath? He would hate the idea of her marrying Mick, and Rose couldn't bear to make him unhappy.

Torn between Mick's frustration and her

father's prejudices, Rose was left with a permanent tension headache.

There were no letters on the mat so she opened the door in case the post boy was still sorting through his bag. Before the war, she would never have opened the door herself. She would have waited for their maid to bring any letters in on a tray. It was like remembering another world. Rose could only wonder now that she had not expired of boredom.

The doorstep was as empty as the mat. So who had come in the gate? Rose went into the kitchen to see what Dot knew.

Edith Haywood had eventually managed to find a maid, a shy young girl called Marjorie who was the niece of Janet Airey's cousin, or some such complicated relationship. Marjorie could clean but she had little experience of cooking and her meals were hardly better than Edith's, which was saying something, Rose thought. Not that she could talk; she couldn't cook either.

In the end, the vicar had succumbed to the longing for a decent dinner and had agreed to Dot coming to the vicarage every morning to prepare a meal. Dot had driven a hard bargain: she would cook, but she wouldn't clean and she wouldn't carry in trays of tea and she wouldn't open the door. Papa didn't like it, but Rose admired the way Dot knew exactly what she wanted and refused to let herself be intimidated into doing anything else.

She would be outside smoking a cigarette, Rose thought, putting her head round the kitchen door and seeing an empty kitchen. The vicar disapproved strongly of women smoking and had expressly forbidden Dot to smoke in the vicarage but Dot didn't care. She knew Rose's father was enjoying his dinners again and she did what she wanted.

Rose wished she were as brave as Dot.

She could hear Marjorie brushing the stairs so wandered through the kitchen and scullery and out the back door. She missed her conversations with Dot as they walked to and from the hospital. Like so much else, life seemed to be reverting back to the way it had been before the war. Class distinctions hadn't seemed to matter so much during the war, and Rose hated the way they were all becoming more aware of them again.

'Dot?' she called.

'Round here,' came the reply and Rose followed the sound of Dot's voice around the wood store to the kitchen garden where Dot was sitting on a low wall, her hair tied up in a scarf, a coat slung around her shoulders against the cool air. A thin spiral of smoke drifted up from the cigarette she held in right hand.

She was not alone.

Mick sat beside her on the wall, looking completely at home. He wore a tweed cap and jacket and his shirt was open at the neck. His legs were spread, his feet planted firmly in their boots and he leant forward on his knees, his own cigarette wedged between his thumb and forefinger.

It struck Rose how comfortable Dot and Mick looked together. They had much more in common than she and Mick did, she thought with a pang. Dot's mother would probably be delighted if Dot wanted to marry Mick.

Dot thought of herself as plain, but Rose didn't think she was plain at all. True, her features were unremarkable but she had beautiful skin and her eyes were bright, like a little bird's. And while she might not be tall, there was something defiant about the set of her chin. She held herself like a challenge, as if defying anyone to ignore her. Rose could easily imagine a man like Mick finding Dot taking.

Neither of them looked embarrassed to be caught talking together. 'Hello, there,' said Dot casually, and Mick got to his feet with a smile.

'What are you doing here?' Rose could hear the sharpness in own voice and winced inwardly. It was ridiculous to feel excluded, she knew that, but she couldn't help it.

'I was hoping to see you,' he said, his smile fading. 'Are you free this afternoon?'

'I'm having tea at Miffield Hall,' she said. She glanced over her shoulder. 'You shouldn't come here like this, Mick,' she whispered. 'If Papa sees you, how will we explain it?'

'We'll tell him the truth, that I've come to see Dot here.' A coolness crept into Mick's voice. 'I've got a proposition to put to her.'

'I haven't agreed yet, mind,' Dot put in.

'What sort of proposition?' Rose asked stiffly.

Dot patted the wall beside her. 'Sit down and Mick'll tell you.'

'I've had a letter from Jonah,' Mick said at the same time, and Rose firmly quashed the sulky realisation that he had told Dot before her.

'He hasn't changed his mind about investing in

the garage, has he?'

'The opposite,' said Mick with a return to some of his old ebullience. 'He wants to come up and see what I've done so far.'

'Where's he going to stay?'

'That's just it. He'll have to stay with me at the smithy. There isn't anywhere else now the Woolpack is no more.'

'Can't Levi put him up? It's not as if he doesn't have room. He could put up half an army of cousins in there!'

Mick hunched a shoulder. 'Levi's got other stuff going on at the moment.'

'So he's said no? When are you going to realise that he won't lift a finger to help you, Mick,' said Rose in frustration.

'Don't start this again, Rose,' said Mick defensively. 'Levi's got his own life. He's not interested in the garage, and why should he be?'

'He should be prepared to help his own brother.' Rose couldn't understand why Mick was so blind to Levi's faults.

'Look, it's not a problem. Jonah can stay with me at the smithy, but he won't enjoy my cooking very much. So I've asked Dot if she'll prepare some meals for me, same as she does here at the vicarage.'

'I'll prepare the meals for you to heat up later, but I'm not doing any washing up or clearing away,' Dot said.

'Now, Dot, is washing up not part of cooking?' Mick countered with a cajoling look. The kind of teasing look he had once given Rose to make her laugh.

128

Dot was having none of it. 'That's the deal. Take it or leave it.'

'Sure, you're a hard woman,' Mick said, but he was smiling.

Left out of their banter, Rose had a chance to think about the implications of Dot's new arrangement with Mick.

'You're not going to leave us, are you, Dot?' she asked in dismay, thinking of how much the vicarage meals had improved lately.

'No, I reckon I can manage both houses easily,' Dot said. 'I'll come here first, then nip round to smithy and do some cooking there. I might do some at home,' she added, thinking about it. 'I'll have to work out the rationing, of course, but I don't mind working hard and earning more.'

'You're a gem, Dot.'

Rose bit her lip. She couldn't imagine ever being confident enough in the kitchen to do what Dot was doing. She would never be a gem, but if she and Mick ever got married, she would have to learn how to cook and keep house for him.

If.

It was getting harder and harder to imagine it.

Dot and Mick were in the middle of a good-humoured negotiation about what the new arrangement would cost. Rose was sitting on the wall and feeling ridiculously excluded once more when her father's booming voice made them all jump.

'What on earth is going on out here?' he demanded.

He had appeared without warning around the side of the vicarage, and Rose got to her feet,

129

horribly conscious of how guilty she looked.

'Nothing's going on, Papa,' she said. 'I was just ... having a word with Dot.'

'And what is that fellow doing here?' Her father glared at Mick, who had pulled off his cap deferentially, although there was nothing cringing about the way he stood and met the vicar's eyes.

'Be off with you!' Charles Haywood glowered. 'You've got no business being here!'

'Begging your pardon, Vicar, but I had some business to discuss with Miss Colton here.'

'Miss Colton can discuss business with you in her own time,' Rose's father snapped. 'I know who you are, Dingle. You and your brother have brought nothing but trouble to Beckindale!'

There was a dangerous silence before Mick deliberately dropped the stub of his cigarette and ground it out with the heel of his boot.

His normally good-humoured face was hard and his voice colder than she had ever heard it. 'I'm sorry if I've caused trouble for you, Dot,' he said. 'We'll talk later.' He put his cap back on and offered a brisk nod of farewell. 'Miss Haywood, Vicar,' he said and walked off, but being Mick he took his own good time.

Bristling with outrage, her father watched him go. 'Damned insolent fellow!'

'What did he say that was insolent?' Rose demanded, almost in tears of humiliation.

'It's not what he says, it's the way he stands there! You saw the way he sauntered off! Typical Irish,' the vicar said, still scowling. 'They don't know their place. I don't want to find him hanging around here again, Dot, do you hear me?'

'Oh, aye,' said Dot, stubbing out her cigarette on the wall. 'I hear you.'

'Papa–'

'That's enough, Rose. I don't want to discuss this any more. What are you doing out here anyway? Come inside at once.'

Miserably, Rose followed her father in. There was no use arguing with him when he was in that mood, but she was mortified at the way he had treated both Mick and Dot, and ashamed of herself at not standing up for them more effectively.

Mick had been angry at the way her father had spoken to him and Rose didn't blame him, but he didn't understand the terrible strain Papa was under or the awful guilt he felt for having encouraged Arthur to go to war.

She was torn between the two men she loved, and at the same time she felt increasingly as if she didn't belong anywhere. She didn't belong at the vicarage, she didn't belong smoking with Dot, and she was starting to wonder if she really did belong with Mick.

She didn't belong at Miffield Hall that afternoon either. By the time she had listened to Violet Verney complaining for an hour of the damage that the hospital had done to the Hall, Rose's excuse of a headache was real.

'I'll walk home,' she told her mother when a groom had brought round the vicarage's pony and trap.

Walking home had once been a favourite excuse to slip off and meet Mick, Rose remembered. Everything had seemed so much simpler then, in spite of the war. What had happened to

131

that fizz of anticipation when she hurried to meet him? Now all she felt was a dull dread at how resentful he would be at the way her father had spoken to him, and shame at how spineless she must have seemed.

Rose dawdled at the end of the lane leading up to the smithy to check that the coast was clear, then walked briskly up and along the track so that she could slip into the smithy the back way. Listening at the door to the workshop, she couldn't hear any voices, so she pushed it open. 'Mick?'

In the workshop, all that could be seen of Mick were the legs sticking out from underneath a chassis.

'Come to slum it after your tea at the Hall?'

Rose bit her lip at the bitterness of the disembodied voice. 'It's not like that.'

'Isn't it? That's what it feels like to me.'

'Can you come out?' she said with a sigh. 'I can't talk to you when I can only see your legs.'

Mick sighed and pushed himself out from underneath the car. Climbing to his feet, he wiped his oily hands on a rag. 'So you're happy to talk now?' he said, clearly not ready to let go of his resentment. 'You couldn't wait to get rid of me earlier.'

'You know we can't talk at the vicarage,' she began, but he cut her off.

'Why not? Because your precious papa might see you talking to me? Why don't you just admit it, Rose: you're ashamed of me.'

'I'm not!' she said hotly.

'Then why won't you stand up and tell your

132

father that I'm the man you love and want to marry?'

'It's a hard time for him at the moment,' Rose said. 'Arthur–'

'You know what, Rose?' Mick interrupted her again. 'I don't want to hear any more about Arthur,' he said. 'I'm sorry your brother is dead, but he's not the only boy who died in this war. It's a hard time for everyone. The question is, are you prepared to make it better? Or do you just want to keep me hanging on until you're ready to give up your comfortable life in the vicarage?'

'That's not fair!'

'Isn't it? It's the way it looks to me. You should have seen yourself this morning, Rose, terrified in case your parents saw you mixing with the riff raff.'

'It's so easy for you,' Rose said, as angry as Mick by then. 'You've only got to think about what *you* want. I love my parents. Is it so wrong that I don't want to upset them? But you keep pushing me to choose between you. That's what's not fair, Mick!'

'Then choose one or the other, Rose,' said Mick. He turned away with an exclamation of disgust. 'I'm sick of this. You can't keep both of us happy.'

She stared at him. 'So what are you saying? It's you or Papa?'

'I'm saying, decide what it is you really want and what you're prepared to do for it. It's up to you, Rose,' he said. 'I'm not going to ask you any more. I don't have much to offer you at the moment, but if you want me, I'm yours.' Dropping back to the ground, he wriggled into position so that he could slide under the car once more. 'Come back when you've made up your mind and let me know what you've decided.'

Chapter Thirteen

Slamming the workshop door behind her, Rose stormed down the track, twin flags of hectic colour in her cheeks, and brown eyes blazing. How dare Mick accuse her of being ashamed of him?! How dare he lay down ultimatums and make her choose between him and her beloved father! He was rude and pig-headed and selfish and if he thought she would go crawling back to the smithy and beg him to come out from under some wretched car, he had another think coming!

Sheer rage drove her down the lane and as far as the turning towards the village, where she hesitated. She couldn't go home in this temper. But where else could she go? All her favourite places were associated with Mick now.

Gazing hopelessly around, Rose's eyes fell on Emmerdale Farm, nestled in the fold of hillside on the far side of river. Maggie would understand. Relieved to have a destination, she marched on, and when she heard a motor car behind her, she moved onto the verge to let it pass. She turned her face away as if interested in the brambles growing over the drystone wall. She knew that she must look flushed and upset and she didn't want anyone to see her like this.

Instead of passing, the car slowed to a stop beside her, and before Rose heard the voice she knew with a sinking heart who it would be. Levi Dingle. As if this day wasn't bad enough!

'Why, Rose,' he said, 'what are you doing out here all alone?'

'Taking a walk,' she said shortly.

'Jump in. I'll take you for a spin.'

'No, thank you.' She couldn't deal with Levi right now. Rose started to walk briskly again, but Levi kept pace in the car.

'Oh, dear, you look very upset, Rose,' he said. 'The two lovebirds haven't had a row have they?'

Ignoring him, Rose strode on, her face set.

'What's Mick done? Has he hurt you? Do you want me to go and talk to him for you?'

'Please stop following me, Levi.'

'But I can't leave you when you're like this,' Levi protested as the car crawled along beside her. 'Let me take you home at least.'

'I'm not going home. I'm going to Emmerdale Farm.'

'Then I'll take you there.'

He was quite capable of creeping beside her all the way, Rose realised. She felt ridiculous, marching along with the great car inching beside her. Besides, she still had on the shoes she had worn to tea at Miffield Hall and they were pinching her toes.

Exasperated, she swung round 'Oh, all *right*,' she said ungraciously.

Unperturbed by her rudeness, Levi leapt out to open the passenger door for her with a delighted smile. Sweeping past him, Rose thumped into the seat and sat staring grimly forwards. He had practically forced her into the car; she didn't see why she should make polite conversation too.

'There now, that's much more comfortable, isn't it?'

Levi put the car into gear and it jerked forward. Rose had to put out a hand to brace herself against the polished walnut dashboard to stop herself pitching into the windscreen.

'Sorry!' said Levi gaily. 'I must get Mick to look at the clutch. He could probably do with me putting some business his way.' He slid a sideways glance at Rose. 'The garage doesn't seem to be doing very well, does it?'

Rose wasn't going to discuss Mick with Levi. She turned her head away and looked at the fields rushing past.

'What have you and Mick been arguing about?'

'It's none of your business, Levi.'

'I hate seeing you upset,' he said fervently.

'If you cross the bridge here, you can take the road up on the left,' was all Rose could say in reply.

'I've missed you,' Levi tried again. 'You've never been to see my house and you *promised* you would.' He glanced at her with a grotesque little pout.

'I've been busy,' said Rose.

'What with?'

'With the hospital closing and ... other things.'

'I can't help feeling hurt,' he said. 'I *thought* we had an agreement. We wouldn't want your dear papa to know you were a girl who doesn't keep

136

her word, would we?'

Rose's lips tightened. She was tempted to tell Levi to tell her father whatever he liked. If Mick was going to be pig-headed, then perhaps she should accept now that the social gap between them was too big to bridge.

But Levi might not just tell her father.

He might tell the police.

He might tell them anything. He might lie. He might tell them that he had burnt down the Woolpack at her instigation. Of course, the police would be far more likely to believe a vicar's daughter than Levi, whose business dealings flirted on the wrong side of the law, but still, she would have to answer questions. The suspicion would always be there and the shame it would bring to her family would destroy her father.

Rose's heart was thudding painfully in her chest. Why would Levi confess to such a crime? He would be punished more than she would. But he was so strange, he might do anything. She couldn't risk it.

'I'll come and see your house tomorrow,' she said in a flat voice as the car drew up at Emmerdale Farm.

'What time?'

'Eleven o'clock.'

'I'll be waiting for you,' said Levi, satisfaction mingling with menace in his voice.

Rose didn't look at him as she got out of the car and walked towards the gate. The knowledge that Levi would hold the fire at the Woolpack over her head as long as he wanted made her breath shorten with panic. She would never be free of him, she thought bleakly.

She found Maggie in the field behind the farm-house where lambing was in full swing. Watching the tiny lambs staggering after their mothers on unsteady legs made Rose's chest hurt in a way she couldn't explain.

Maggie was in her farming trousers, bending over a sheep. She looked up and smiled when she noticed Rose leaning on the gate, and came over.

'How's it going?' Rose asked, nodding at the lambing field.

'Not too bad. We lost a couple of lambs to foxes but we've had some twins too.' Maggie looked pale and tired but when she glanced at Rose, her pale grey eyes were as keen as ever. 'What is it?'

Rose pulled her gloves through her hands, irre-solute. 'Oh, it's nothing. I shouldn't bother you when you're so busy.'

'That's all right. I wouldn't mind a break.' Mag-gie leant against the drystone wall by the gate and turned her face up to the weak spring sun, but she didn't ask any more. There was silence for a while. Rose rested her arms on the gate and listened to the plaintive bleating of the lambs and felt calmer.

'I thought once the war was over and Mick was safely back that I'd have nothing to complain about,' she said at last. 'But here I am feeling miserable. I just thought things would be differ-ent somehow,' she said, knowing that she wasn't expressing herself very well, 'but they aren't. The hospital has closed, the patients have gone home or been moved on. Lord and Lady Verney are back at Miffield Hall. We've all gone back to the way we were.'

'Except we're not the same, are we?' said Maggie. 'I know I'm not. I don't think any of us are.'

'Papa is.'

'Is he?'

Rose thought about it. 'He's changed in some ways, but not others.'

'We're all adjusting after the war,' said Maggie. 'It's not easy.'

And harder for Maggie than most, Rose thought guiltily. Maggie had lost both men she had loved, first Ralph Verney and then Hugo, and was still trapped in a marriage with the husband she had hated while she struggled to support her son and keep Emmerdale Farm going. What did Rose have to complain about in comparison?

'How is it with Joe?' she asked.

'Better,' said Maggie after a moment. 'He still hasn't remembered anything, thank goodness. He's learnt my name and Jacob's, and I think he knows Grace and Molly now. He seems to remember how to do things around the farm. He can harness Blossom and he's been ploughing the lower field. The first time I went to show him what to do and there was a kind of flicker in his face, as if he almost remembered.

'It's strange,' she said. 'Joe always used to complain about farming, but now he seems to find it comforting to have a job to do, and he likes being with the animals – all except Fly, of course. He can obviously sense her fear of him, but Laddie loves him. It's so hard to know what he thinks about anything, though.'

'Does he talk?'

'Very little,' said Maggie, 'and it's an effort for

139

him. Still, it's much better than when he just sat with that vacant expression.' She shuddered at the memory. 'Now at least he can be useful. That makes a difference.' She glanced at Rose. 'Especially as I'm going to have another baby.'

Rose's mouth fell open. 'A baby? Is it–?'

'It's Hugo's.'

'Oh, Maggie...' Rose didn't know what to say.

'I know it was wrong,' said Maggie. 'I'm an adulteress.' She said it firmly. 'My husband and my child were in the house and I was in the stable with another man. How shameless can you be? But I don't feel ashamed. I just wanted some happiness, something I could remember Hugo by.' She sighed. 'I knew I'd have to say goodbye but I didn't care, and it was so...'

Her voice failed her and she looked away. 'The next morning I went into the stable and Hugo was dying. It was so ... *unfair.* And then I realised I was pregnant and it feels like a parting gift from him.'

Rose was trying hard not to be shocked. She had been a nurse for three years, but she knew that she was still an innocent in many ways. 'What are you going to do?'

'What can I do?' said Maggie. 'I'm having it, one way or another.' She laid a protective hand on her stomach. 'And I'm keeping it. This child is all I have of Hugo now.'

'But what about Joe?'

Maggie's eyes slid away. 'I don't know. I'm not sure he would understand. He's gentle with Jacob, and Jacob loves him. I'm glad about that. I hope he'll be the same with this child. As far as the rest of the world is concerned, this will be

Joe's child, but for me it will always be Hugo's. Hugo's and mine.'

Rose was thinking about Maggie as she made her way to Levi's house the next morning. Everybody in Beckindale knew where it was, of course. It stood on the edge of the village, but completely apart. Instead of the cosy grey stone cottages and the sturdy elegance of the vicarage and other houses, Levi's house was built in a starkly modern style, with pebbledash walls painted white, and huge windows. The gardens had yet to be land-scaped and the house stood in a sea of mud and weeds, looking cold and isolated.

Better get it over and done with, Rose told herself, but still she hesitated at the gate. She didn't want to be there. She didn't want to go inside. She didn't want to be alone with Levi.

She was tired after a sleepless night going over and over her argument with Mick. He had been so cold, so definite. Her father or him. Rose couldn't understand why Mick didn't see why that was an impossible choice for her to make. It wasn't fair of him to throw down an ultimatum and then hide away under his car. He should be protecting her from his brother, not making her feel guilty.

'Just do it,' Rose said out loud. All she had to do was walk up the drive, ring the bell and let Levi boast about his ghastly house. How hard could that be?

Levi answered the door himself, a triumphant smile on his face. 'At last! Come in, come in.' He ushered her into a large hall tiled in black and white. It had mirrors on the walls and strange, angular furniture. A grand staircase swept up to the first floor.

'I paid for a top designer,' Levi boasted, throwing open the double doors to a drawing room with a flourish. 'Everything is in the latest style.' He looked eagerly at Rose. 'What do you think?'

'It's very ... modern,' she said, regarding the uncomfortable looking sofas and chairs and hard-edged cabinets without enthusiasm.

Levi took that as a compliment and looked pleased. 'Wait till you see upstairs.'

Rose hesitated. She didn't like the idea of going any further into the house alone with Levi, although she was afraid of how he might react to a refusal.

'Do you have any servants at the moment?' It must surely take some staff to look after such a large house.

Levi's face darkened. 'Only one maid. It's hopeless! An agency sends staff from Bradford but they hate the country and won't stay. The last cook left after a day!'

Rose didn't blame them. She wouldn't want to work for Levi either.

'It's hard to get servants nowadays,' she said. 'Nobody wants to be in service any more.'

'You've got a maid at the vicarage. And I heard that Dot Colton is your cook,' he added enviously. 'Everybody says she's a good cook.'

'She is, but she's not our cook. She comes in to prepare some meals but Dot is her own woman. Cooking is a business for her.'

Rose wondered with a pang if Dot was at the smithy now, cooking Mick a decent lunch for a change. Being a *gem*.

Mick would be much better off with someone like Dot, Rose thought bleakly. They were alike in their good-humoured practicality.

'Perhaps I could get her to come and cook for me,' Levi was saying. 'This maid has no idea at all. Her meals are inedible but she's all I can get. Do you think Dot would come here too? I'd pay her good money.'

'I've no idea,' said Rose distantly. 'You'd have to ask her.'

The thought of a maid in the house was somewhat reassuring, but Rose still felt uneasy as Levi insisted on taking her upstairs. The rumours in the village had not been wrong: there were no less than three bathrooms with indoor plumbing, tiled floors and grand marble wash stands, and six bedrooms.

'Electricity too!' Levi switched on the light which sprang glaringly to life, and Rose flinched.

Levi was making her uncomfortable. He was standing too close, looking at her too eagerly.

'So?' he asked.

'It's very impressive,' she said, wishing that he wouldn't stand between her and the door.

'You *do* like it? I'll change anything you don't like.'

His fervent expression chilled Rose. Not for the first time, she wondered if Levi was quite sane. Did he really expect her to take an interest in his house when he had had to blackmail her to come here?

'There's no need to change anything,' she said, edging towards the door.

'I wouldn't mind,' he said without moving. 'Anything you wanted.'

'There's nothing.' Rose summoned a smile. 'Excuse me, Levi. I must go.'

His face fell. 'But I thought you could stay and we could talk properly,' he protested.

'It's not possible today, I'm afraid.' She made herself stay calm but all at once Levi seemed to block the doorway and his eyes had grown cold.

The sound of a door opening below and footsteps on the stairs made her almost dizzy with relief.

'That must be your maid,' she said and pushed past Levi, evading the hand he instinctively put out to stop her.

The maid stopped on the landing, clearly surprised to see her. 'Excuse me, miss,' she said. 'I didn't realise you was here.'

'It's fine.' Rose smiled gratefully at her. 'Thank you for the tour, Levi,' she called over her shoulder as she practically ran down the stairs.

'Rose, wait!'

'Sorry, I must dash,' she said, hurrying towards the door. 'I'll let myself out.'

Chapter Fourteen

'Where's the fire?' said Dot as Rose came round the corner of the newsagent's so quickly they almost collided.

'Fire?' Rose stared fearfully at Dot, thoughts of

the Woolpack swirling in her head.

'You seem to be in a tearing hurry.'

'Oh, yes...' Rose managed a breathless little laugh. 'I suppose I was in a bit of a rush.' She drew a deep breath and let it out unsteadily. 'I wanted to get away.'

'Why, where have you been?'

Rose glanced around. The high street was busy that morning. Outside the chandler, Peter Swales and Tom Teale were conducting a noisy discussion about different kinds of rope, while Polly Warcup, looking harried, was chasing her twin girls who were squealing with laughter.

'Margaret! Rose! Come back here at once!'

Mary Ann Teale and Lizzy Gregson had their heads together outside the post office. Grace Armitage lifted a hand in greeting as she clicked her tongue to gee up old Blossom, and the cart wheels creaked as they trundled past. Jim Airey was leaning against the entrance to the butcher's in his striped apron, chatting up Hannah Rigg's niece, Agatha.

Dot followed Rose's eyes. 'I remember Aggie Rigg playing hopscotch before the war. She were all freckles and pigtails then. Makes me feel old to think she's old enough to flirt,' she said.

While she had been trapped at Levi's, Beckindale had been going about its business on a normal, bustling morning. Rose could hear the shrieks from the school playground, the buzz of chatter mingling with the country sounds so common she barely heard them unless she was listening for them: the distant bleating of sheep, clucking hens, the soft snorts of horses waiting

145

patiently outside the shops, their manes twitching.

Dot was looking curiously at Rose. 'Well?' she demanded.

'I was at Levi Dingle's house,' Rose confessed, lowering her voice.

'What!' Dot sounded appalled. *'Why?'*

'I can't explain,' said Rose wretchedly, 'but I had to go, and it's silly, but I got in a panic. Levi was standing between me and the door and I thought he wasn't going to let me go.' She shivered at the memory. 'Luckily, the maid came along and I escaped.' Pausing, she seemed to listen to what she had said. 'Escaped: that what it felt like.'

Dot frowned. 'What if the maid hadn't been there?'

'I'm sure Levi wouldn't have hurt me,' said Rose, although she could hear that she didn't sound sure at all. 'He just doesn't realise what is and isn't appropriate sometimes.'

'You want to be careful with that one,' Dot said firmly. 'You should tell Mick what he's like.'

'Mick won't listen to me.'

Dot cocked a brow at the snippy note in Rose's voice. 'Had a row, have you?'

'Yesterday. It was awful,' Rose burst out. 'You should have heard the way he spoke to me, Dot. As if he *hated* me!'

'Rose, Mick does not hate you,' said Dot patiently. 'He loves you madly, as you well know.'

'I don't think he loves me any more.' Rose sniffed, but summoned a smile to wish Betty Porter a good morning as she passed.

Betty had ears like a bat, and Dot waited until

146

she was well out of earshot before she replied.

'You don't think you might be overreacting just a little bit?'

'You didn't hear him, Dot,' said Rose tragically. 'I think this time he's had enough and he'll be relieved to have got rid of me.'

'Right, and I suppose relief was why he was like a bear with a sore head when I took him a pie for his dinner just now? When I asked him how he was, he just about bit my head off.'

'I'm surprised he snapped. He likes *you.*'

Dot started to laugh. 'Please tell me you're not jealous!'

'I can't be the only one who's noticed how well suited you and Mick are.'

'Don't be daft,' Dot said bluntly. 'Have you looked in a mirror lately? As if Mick would look at me when he's got you! I've seen the way his face lights up when he looks at you. That's not going to change because you had an argument.'

Horrified at the tears that sprang to her eyes, Rose blinked them away and ran her knuckle under her lashes to dispose of any lingering evidence of her weakness. 'I think this time he's had enough,' she told Dot. 'Mick doesn't want to wait any longer. He's given me a choice. I have to tell my parents about him or it's over. He doesn't understand how *difficult* it is!'

'I don't know, Rose,' said Dot with a sigh. 'Didn't we all have enough waiting during the war? It seems to me if that bloody war taught us anything, it's to take our chances when we have them, or it's too late. Look at Maggie Sugd–'

She broke off as Hannah Rigg bore down on

147

them, like a ship in full sail.

'Good morning, Miss Rigg.'

'Morning, Miss Haywood, morning Dot.' Hannah's eyes were bright with interest. 'You two are having a good chat.'

Nosy old bat, thought Rose. 'Just passing the time of day,' she said, baring her teeth in a smile.

'How's your ma doing, Dot?'

'Better, ta.'

Balked of gossip, Hannah smiled tightly and moved on.

Rose waited until she had gone before turning back to Dot. 'Have you seen Maggie lately? Do you know about...'

'The bairn? Aye, she told me. Not that she'll be able to hide it much longer. That'll give all the old cats summat to gossip about.'

'Will they know it's Hugo's child?'

'They'll have a good guess,' said Dot in a dry voice. 'It wouldn't take the likes of Janet Airey and Mary Ann Teale two seconds to put the truth together.'

'I was quite shocked,' Rose confessed.

'What, that she and the conchie got it together?'

'Well, yes. She *is* married.'

'It were never much of a marriage, even before Joe got blown up,' Dot said. 'Maggie told me that she loved Hugo, and after everything they'd been through, she didn't want to waste her one chance at happiness. And neither should you,' she told Rose. 'I know it'll be difficult to tell your ma and pa, but you're lucky, Rose. Mick's all right, he is,' she said. 'He's survived the war in one piece. He loves you and you love him. Don't throw that away. That really would be daft,' she finished. 'You might end up with a husband like Levi.'

Rose shuddered at the thought.

'Just think about it, that's all I'm saying,' said Dot.

Rose did think about it. She thought about nothing else for three long days as her sulk gradually subsided. She knew Dot was right and that she was lucky. Mick was a good man, and he loved her. If only he would be more understanding about her reluctance to tell her parents about him... Mick's accusation that she was ashamed of him still rankled, but in the bleak early hours when she lay awake, Rose wondered if that might have hurt more because it was partly true. Not completely true, she reassured herself hastily, but the differences between them would make it harder to convince her parents that he would be a good husband.

She had to make a decision. Too restless to sit still, Rose took herself off for a long walk. She had a long list of reasons why it would be better to end everything with Mick right then: Levi, her parents, the differences between them, Mick's refusal to understand her point of view ... oh, ending it was so clearly the sensible thing to do.

On the other side, there was just one reason not to end it: she loved him. The last few days had been wretched, and they would just be a foretaste of life if she went to Mick and told him that it would never work. Dot was right, it was stupid to throw away what they had when so many people had lost so much.

Rose had been more shocked than she wanted to admit to learn that Maggie was carrying Hugo's child. Maggie hadn't been embarrassed or ashamed or any of the things that Rose had been taught that immoral women should feel. She had loved Hugo, she said, and lying with him had been an expression of that love. For Maggie, it hadn't been sinful or shameful. It had felt right.

Rose's steps slowed on the bridge. Drawing the collar of her coat closer around her throat against the chilly wind that was making the daffodils under the walls dip and sway, she stood and looked down into the brown rushing river. The water was so high after a wet winter that the little beach where she had once met Mick had vanished.

Now she made herself remember how she felt when she was with him. She thought about how warm his hands were, how sure his lips. How his kiss made her whole body hum with pleasure.

What if they were to do more than kiss?

Rose was a virgin. She knew hardly anything about what was actually involved in the physical act of love. Doubtless the night before her wedding, her mother would explain it to her.

Or she could find out for herself.

And although she wasn't ready to accept Mick's ultimatum, perhaps there was a compromise...

Before she had a chance to change her mind, Rose made her way to the smithy, barely noticing the beauty of the warm spring evening. Mick was closing up the workshop when she arrived. He looked tired, she thought, as he paused in the middle of shutting the great door that had once opened into the forge. He straightened at the sight of her, watching tensely as she walked towards him.

'Hello Mick.'

'Rose,' he said warily.

'You told me to come back when I'd made a decision.'

'And have you?'

She drew a deep breath. 'I have,' she said. 'Can I come in?'

'Of course.'

They were being formal with each other, but at least Mick wasn't under a car. Rose's heart was beating hard as she stepped into the workshop and Mick pulled the great door to behind them.

The old furnace was cold, and where carthorses had once stood patiently, was now littered with pieces of motorcars; engines and tyres and a couple of doors were propped in one corner, and piles of rubber strips for mending punctures were in another. Cans of petrol were stacked by the door.

'We can't talk here,' said Mick. He led her through to the back of the smithy, where the choice was between a poky kitchen and a parlour that was musty and rarely used. Above were two bedrooms where Will Hutton, the blacksmith, and his son Billy had once lived.

Rose wrinkled her nose at the parlour. 'Let's sit outside at the back,' she suggested, and he nodded with relief, hurrying ahead to open the back door. It led into a scrubby garden, whose only redeeming feature was a stone bench placed to make the most of the evening. 'Can I get you anything?'

'No, I just want to talk.' Rose sat down and patted the bench beside her. 'And I want you to listen.'

Mick dropped heavily onto the bench. 'All right,' he said. 'You may as well get it over with.'

'What do you mean?'

'I've been waiting for you to come and tell me that it's over,' he said, leaning forward to rest his elbows on his knees. 'I don't blame you. I should never have started throwing ultimatums around. Of course you going to choose your parents.'

'I do choose them,' said Rose, 'but I choose you too.'

Mick turned his head to look at her, a glint of hope in his eyes. 'You do?'

'I'm not going to accept your ultimatum. I'm just not ready to tell my parents about you yet, Mick, but I know that's selfish. I hadn't realised how unfair that was on you.'

'What's the point of telling them, anyway?' he said with a sigh. 'Your father will never give me permission to marry you.'

'I'm twenty-one. I don't need his permission.'

'You want it, though.'

'Yes, I would like it,' she acknowledged. 'I love my father, but I love you too, Mick.'

'Do you?'

Her heart ached at the bitterness she heard. 'Yes,' she said. 'I do.'

Nerves fluttered alarmingly in her stomach as she reached for his hand. 'I'm not ashamed of you, Mick. I want to be your wife one day, and I will be, whatever my father says. But I'd like to wait a bit longer before I tell them about you.'

'I don't mind waiting,' he said quickly. 'Anything would be better than these last few days when I've had to contemplate life without you.'

'I've been doing the same,' Rose agreed. Lifting their entwined hands, she kissed his fingers. 'We're so lucky to have each other. Let's not spoil things by arguing.'

'No, you're right.' Mick's smile was brilliant with relief. 'Whatever you want, *acushla*. I'll do anything as long as you don't leave me again. We'll wait till you're ready to talk to your parents.'

'We may have to wait for the wedding, but we don't have to wait for everything.' Moistening her lips, Rose let go of Mick's hand and turned towards him. Very deliberately, she began to unfasten the buttons on her lawn blouse.

Mick's eyes darkened. 'You don't know what you're doing,' he said almost harshly.

'No,' Rose agreed, still fumbling with the buttons. 'I'm counting on you to show me.'

'Rose...' His voice was hoarse, and she drew confidence from it. 'You don't need to do this.'

'I do. I want to. I don't want to wait any longer, Mick. I want to love you now.'

He looked down at his stained overalls, the hands that were black with oil. 'I'm all dirty.'

'I like you dirty.'

Mick smiled at that. 'You might regret you said that,' he said.

Getting to his feet, he reached down to pull her up beside him. 'Come upstairs, *asthore*,' he said. 'Let me show you how much I love you.'

Trembling with nerves and excitement, Rose let him lead her up the rickety wooden stairs to the room above the workshop. It was plainly furnished with an iron bedstead, a chest of drawers and a rag rug on the floor. Mick went over to the window and closed the shutters, leaving only a strip of sunlight falling across the pillow.

He smiled as he turned to Rose and she smiled back, her nerves vanishing in the dark pulse of desire. Mick's hands were warm and sure as he undressed her, his lips grazing her skin as he went, and with every touch, Rose felt herself dissolving. Her breath shortened when he drew the blouse from her shoulders and tugged it free of her arms, and when he pressed his mouth to her shoulder, she gave an inarticulate gasp.

Mick's hands grew more insistent as he unfastened her skirt. It fell in a puddle of fabric on the floor. Rose stepped out of it in her petticoat.

'Now you,' she said, stepping forward to kiss the base of his throat and lifting her hands to the buttons on his overalls.

With a low sound almost like a growl, Mick shrugged off the overalls and let Rose undo his shirt, pulling it free of his trousers and laying her hands on his bare chest with a shiver of possession.

'You don't know how I've dreamed of this, *asthore*,' he said unsteadily and swept her up into his arms to lay her on the bed beneath him.

Her brown eyes were glowing as she linked her arms around his neck. 'Make love to me, Mick,' she said as she smiled and he bent to kiss her, pressing her down into the mattress with the weight of his body. Rose gave herself up to the sheer pleasure of touch and taste, to the swirl of sensations that pushed her to hold him tighter, kiss him more deeply, to want more and more and more.

Murmuring endearments against her flesh, Mick kissed his way down her body while she writhed and gasped. Her petticoat slithered over her skin, his hand slid insistently under the fine material, making her arch beneath him. Absorbed in each other, they didn't hear the sound of a motor approaching and Mick was deftly peeling off her petticoat when a loud banging on the door made Rose gasp with fright.

'Maybe they'll go away,' he whispered.

But the banging continued. 'Mick Dingle, are you there? Open up!'

'You'd better go and see,' Rose whispered back, terrified in case her father had somehow divined where she was and sent a posse to rescue her.

Cursing fluently under his breath, Mick rolled off Rose and groped for his trousers. Hair tousled, eyes dark with frustration, he threw open the shutters and glowered out. 'Holy Mother of God, somebody had better be about to die!' he growled.

'Ah, Mick, there you are!' Rose heard the voice say as she clutched the sheet over her bare breasts. 'You haven't forgotten me already have you? I'm your cousin Jonah.'

Chapter Fifteen

While Rose was standing on the bridge and trying to decide what to do about Mick, Dot perched on the wall opposite the Woolpack and lit a cigarette, ignoring Betty Porter's disapproving looks as she weeded her front garden further down the street. It was six o'clock on a May evening. The shops were closed, the farm work largely done. The residents of Beckindale were at home eating supper or, like Betty, tending their gardens. Dot blew out a defiant cloud of smoke. What was there to do here apart from smoke?

It was lonely being the only modern girl in Beckindale. Oh, there were other young women here, of course, but none of them had lived in a city. None of them smoked and none of them drank. They didn't know about finishing work and going out in the evening with a group of friends. Dot let out a little sigh remembering some of the laughs she and her pals had had in Bradford during the war. Perhaps they had had a drink or two too many sometimes, but it had been fun.

She wished Ellen had come home after the war. She and Ellen had left Beckindale to work at the munitions factory together, and they had done everything together in Bradford. At least Ellen would have understood. But Ellen had opted to stay in Bradford where she had married a tram driver who had been invalided back from the front in early 1918.

Rose Haywood was nice but there was no way the vicar would let her out in the evening even if there was somewhere to go, and he certainly wouldn't approve of his daughter socialising with the likes of Dot.

Taking another drag of her cigarette, Dot contemplated the pub. It was clear that she would need to be in Beckindale for some time, and she'd had her eye on the Woolpack for a while now. Every time she walked past the blackened ruin, she imagined how the pub could be if it was restored. She had even asked around about the owner, Jack Micklethwaite, and whether he might be prepared to sell, but the word was that Jack wouldn't deal with a woman.

Dot had set her teeth and refused to give up. She would get round him somehow, and in the meantime, she was taking all the work she could, even from that creep, Levi Dingle. He swept the car to a stop beside her the day after she met Rose and asked if she would cook for him on the same basis as the vicarage. Dot named a price so steep that she was certain he would laugh at her and drive off. Instead he accepted it without a blink. Some businessman *he* was! How had Levi managed to accumulate so much money when he was daft enough to pay that for a cook? With Levi it was all about appearances and showing off, Dot decided.

Between her cooking jobs, she was managing to put a little aside every week, but it would take years to earn enough to get the Woolpack up and running again. She needed an investor, though

Dot couldn't imagine who would invest in a one-time munitionette and farm girl, no matter how light her pastry.

Still, it was good to have something to dream about. Dot ground out her cigarette on the wall and wandered over to have a closer look. The high street was rutted and potholed after the long winter, and hadn't had much in the way of repairs during the war either, so it was in a bad way. It was a soft May evening, but yesterday's rain had left large puddles gleaming and Dot stepped carefully between them, picking her way past great splatters of horse dung and soggy straw.

One of Walter Dinsdale's hens pecked at the edges of the puddles and a black and white cat lay indolently on the bench that had survived the fire and still sat outside the Woolpack. Two black-birds were chittering fiercely somewhere nearby.

As if to mock the tranquillity of the evening, there was a full throated roar of an engine changing gear as it came over the bridge, and before Dot could react, a motorcycle had come sweeping round the corner, scattering hens, setting a dog barking furiously and making the cat leap for cover. Dot herself jumped out of the road, but not quickly enough to avoid a spray of muddy water as the wheel of the sidecar rattled into a deep puddle beside her.

'You bloody bugger!' Incandescent with rage, Dot shook her fist after the driver who had screeched to a halt at the junction with the lane, although obviously not in response to her. Evidently he hadn't seen her at all, and was simply lost.

He stood astride the motorcycle and was looking up and down the road. After a moment, he swung a long leg over the engine and stood up, lifting his goggles onto his forehead with gloved hands. Looking around, he spotted Dot, glaring at him from outside the Woolpack, and came towards her with a long, easy stride. In his flying jacket and helmet, he was the epitome of glamour, bizarrely out of place in Beckindale.

Dot watched him approach with a fulminating gaze.

'Excuse me,' he began and she could practically see him calculating how awed she would be to speak to him. He probably thought of himself as a god, dropping in from another world to thrill and awe the local inhabitants.

Dot had no intention of being thrilled or awed. 'No, I bloody won't excuse you,' she snapped. She gestured down at the serviceable brown skirt she wore when cooking. 'I'm covered in mud thanks to you!'

His brows rose in amusement, as if a mouse had stood up and roared at him. As he came closer she could see that he had pale piercing eyes, green like a cat's. That arrogant stare and careless grace belonged in the Verneys' set at Miffield Hall, not in the middle of Beckindale.

'I'm sorry,' he said, not sounding sorry at all. 'I didn't see you.'

'That's no excuse,' she said. 'You should have been going slow enough to see me, instead of showing off. What if I'd been in t'middle of t'road? You would have knocked me down.'

'I'd hope people in Yorkshire didn't make a

habit of standing in the middle of the road.'

'We certainly don't make a habit of letting arrogant toss-pots drive around without looking where they're going,' Dot snapped back.

His jaw tightened. She had the impression that he wasn't used to being answered back but he swallowed any retort he might have been about to make. 'I'm sorry,' he said grudgingly again. 'It's been a long drive and I've got lost several times trying to find this village. I'm impatient to get there, so I apologise.'

Far from mollified, Dot jerked her head in the direction from which he had come. 'If you're looking for Miffield Hall, you missed the turning before the bridge.'

'I don't want the Hall. I'm looking for the smithy.'

'The smithy?' Dot's jaw actually dropped. *'You're* Jonah Dingle?' When Mick had talked about his cousin who he hoped would invest in his garage, she had imagined a middle-aged businessman, not this lean, tough-looking man.

'I am.' Jonah lifted his brows at the surprise in her voice. 'You know Mick, then.'

'My name's Dot. Mick's arranged for me to cook for you both while you're here.'

'Has he now? That's very thoughtful of him.' Jonah Dingle studied her with those unsettling eyes, a ghost of a smile hovering around his mouth, and Dot was mortified to find her cheeks warming.

She wasn't striking like Maggie Sugden or beautiful like Rose Haywood. She was just ordinary: ordinary features, ordinary brown hair, ordinary

160

eyes that were not quite grey and not quite blue. Ordinary, just like almost everybody else in Beckindale. She wasn't plain, exactly. She was just ... ordinary. She wasn't the kind of girl men fell madly in love with, or tried to charm. Dot was used to being treated as a pal. She wasn't used to being not-quite-smiled at in a way perfectly designed to make her think that he was intrigued and amused by her.

Not that she *would* be fool enough to fall for that, Dot reminded herself sternly. For reasons best known to himself, Jonah Dingle was trying to fluster her.

He must know perfectly well how attractive he was. He was tall and lean with dark, uncompromising features and a hard mouth softened by that glimmer of amusement. Mick was Dot's idea of an Irishman, warm and humorous and charming, but Jonah Dingle wasn't like that at all. He struck Dot as tough and impatient with the innate arrogance of a man who was used to most women crumbling to his will at the merest hint of a smile.

Dot had no intention of being one of them.

Refusing to let him see that he had discomposed her, she lifted her chin and stared back at him. 'Mick didn't say he was expecting you today.'

That annoyingly intriguing dent at the corner of his mouth only deepened at her accusing tone. Dot wrenched her eyes from it. 'I only decided to drive up yesterday,' he said carelessly. 'I spent last night at Stamford and thought I might go to York but this morning it was such a nice day, I decided to come all the way.'

161

Something about the casual assumption that everyone would put themselves out for him raised Dot's hackles. 'You didn't think to send a telegram?' she asked sharply.

He seemed surprised by the question. 'I didn't need to be met off a train.'

'Mick might have liked to know that you were coming.'

Jonah did smile at that, a devastating smile that she felt down to her toes. 'Mick didn't strike me as a man who worried about putting flowers on the table.'

That was true, but he had been waiting anxiously to hear from Jonah and Dot knew he would have wanted to be ready to welcome him. As it was, she had only left him some bacon cakes for his supper that night. She had a rabbit pie at home, she thought. She could drop that round later.

'Look, since you obviously know Mick, perhaps you could direct me to the smithy?' said Jonah after a moment.

Dot was tempted to tell him to find his own way, but she didn't want to make things difficult for Mick. So she turned and pointed down the street. 'Turn right at the end there, and follow the road until it bends round to the left,' she gabbled. 'You'll see a lane there, and then a track off it–'

She broke off as Jonah lifted a hand. 'I'm afraid I don't speak Yorkshire. Do you think you could show me the way?'

Dot rolled her eyes. 'Oh, all right,' she sighed, and started walking down the street.

'I meant in the sidecar,' said Jonah. 'Or did you

think I was going to creep along behind you?'

'It's not that far...'

'Nevertheless,' he said firmly. 'I have a constitutional dislike of looking a fool.'

'It wouldn't do you any harm to go at walking speed,' grumbled Dot but she followed him back to the motorcycle. 'I've never been in one of them contraptions before,' she said, eyeing the sidecar dubiously.

'It's perfectly safe,' he said with a hint of impatience as he opened the door. 'Here,' he added, holding out a hand, but Dot refused to take it.

'I can manage,' she said shortly, and then had to prove it. It meant folding herself up and wriggling awkwardly into the space, while Jonah watched her with barely disguised amusement.

'Ready?' he said when she was settled at last.

Dot put up her chin. 'Yes, thank you.'

Jonah shut the door with an exaggerated flourish and went round to climb onto the motorcycle once more and start the engine with a practised kick. The motor sprang to life with a deafening roar. Lowering his goggles, he pulled on his gloves and turned to Dot.

It was clear he wasn't going to be able to hear her over the noise of the engine, so Dot jerked her thumb to indicate that he should turn round. She kept her expression neutral but the sidecar felt very low on the road and it juddered around her in time with the engine.

At the end of the road, she pointed right and then, as Jonah roared towards the bend, she waved frantically to indicate that he should turn right again. The narrow lane slowed him down somewhat, and the rough track leading up to the smithy even more, but Dot was still glad when they pulled up in front of the old forge. The speed had blown her hair into wild confusion, and her eyes were stinging.

Jonah cut the engine and the silence dropped blissfully over them like a blanket. Dot had always liked the noise and bustle of the city, but the short ride in the sidecar had left her cars ringing and her whole body feeling jolted.

Before she could protest, Jonah had swung off the motorcycle, stripped off his gloves and was opening the door of the sidecar, holding down a hand to help Dot out. She had little choice but to take it. Getting in had been bad enough, but getting out was almost impossible without help and even then hard enough to do with dignity. Dot was very aware of Jonah's strong grasp and the warmth of his fingers around hers, and she snatched her hand back as soon as she could, feeling distinctly ruffled as she straightened her skirt.

Pushing his goggles up onto his head once more, Jonah was striding over to the big door of the smithy which was firmly closed. 'Are you sure this is the right place?'

Dot threw him a withering look. 'Of course I'm sure.'

Jonah pounded on the door. 'Mick Dingle, are you there? Open up!'

There was a sound of muffled cursing, and then the shutters above the workshop were flung open. 'Holy Mother of God, somebody had better be about to die!' said Mick scowling down at them.

'Ah, Mick, there you are,' said Jonah. 'You

164

haven't forgotten me already have you? I'm your cousin Jonah.'

'Jonah!' Mick blinked down at him. 'I didn't know you were coming today!'

'Is it a problem?' asked Jonah lightly.

'No, no, of course not. Just a minute, I'll come down.'

Dot and Jonah could hear him muttering to someone.

'We seem to have interrupted something,' said Jonah. He glanced at Dot. 'Go on.'

'What?'

'Say "I told you so".'

She sniffed. 'I told you so.'

A few moments later, Mick appeared, pulling back the great door to the workshop with one hand and tucking his shirt into his trousers with the other.

'Jonah Dingle, is that really you?'

'It is. I'm sorry, did I come at a bad time?'

'Ah, no, you're welcome at any time, to be sure,' said Mick, although he looked a little harried.

'I'll be off then,' said Dot. 'I've got a pie I can bring round for you later, Mick.'

'I'll drive you back,' said Jonah.

'There's no need,' she said stiffly.

'Of course there is. I've brought you out of your way. And now I'll be able to find my way back easily—'

Jonah broke off as Rose came through the workshop, looking faintly dishevelled. She was wearing a pale green blouse with the buttons all askew and her skirt looked decidedly rumpled. Her beautiful skin was flushed, her eyes glowing, the golden

165

hair so hastily pinned up that it was coming un-done already.

It was instantly clear what she and Mick had been doing when Jonah had driven up, and an awkward silence fell.

Mick cleared his throat. 'Rose, this is my cousin, Jonah.'

Rose's blush deepened. 'How do you do?' she managed.

'I'm delighted to meet you,' said Jonah, pale eyes alight with appreciation. 'I'm so sorry to interrupt.'

'Not at all.' Rose was clearly flustered, and Dot didn't blame her. 'We were just, er...'

'Discussing the wedding,' Mick put in.

'Congratulations,' said Jonah. 'When is it to be?'

'That's what we were discussing,' Mick said firmly.

'Rose,' said Dot, taking pity on her. 'I'm walk-ing back to Beckindale. Do you want to come with me and leave Mick and his cousin to catch up?'

'Oh, yes,' said Rose gratefully. 'Yes, what a good idea.'

Mick was clearly torn between wanting to wel-come Jonah and not wanting to let Rose go. 'We'll finish that discussion another time,' he promised and Rose turned scarlet, and shot past Dot out of the door.

Dot caught up with Rose halfway down the track. For a while they walked together in silence. Rose was very straight-backed, bright patches of colour in her cheeks, while Dot preserved an innocent face.

As they turned into the lane, Dot risked a sideways glance. 'So, you and Mick, eh?' she said. 'You actually doing it?'

'Dot!'

'You are, aren't you?' Dot grinned.

Rose stopped dead and pressed her hands to her cheeks. 'I must be mad!'

'Or in love.'

'Yes...' Rose let out a sigh, as if she had been punctured. 'Yes, or that.'

Chapter Sixteen

Dot was cutting lard into a bowl of flour when she heard a knock at the door and she frowned. Who knocked at the door? The post boy had used to knock with a telegram from the Army but those days were gone, thank goodness. Their neighbours would just walk in. It wasn't as if the door was ever locked.

Dot's mother had gone next door to drink tea with Mary Ann Teale while Dot took over the kitchen. She was making bulk quantities of pastry at home to make fruit pies for the vicarage, Mick and Levi, who she thought of as her customers, as well as one for Janet Airey who was suffering with arthritis and not forgetting one for her mother and herself. It was a lot of cooking, but Dot liked the idea of running a little business on her own terms.

A second, more impatient, knock made her raise her voice. 'Come in!' she shouted, and plunged her hands into the bowl to start rubbing the fat into the flour.

The next thing she knew, Jonah Dingle was ducking his head under the kitchen door. 'Good morning, Dot,' he said and Dot's heart lurched alarmingly into her throat. She was already cross with herself for lying awake the night before, unable to get the memory of that mocking, almost-smile out of her mind. Aware of a stirring deep in her belly, a fizz of unwanted attraction.

Dot had been forced to give herself a good scold before she could put Jonah from her mind and go to sleep, and now here he was, filling her kitchen and making it hard to breathe again. She might as well have spared herself the effort.

'Morning,' she said, and then, hearing the curtness in her voice, summoned a more pleasant tone. 'What can I do for you, Mr Dingle?'

'You can call me Jonah, for a start.' He moved into the kitchen, perfectly at ease, Dot noted resentfully when her own heart was knocking almost painfully against her ribs. 'What are you doing?' he added and Dot realised that she was just standing like a great gowk with her hands in the bowl of flour.

'Making pastry,' she said. 'Mind if I carry on while you're talking?'

'No, not at all. I'm not sure if I've seen anyone actually make pastry before,' he said, watching as her hands moved busily, rubbing the butter into the flour with quick, fluttering movements.

'Your ma not much of a cook, was she?'

168

A strange expression crossed Jonah's face. 'You could say that. In fact, I don't think I ever saw her in the kitchen. We had a cook, a very bad-tempered one called Maureen. I was terrified of her.'

Dot didn't believe that for a minute. Jonah Dingle looked like the kind of man who had never been afraid of anything.

'Sit down,' she said, determinedly unimpressed, 'and tell me what I can do for you.'

'I've got a proposition for you.'

She looked at him suspiciously over the bowl. 'What kind of proposition?'

'A business one.'

Of course it was a business one. Jonah Dingle wasn't likely to offer her any other kind of proposition, was he?

She shook the bowl to bring any larger lumps of fat to the surface. 'I'm always interested in discussing business,' she said, brushing the flour from her hands. 'You may as well have a cup of tea as you're here,' she added and turned to put the kettle on the range.

It was a less than gracious invitation even for one as blunt-speaking as Dot, but Jonah didn't seem to mind. He pulled out a chair and sat at the table, evidently unconcerned by her grudging welcome. Under his waistcoat he wore a plain white shirt with the sleeves rolled up above his wrists. It was exactly what her father or Olly might have worn on a summer day but Jonah managed to look tough and faintly dangerous.

Dot made the tea in a pot, poured out two cups strong enough to stand a spoon in, and went back to her pastry, pouring water into the bowl. 'So, tell me about this proposition of yours,' she said as she deftly gathered the dough together into a ball before turning it out onto the floury surface.

Jonah watched her deft movements as she kneaded the pastry briefly. 'Have you ever considered having a lodger?' he asked.

Dot was taken aback. 'I've never thought about it,' she said. 'Who would want to rent a room?'

'I would.'

'You? But aren't you staying with Mick?'

'That was the plan,' Jonah agreed, 'but Mick, as you no doubt also realised last night, is engaged in, er, intimate relations with his Rose. I've got no intention of playing gooseberry. Not to mention that the smithy is not exactly comfortable and that Mick is the world's worst cook. He couldn't even manage to boil some potatoes to go with your pie last night.'

Dot took the first batch of pastry to the larder and came back with some more lard which she cut briskly into the flour. 'What makes you think you would be more comfortable here?' she asked, plunging her hands back into the bowl and feathering the flour and fat through her fingers.

'You do. You seem a very competent, practical young woman. I can't imagine you would run an uncomfortable house.'

Competent. Practical. That was her fate, Dot decided with an inward sigh.

'Careful, you'll sweep me off my feet with that sweet talking,' she said, not bothering to hide her sarcasm.

'You also seem like a woman who would appreciate straight-talking,' Jonah explained.

'Well, that's more of a compliment,' she said, mollified.

'Compliments are easy,' he said. 'I'm trying to work out what would appeal to you most. I thought flowery compliments and flattery would go down less well than a businesslike approach.'

'You think you've got me pegged, don't you?' said Dot with a sour look, but she was already calculating how much she could charge him.

It had never occurred to her to have a lodger. There was little enough call for accommodation in a village like Beckindale but now the Woolpack was in ruins there was nowhere for anyone to stay.

And thinking of the Woolpack gave Dot an idea. Mindlessly she rubbed the fat in the flour while her mind ran busily over her options. When she looked up at last, she found Jonah watching her with an amused expression.

'You've been looking very intent,' he said. 'What are you thinking?'

Dot studied him for a minute before pushing the bowl aside and wiping her hands on her apron. 'That I might have a proposition for *you*.'

His brows rose. 'Is that so?'

'You'd better come and look at the room,' she said. 'If it suits you, then we can talk.'

It was strange seeing the cottage through his eyes. For the first time Dot noticed the unpretentious rooms, the plain but serviceable furniture. Olly's bedroom was little changed from her brother's last visit, she guessed. She had been in

Bradford then and she hadn't seen him. Hadn't made the effort to come to Beckindale and see him. Dot was sorry about that now.

There was a bed and a wooden chair and a small window that looked out over the fields to the fells. Dead flies littered the windowsill but otherwise the room was clean enough. Olly's cap had been returned to her parents and it sat forlornly on top of a battered chest of drawers. Dot picked it up and turned it in her hands as she looked around, remembering Olly as a small, gaptoothed boy and later as a gangly youth. Now lying in an unmarked grave somewhere in France.

'Will your mother mind you letting your brother's room?' Jonah asked, glancing at the cap Dot held, and she sighed.

'Ma doesn't mind much at the moment. She lost heart when Olly died, and after Pa got the flu she's just given up.' She lifted her shoulders and let them drop. 'She used to be a busy, bustling women but now ... it's like she doesn't care any more.'

Jonah had been bending to look at the view through the window but now he turned. 'I'm sorry,' he said.

'Aye, well, we've all got our sad stories,' said Dot, prickling at the sympathy in his face. 'You too, I daresay. We've just got to get on wi' it.' She looked around the room once more. 'So, what do you reckon to t'room? It'd look better with a clean and a dust but I know it's not much.'

'It's fine,' said Jonah.

'There's a privy out t'back,' she told him, 'and you could use the parlour if you wanted. Ma and

172

I spend our time in the kitchen. You can eat with us there if you want or in t'parlour: I'm not carrying trays up and down them stairs.'

Jonah's face relaxed into a smile that made Dot's cheeks tingle annoyingly. 'I won't ask for any trays, I promise.'

'Well, then, let's go down and we can talk terms,' said Dot.

This time she sat across from him in the kitchen. The tea had grown cold and she pushed it aside to fold her hands on the table. She might have one chance to do this, and she didn't want to betray her nervousness.

'So,' said Jonah, 'shall we negotiate?'

'All right. I'll let you have room and board for free,' she said, and his eyes narrowed.

'In return for...?'

'Investment.'

Jonah's expression was impassive. 'Investment in what?'

'The Woolpack.'

'The pub? Mick said it was a ruin.'

'It is,' said Dot. 'It burned down three years ago and nobody's done anything with it since. It's just sitting there, a black hole in the middle of the village, when it could be the centre of things.' She leant forward in her eagerness to explain. 'Church or chapel is the only place to go here. The Woolpack could be a friendly, welcoming place, somewhere everyone can go if they feel like a bit of company.'

'And you think you could make it that?'

'I know I could.'

'What do you know about running a pub, Dot?'

'Nothing,' she was forced to admit. 'But I know what makes a good pub and what doesn't. I'm a good cook and I've got a head for business.'

'When did you get familiar with pubs?' There was an undercurrent of disapproval in Jonah's voice but Dot refused to let herself be discouraged. She had started this, and it was too late to back down now.

'When I worked in Bradford during the war. The other girls and I were earning a decent wage, and we spent most of it in t'pub after work. It were good to unwind after being in that factory all day.'

'It's not the war now,' said Jonah, clearly unimpressed.

'No, but things have changed,' she said. 'It's not a terrible thing for a woman to go to a pub now, and we don't need no man to take us neither.'

He made a face. 'I don't think things have changed that much,' he said frankly. 'What might have been accepted during the war won't be now, and I don't see people around here liking you taking over the pub as single woman.'

'That's the thing, I wouldn't be taking it over,' said Dot. 'You would. Jack Micklethwaite still owns the lease but he's old school. He wouldn't deal with a woman. But he'd deal with you,' she said persuasively. 'I've heard he'd be glad to be rid of the Woolpack now so you could drive a hard bargain, I reckon. Buy the lease from him outright, even.'

'What would I do with a pub?' Jonah's expression was dubious. 'I've never even bought a house. I don't do settling down, and I certainly

174

don't plan on staying in Beckindale.'

'I wouldn't want you to stay,' said Dot.

'You just want my money, is that it?'

'Isn't that the point of being an investor? What else are you going to do with it?'

A smile lit his eyes. 'Now, that is a good question, Dot. But there must be a thousand things more exciting to do with my money than taking on a charred ruin!'

'It *would* be exciting,' she said stubbornly. 'Taking a big mess, sorting it out and making something of it. *I* think it would be exciting, anyway. Look, I'm prepared to keep working my socks off, and I've saved what I can, but there's no way I'd ever be able to afford to fix the roof and do the other structural repairs. Whereas *you*,' she said with what she hoped was a winning smile, 'I heard you found a great lump of gold and have got money to burn. It's not as if I'm asking for a handout,' she added. 'It would be a business loan, just like you're giving Mick. I'd repay you as soon as I made a profit.'

Jonah didn't say anything for a moment. He studied Dot across the table. 'You're talking about a lot of work, Dot. Why do you want to do it? Wouldn't it be easier to get married?'

'I don't want to get married,' she said, bristling. 'Why should I hand myself over to a man when I can look after myself? The war taught us that women can do anything men can do. I want a chance to live on my own terms,' she told him. 'I'd be doing up the Woolpack for myself as much as for the village. I loved going into the pubs in Bradford in the war. They were places you could forget about everything horrible that was going on. There's nowhere like that in Beckindale.'

Dot looked directly into Jonah's green eyes. 'I know I could make the Woolpack somewhere special,' she said. 'I'll do all the work, but I just need you to help me get going. And in return, you'll get bed and board for as long as you're in Beckindale, and Mick gets his privacy. It's a good deal for all of us.' She paused. She didn't want to overdo it, and she was damned if she was going to beg. 'What do you think?'

'Frankly, I think it's a mad idea,' said Jonah and her heart plummeted. 'But then mad ideas have always appealed to me. The truth is, I've been bored since the end of the war. I'm glad I came to Beckindale. Between you and Mick, you've given me something to keep me busy for a few months.' He grinned suddenly, and Dot's spirits shot upwards once more. 'I think you'll have a fight on your hands to get the Woolpack up and running again, Dot, but if you're up for it, I am too.'

Chapter Seventeen

Rose curled into Mick, listening to the steady beat of his heart, feeling his chest rise and fall beneath her hand as he breathed. She had finally lost her virginity one wet afternoon when Mick had closed the garage and promised that the King himself could come knocking and he wouldn't answer. The once dreary sound of raindrops beating against the window would for ever after be associated with the bone-melting pleasure he had shown her, with the memory of his hands curving over her body, of the way he had smiled against her skin.

Since then, she had slipped away to the smithy whenever she could, but sometimes Mick had customers and she would have to pretend that she was just walking past. Sometimes, too, she had obligations at the vicarage and couldn't get away. It was frustrating for both of them, but today was a Sunday, her father was dozing after lunch and Rose had told her mother that it was such a lovely day that she felt like a long walk.

Now Mick sighed and dropped a kiss on the top of Rose's head. 'We'd better get up,' he said reluctantly.

'Do we have to?'

'If you don't want your parents sending out a search party.' He sat naked on the side of the bed and reached for his trousers. 'How much longer is it going to be like this, Rose?' he asked. 'I know I said I'd wait, but I'm tired of sneaking around. I want to be together all the time.' Standing up, he shrugged on his shirt and tucked it into his trousers. 'Sometimes it feels as if we'll never get married, that we'll still be creeping around, closing doors and slipping in the back way when we're fifty!'

'I'm tired of it too, Mick.' With a sigh, Rose sat up against the pillows. 'It's just never the right time for me to talk to Papa. We used to be a close family, but since Arthur ... oh everybody's cross. Today Papa was upset about John. He was shouting at him when I left, and John was saying nothing which just makes Papa worse.'

'What is he angry with John about?'

'He wants John to move back to the vicarage. He's been looking after Robert Carr since his mother died and the hospital closed. Robert was his batman and he's suffering from awful shellshock. He can't stop trembling, and there's no way he could look after himself but Papa won't see that. He says it's "not fitting" for John to look after him. He says John's a gentleman who should finish his degree and go into the church like he planned, but John won't leave Robert.' She hesitated. 'I think Papa's afraid that John's feelings for Robert might not be ... natural.'

'When you've been through that war, it's hard to know what's natural and what isn't,' said Mick. 'Your papa probably thinks your feelings for me aren't natural either,' he added with a wry smile.

'I just wish we could find out what happened to Arthur, and then we could all move forward.'

Mick sighed. 'Rose, I wish you would trust me about this. I wish you would trust me about a lot of things.'

'I do trust you,' she said, taken aback.

'No, you don't. Not really.' Mick shook his head. 'You didn't trust me to come back after the war, did you?'

'Yes, I did! Who told you I didn't?' Rose sat bolt upright, golden hair tumbling around her shoulders, brown eyes sparkling with indignation. 'It was Levi, wasn't it?'

'He mentioned it, yes. I don't blame you,' Mick added quickly. 'I'm not much of a writer. It was hard for you to believe in me.'

'That's not true,' Rose said, wrapping the sheet round her so that she could get out of bed and find her clothes. 'Levi had no business saying that. He's just trying to make trouble, Mick. I've *always* trusted you.'

'Then why won't you trust me now about Arthur?'

'Because that's different,' she said in frustration.

'It feels like you're using his death as an excuse not to talk to your parents.'

'It's not an *excuse!*' Angry with Mick for spoiling the pleasure of the afternoon, Rose made herself stop and take a deep breath. 'Please, let's not quarrel, Mick. It's such a lovely day.'

The words were barely out of her mouth before the peace of the afternoon was broken by the sound of an approaching motor. 'Someone's coming,' she said in dismay. 'Is it Jonah?'

'Jonah doesn't crash his gears like that.' Mick frowned and went over to open the shutters. 'It might be a customer.'

'You should go down,' said Rose, knowing he couldn't afford to turn customers away, Sunday or no Sunday. 'I'll get dressed and slip out the back.'

Mick hesitated, as if he would have argued, but after a moment, he nodded and clattered down the stairs and into the garage below.

Rose dressed slowly, wishing they didn't always seem to end their meetings on a tense note. The truth was that she was enjoying this time without any responsibilities. Whenever she came to the garage, she couldn't help imagining what it would be like to live there with Mick.

The kitchen was a dark, cramped room looking out onto a rough field where once the horses waiting to be shod had been tethered. If she married Mick she would have to learn to cook. She would have to spend half her day in that dreary room, and the other half cleaning the equally charmless parlour and the bedrooms upstairs. There would be no indoor bathroom as at the vicarage. There was a privy outside, and a tub in front of the fire would have to do for a bath.

It would be a very different life. It had been easy to ignore that when Mick was in France but now that he was home the idea of being married and what that would mean had become somehow more ... real. When Mick made love to her, everything else faded away, but Rose could see that they couldn't make love all the time, and what would she do then?

'Rose!' Mick shouted up the stairs. 'Come on down. It's Levi!'

Her heart jolted. She had managed to avoid Levi since escaping from his house that day. He was the last person she wanted to see, but Mick was so eager to mend fences with his brother that she couldn't bring herself to tell him how Levi had behaved.

Hastily pinning up her hair, Rose twitched her skirt straight and made sure all her buttons were done up in the right order. Mick was right: they couldn't go on being interrupted like this and feeling embarrassed.

When she went downstairs, Levi and Mick

were standing outside the workshop door in the sunshine. Rose summoned a stiff smile.

'Hello, Levi.'

He turned. It must have been obvious what she and Mick had been doing and just as obviously, Levi was displeased.

'Rose,' he acknowledged her, a warning muscle twitching under one eye

'Levi's brought a visitor,' said Mick, oblivious to any undercurrents, and Levi stepped back so that Rose could see the young woman standing beside him.

'May I introduce Miss Cora Ramage?' he said grandly. 'My fiancée.'

There was an astounded silence. Mick recovered first. 'Well, now that's grand news, grand! Welcome, Miss Ramage. This is an unexpected pleasure! I'm Levi's big brother, Mick, and this is my fiancée, Rose Haywood.'

'Fiancée?' echoed Levi sharply. 'I didn't think you'd been able to get engaged yet?'

'It's only a matter of time,' said Mick, looking on fondly as Rose offered Cora her hand. 'Congratulations, Miss Ramage,' she said, beaming. 'This is exciting news! I'm so happy for you.'

Cora simpered and adjusted the fur stole around her neck. 'Pleased to meet you, I'm sure.' The strangled vowels were not quite sufficient to disguise a strong Bradford accent. She had tightly waved hair beneath a chic little hat and bright red lips, and she was wearing a short chiffon dress in lemon yellow with a wide ruched waistband and a flounced hem.

Rose was too elated at the news that Levi was

getting married to care how out of place Cora looked. 'We must celebrate,' she said with enthusiasm. 'Mick, what can we offer them?'

She fussed around, sending Mick to bring some chairs outside so they didn't have to sit in the musty parlour, and making tea which she carried out on a tray. 'I wish we'd known you were coming,' she said. 'We could have given you a proper welcome.'

'We only got engaged this morning,' Cora said. 'Levi couldn't wait to bring me out to meet you both,' she added.

'Well, I'm glad he did!' Mick beamed at her as they all settled onto the chairs at last and Rose poured out the tea. 'Have you two known each other long?'

'I've been an associate of Cora's father for a couple of years now,' said Levi importantly.

'Pa has only let me meet his business associates since I've been out,' Cora added. 'Levi swept me off my feet.'

'I want to tell the world,' said Levi. He slid a glance from Mick to Rose. 'I couldn't bear Cora to be a secret, as if I were ashamed of her.'

Rose saw Mick's smile stiffen. Even he couldn't misunderstand Levi's dig. She was torn, hating to see him hurt but glad when he got a glimpse of the Levi she saw.

'So, when are you getting married?' she asked to fill the taut silence.

'Very soon,' smirked Cora. She patted Levi's hand. 'Levi doesn't want to wait.'

'I just need to talk to your father,' Levi said to Rose, ignoring Cora's hand.

'To Papa?' said Rose, puzzled.

'We want to get married in St Mary's.'

Mick frowned. 'St Mary's isn't a Catholic church. Mammy will be turning in her grave.' Mick's attempt at humour didn't go down well with Levi.

'That was Ireland, Mick,' he snapped. 'That's all in the past. We're in Yorkshire now, and Beckindale will be our home.'

Rose turned quickly to Cora. 'Have you lived in the country before?'

'No.' Cora shifted the fur she wore around her neck in spite of the warmth of the afternoon and Rose realised with a shiver of horror that it was a dead fox complete with brush and glassy eyes that stared back at her.

Cora was looking at the view from the front of the smithy. The air was rich with the scent of long grass and blossom, and a skylark let loose its glorious song as it rose and fell over the heather on the fell.

'It's messy, isn't it?' she said, evidently unimpressed.

The grass under the drystone walls was lush, flecked with cuckoo spit and bright with colourful wildflowers: yellow buttercups, white cow parsley, blue speedwell, the vivid pink of cranesbill. The warm air had brought out the heady scent of the honeysuckle and wild roses that scrambled over the hedges while a wren darted along the wall in search of insects. It was true that the track was rutted and tangled with grass and that outside the smithy bits of cars were strewn around in a haphazard way but Rose marvelled that Cora could look so unimpressed.

'I love your dress,' she tried again.

Cora looked complacently down at herself. 'This is the latest fashion,' she said. 'I think it's important to look nice now I'm engaged.'

'Well, you certainly do,' said Rose. She glanced at Cora's shoes, with their pointed toes and heels. 'You might find boots more useful when you're living in country, though,' she suggested tactfully. 'Especially in the winter. Those shoes are lovely but they won't last long when you're walking down to the village shop.'

'Oh, I won't be walking anywhere,' said Cora, pale blue eyes widening. 'Levi's going to buy me my own car.'

'I hope he's not going to teach you to drive it,' said Mick, stretching his legs out in front of him with a grin. 'Levi's got no feel for an engine. I keep telling him he should have stuck with horses,' he went on, apparently oblivious to the fact that Levi was looking daggers at him. 'You come to me if you want to learn to drive, Cora.'

Oblivious to Levi's resentment, Cora was soon tittering at Mick's jokes. Rose wondered if she had any idea of the kind of man Levi was. Why would Cora suspect that her fiancé was capable of burning down a pub and killing a woman without regret, of forcing a kiss on Rose and holding a threat over her head?

Rose's first gushing enthusiasm for the news of Levi's engagement was rapidly fading. She had so hoped Levi would be in love with Cora, or at least transfer his obsession to her, but there was no warmth in his expression when he looked at his fiancée, just a calculating look that chilled Rose to the bone.

But what could she do about it? Cora was clearly so pleased with her status as an engaged woman, with her smart clothes and the prospect of living in Levi's big house. She would never believe Rose if she tried to warn her.

'I'll get some more tea,' she murmured, only to regret it the next instant when Levi leapt up.

'I'll give you a hand.'

'It's fine, Levi,' she tried. 'You and Cora are the guests of honour.'

But he insisted on following her into the kitchen, where he stood in the way and made her squeeze past him to get to the range.

Rose forced herself to smile. 'Cora seems very nice.'

'I'm sorry if the news was a shock,' said Levi, moving closer so that she stepped back until she came up against the table.

'A good one,' she said. 'I'm delighted for you.'

'And just a teeny bit jealous, hmm?'

She laughed nervously. 'Of course not!'

'I don't mind if you are. I was jealous of you being here with Mick,' said Levi and before she could move, he had grabbed her and was smothering slobbery kisses over her face and neck.

'Levi, stop it!' Breathless with disgust and fright, Rose wrenched herself free and put the table between them.

'Cora won't make any difference to us, Rose, I promise you that.'

'Levi.' Rose kept her voice low and firm. 'You have to stop this. I'm engaged to Mick, you're engaged to Cora, and that's all there can ever be between us. Now, go back outside, I'll bring the tea in just a minute.'

He sauntered off, and she pressed a fist to her chest, trying to calm her breathing. She would have to find a way of talking to Mick about his brother.

When she carried the teapot back outside, Levi was talking loudly about the plans for the wedding and how he was going to invite the whole village. Cora sent Rose a sharp glance and Rose wondered what Levi had said about her to his fiancée. Nothing good, by the look of it.

'Would you like to see my ring?' she asked Rose, sticking her hand out.

Dutifully Rose inspected the ostentatious ruby surrounded by diamonds. 'Very nice,' she said.

'I see you're not wearing a ring,' said Cora. 'I thought you and Mick were engaged.'

'We are,' said Rose composedly. 'I don't need a ring to feel engaged. Mick knows I love him.'

'That's the spirit, *acushla!*' Mick grinned at her, and Rose relaxed and smiled back at him in a private moment of understanding.

Levi stood up abruptly. 'Come on, Cora, we need to go.'

'Mother of God, when is Levi going to learn to use a clutch?' Mick shook his head as they watched Levi drive the car jerkily away.

She should tell him about Levi now, Rose resolved, but Mick was turning to her.

'Do you mind about not having a ring?' he asked abruptly and she took his hand.

186

'I really don't,' she said and she smiled at him. 'I don't need a ring, I just need you. Let's get married, Mick.' Surely if she and Mick were married, Levi would give up?

To her surprise, he hesitated. 'Do you think knowing the truth about Arthur would make a difference to your parents?'

'I do, yes.'

He drew her over to the chairs. 'Then sit down, Rose. I've got something to tell you.'

Chapter Eighteen

'What on earth are you doing?'

Startled by the sound of Jonah's voice, Dot looked up from her broom. She was happily sweeping in what had once been the front bar of the Woolpack. Her hair was tied up in a scarf and she was wearing an old smock that swamped her but at least protected her from the worst of the dust.

'I thought I'd start tidying up,' she said.

Jonah looked around the room. The walls were still charred but Dot had dragged as much debris as she could out into the yard behind and was brushing up three years of accumulated rubbish: ashes, dust, plaster, leaves, bird and mouse droppings and the weeds that had started to take root in the mess.

'The roofers won't start until next week,' he pointed out. 'There's not much point in tidying until they've finished.'

'I can't wait to get going,' Dot confessed.

She was too excited to sit around and wait for the men to do their bit. The day before, she had gone with Jonah to see Jack Micklethwaite about purchasing the lease to the Woolpack. Reluctantly accepting that Jack would have nothing to do with a woman, Dot had let Jonah do the talking while she posed as his assistant. She had been secretly impressed by the way Jonah had bargained with Jack. Not that Dot had any intention of telling Jonah that. He had a high enough opinion of himself already, she reckoned.

After Jack and Jonah had shaken hands on the deal, Dot had contained herself long enough to get outside, at which point she had hugged Jonah. 'We did it! We've got the Woolpack!'

Later, of course, she had been mortified at the way she had thrown herself at him, but at the time she had been too excited to think clearly. Jonah's arms had closed around her and he had lifted her up and swung her round, laughing at her exuberance. When he set her down, she had still been smiling, but she was suddenly acutely aware of the strength of his arms and the solidity of his lean male body, and she had stepped back while she cleared her throat awkwardly.

'You won't regret it,' she had told him, and Jonah had looked down into her bright face.

'I'm beginning to think I won't,' he agreed.

Dot was impatient to get going on the renovation. 'Since you're here, you can give me a hand,' she said, propping her broom against the wall and pointing at an old iron bedstead that had fallen through from the floor above. 'Help me drag this outside, will you?'

'Shouldn't you be at home cooking my supper?' said Jonah, but he came into the room and took hold of one end of the bedstead.

'It's all done.'

'I thought my role was investing, not dragging furniture around,' he grumbled.

'A bit of lifting won't kill you.'

Dot put her shoulder to the bedstead and pushed while Jonah dragged from the front, and together they managed to get it out into the yard, abusing each other like old friends.

It was surprising how quickly she had got used to having Jonah around. Agnes Colton had been reluctant to consider having a lodger at first. 'What will Mary Ann say?' she had asked.

Mary Ann, when consulted, had opined that it would be good for Agnes and Dot to have a man about the house. She was less keen when she discovered that the lodger would be Jonah.

'One of them Dingles?' She had pursed her lips. 'Irish,' she had added darkly. 'You can't trust the Irish.'

When Mary Ann heard that Jonah was buying the Woolpack, she was torn. On the one hand, it would be good to have the pub restored. It was an unsightly blot on the village, and her Tom would be glad to have a quiet pint once more. On the other, Jonah was a Dingle, and Mary Ann had little time for the Dingles.

'Jonah's not like Levi,' Dot had tried to argue, but Mary Ann was unconvinced. 'What do you really know about him, Dot? There's rumours going around that he found a lump of gold! Sounds like a fairy story to me,' sniffed Mary Ann, 'and you don't want to start believing in fairy stories now.'

There was worse to come when Mary Ann found out that Dot was planning to get involved in the Woolpack. 'I wonder that you let her, Agnes,' she said in front of Dot. 'A girl running a pub? Whoever heard of such a thing? It's not fitting.'

Of course, once Mary Ann had set her face against it, all the other women followed. Janet Airey, Betty Porter, Lizzy Gregson, Hannah Rigg and all the other village gossips shook their heads and clicked their tongues and informed anyone who would listen that no good would come of it.

Dot refused to be daunted. They would come round, she vowed. They would have to if she were to convince Jonah to leave her in charge. In the meantime, she was grateful to him for setting out to charm her mother. Agnes was adamantly against her daughter working in a pub, but she had admitted to Dot that she liked having a man around the house again, and Dot thought she seemed much brighter since Jonah had arrived.

He had soon given up sitting in the parlour in the evening and joined Dot and her mother in the kitchen. He was good company, and although he never talked about his family and rarely about the war, he was full of stories about his time prospecting in Australia and hair-raising tales about learning to fly. After supper Dot would sit out on the back step with him and share a cigarette, ignoring her mother's disapproving looks. Only now did she realise how lonely she had been. Jonah wouldn't stay long, she knew that, but in the meantime it felt as if she had found a friend.

Now she brushed her hands together with satisfaction as she studied the growing pile of old furniture in the yard. 'We might as well get rid of that settle while you're here too.'

'Don't you ever rest, woman?' Jonah grumbled but he manoeuvred the settle into the yard as directed by Dot.

'This is ruining my suit,' he complained.

'Why are you dressed up like that anyway?' said Dot, eyeing his smart suit with disfavour.

'I've been talking to the Honourable Freddie Winstruther,' he said, and Dot grinned at the affected voice he put on.

'Oh, aye? And how do you get to know an Honourable?'

'He went to school with someone I knew in the Flying Corps, and it turns out he's a handy fellow to know. He invited a whole lot of other Hons to meet me this morning, and I sold three cars.'

Dot picked up her broom once more. 'Mick'll be pleased about that.'

'I thought it deserved a celebration.'

'I'd offer you a drink,' she said and cast a glance at the charred remnants of the bar. 'Unfortunately, we're not *quite* ready to open!'

'What about dinner instead?'

She pursed her lips as she ran her mind over the contents of the larder. 'We'd need something a bit special for a celebration. It's a bit late to see what the butcher has under the counter ... I could kill one of the hens?'

Jonah held up a hand. 'I was thinking it would be nice for you to eat a meal someone else has cooked for a change.'

'*You're* planning to cook?' Dot asked in surprise.

'No,' said Jonah with exaggerated patience. 'There are these places called hotels with restaurants, remember those? I'm suggesting that I take you out for meal in Ilkley tonight. I'll borrow one of Mick's cars. It's a beautiful evening, not that you'd notice stuck in this ruined pub all day, and it'll be a nice drive.'

She stared at him. 'You're inviting *me* out to supper?'

'I am.'

'Why?'

'Because I feel like celebrating and I would like your company.'

Dot hesitated, flummoxed. She wasn't the kind of person who got invited out to dine in a hotel. Still, in Bradford she had loved going out in the evening. It felt like a long time since she had had any fun.

'I'd have to dress up for a restaurant,' she said doubtfully, mentally reviewing her extremely limited wardrobe.

'You might want to change,' he agreed, glancing at her grubby smock.

Lifting a hand, he wiped a smudge from her cheek with his thumb and her skin burned at the casual graze of his fingers. 'And wash your face, too, perhaps.'

Furious at her own reaction, Dot stepped smartly out of reach. Jonah was a friend, and she wanted him to stay that way. She had no intention of getting all daft about him, and she certainly wasn't going to go all coy and turn down a chance of dinner because of this uncomfortable awareness that hit her every now and then.

'I could mebbe borrow summat to wear,' she said.

'Excellent,' said Jonah. 'Be ready to leave at half past six.'

Nervously, Dot smoothed down the embroidered lawn dress that Rose Haywood had lent her. It was longer than was now fashionable, Rose said, but Dot thought it was the most beautiful thing she had ever worn. A pale, pretty blue, the dress had loose sleeves gathered at the cuffs, tiny lawn-covered buttons and loops that took for ever to do up, a bobbled fringe under the neckline and at the hem, and a contrasting ribbon at the waist.

She looked almost pretty, Dot realised, disconcerted by her reflection. It was a faintly alarming thought. She didn't feel like herself at all.

Did she look as if she were trying too hard? A worse thought struck her. What if Jonah thought she was trying to attract him? Why, oh why, had she asked Rose if she could borrow a dress? She should just have worn her Sunday best skirt and blouse and been done with it.

But it was too late to change now. Jonah would be waiting.

Grabbing a straw hat and a scarf Rose had lent her, Dot went downstairs and out to where Jonah had brought the car he had borrowed from the garage.

As she stepped outside into the street she had lived in her whole life, Dot was conscious of a sudden silence. It was, as Jonah had said, a lovely late spring evening, and it seemed that every single one of her neighbours was outside enjoying the sunshine. Women were sitting in doorways or leaning over the gate for a natter. Small children ran around in the street, playing a noisy game of tag. Girls whispered together on the corner and giggled to make the lads watching them blush. Older men were tending their gardens while the younger ones and small boys crowded around a car parked right outside Dot's cottage.

And every single one of them, it seemed to Dot, stopped what they were doing to stare at her as she walked out in her borrowed dress.

The circle of men and boys backed away to reveal Jonah, leaning against the bonnet of the car, which was painted a glossy maroon colour and had a polished wood trim. At the sight of Dot, he straightened and smiled.

'You look nice.'

Dot's cheeks were burning. 'Why's everybody staring at me?'

'Because you look nice.'

'Can we just go?' she muttered and he opened the passenger door with a flourish. 'Stop it,' she hissed.

'Stop what?'

'I can get in the car by myself! Stop treating me like a lady.'

'You shouldn't look like a lady if you don't want to be treated like one,' said Jonah, amused.

Dot glowered. She had known this dress was a

194

mistake. 'It'd take more than a dress to make a lady out of me,' she said, and scowled through the windscreen as Jonah got into the driving seat and pressed the starter button. 'Let's get out of here!'

She kept her gaze fixed firmly ahead as Jonah drove along the street. The children stopped playing and ran after them, shouting, instead. Dot was burningly conscious of her neighbours' knowing gazes following her. She could practically hear what they would say the moment the car was out of sight:

Who does that Dot Colton think she is?

Did you see her all tarted up?

She'll be making a play for that Dingle lad, you mark my words.

Her cheeks stung. She was so embarrassed that she couldn't enjoy the drive to Ilkley, although she had been looking forward to it. She had a blurred impression of high ceilings, crisp tablecloths and the subdued murmur of conversation and cutlery as they were shown to their table in the Royal Hotel. They ordered asparagus soup, baked haddock with a sharp sauce and roast duckling with green peas, and gradually Dot began to relax.

'Feeling better?' asked Jonah when the waiter had taken away their soup bowls, and Dot gave a shame-faced laugh.

'Sorry, I haven't been good company, have I? I'm just so embarrassed about the way everybody stared when we left. You'd think they'd never seen a motor car before!'

'I think they were more interested in you than the car,' said Jonah, smiling when she made a

195

face. 'That's why I could never live in a village. I'd suffocate with everybody knowing my business.'

'I know,' Dot said with feeling. 'It's so hard to get Beckindale to accept change, too. Oh, they got through the war, but most of them want everything to go back to exactly the way it was before.'

Jonah hesitated. 'Are you sure you want to run the Woolpack, Dot? You're going to meet a lot of resistance. Wouldn't you be better trying in a city? Leeds or Bradford, maybe?'

'Nobody would give me a chance in an established pub,' she said flatly. 'It's only because the Woolpack's in such a state and that you've come along that I've got the opportunity to have a go at all. I know it'll be hard, but I can do it. I know I can. Besides,' she added, 'I need to stay in Beckindale for Ma. Family's important, isn't it?'

'Is it?' said Jonah. 'Mine isn't important to me.'

'You're supporting Mick,' she pointed out. 'You wouldn't do that if he wasn't important to you.'

'I'm supporting Mick because I like him, not because he's my cousin.'

Dot sat back in her chair and studied him. 'You never talk about your family. I assumed they were dead.'

'No, my parents are alive and living in Dublin.' Jonah picked up a spoon and idly balanced it between his fingers. 'As far as I know, anyway.'

She found it hard to believe that he couldn't care. 'Don't you worry about them?'

He shrugged. 'They cut me off without a second thought, just like my father cut off the rest of his family in Ballybeg when it suited him. He grew up there with Mick's father and a whole lot of other brothers and sisters but he left when he was fifteen, and he never went back. He re-invented himself in Dublin as a successful busi-nessman and married my mother, which was a huge step up socially for him. I think he was ashamed of his origins in Ballybeg so he never took us there.'

'Us?'

'My brother and I. Adam was the favoured son,' said Jonah with a faint smile. 'A lot of Irish families have a favourite, and Adam was my par-ents', no question. He deserved it. He was hand-some, charming, clever, dutiful, *good* ... but damn it, he was nice too,' Jonah finished but not before Dot had seen the sorrow in his eyes.

'And you?' she asked.

'Oh, I was the rebel, of course,' he said easily. 'I was the bad son. I bunked off school and broke all the rules. I did everything I could to disappoint my father, and the more he punished me, the worse I behaved. But I was the lucky one,' he said. 'They suffocated Adam with their love and their expectations. Adam was to take over the family business in spite of the fact that what he really loved was music. Adam was to marry well. Adam was to be a pillar of society.'

'What happened to him?' Dot asked.

'He died of septicaemia in 1904. It was just a scratch but it wouldn't heal and then the infec-tion spread... I was away, behaving badly some-where, but I went home when I heard he was ill. He died about an hour before I got there. He was only eighteen.'

'I'm sorry,' said Dot.

Jonah dropped the spoon on the tablecloth as if discarding a bad memory. 'When my mother saw me, she fell on me and started beating my chest with her fists. The wrong son had died, she cried. Why hadn't it been me?'

Dot was shocked. 'That's not fair!'

'My father told me they couldn't bear the sight of me, knowing I'd survived instead of Adam,' Jonah said. 'He asked me to go rather than distress my mother any more. So I went,' he said. 'I walked out with nothing, the clothes on my back and a few shillings in my pocket, and I've never been back.

'That was the end of my experience of family,' he said. 'I vowed then I'd never have one of my own. I'm not putting anyone else through that. I'm not getting married, not settling down, not having children. None of it,' he said fiercely as the waiter set their fish in front of them.

Dot picked up her fish knife and fork. 'You warning me off, Jonah?' she asked.

He looked taken aback. 'No, of course not.'

'Good,' said Dot, 'because it's not necessary. I've got no intention of tying myself to some man, no matter how many lumps of gold he's got. I want to make something of myself and not account to anybody for it. I may have put on a pretty dress tonight,' she said, 'but you don't need to worry about me getting ideas, whatever the neighbours say.'

Jonah hadn't started his fish. He watched as Dot calmly cut into hers and took a mouthful.

'You're very blunt,' he said, half a smile hovering around his mouth.

'I'm just saying it how it is,' said Dot. 'It's best we both know where we are, I reckon. I know you won't be staying in Beckindale for long, and I don't blame you but I don't want to spend the time you are here watching my words and feeling awkward in case you think I'm after you or summat.

'Neither of us is interested in any soppy business,' she said, 'so let's agree to be business partners and friends and leave it at that.'

Summer 1919

Chapter Nineteen

Dot saw the Sugdens drive up to the church and went over to help Maggie down from the trap.

'Thanks, Dot,' said Maggie, clambering awkwardly down with the help of Dot's hand. 'Ouf!' she said when she had both feet on the ground. 'Perhaps this wasn't such a good idea.'

There was no disguising the baby now. Maggie's belly was swollen under her cotton dress, and she winced as she pressed her hands to the small of her back.

'I wasn't sure if you'd come,' said Dot.

'I nearly didn't but I was desperate for a change of scene. The baby's been keeping me awake at night lately so I've been tired and cross.' Maggie glanced over her shoulder at Joe who was fitting a nose bag onto the horse. 'A wedding seemed a good time to start getting Joe out and about a bit more, too,' she said, lowering her voice. 'Get people used to seeing him.'

Dot nodded. It was only sensible to get people used to the idea that Joe was the baby's father, although it was still hard to look at his grotesque injuries without flinching. There would be plenty of people who would wonder how Maggie could bear to take him into her bed, but Dot knew that Maggie was banking on the fact that nobody would ask her outright. It wouldn't stop the gossip and speculation, but then, nothing would stop that.

'He still hasn't remembered anything?'

'No,' said Maggie. 'I'm just hoping he never does. Sometimes, I forget he's Joe. He's another man who happens to have the same name. That's how I think of him, anyway. He doesn't speak very well still, but he works hard and he's good with Jacob ... I'm not asking for more than that.'

'Where is Jacob?' Dot asked, peering into the trap to see if the little boy was there.

'I thought I'd spare him sitting through a church service. Grace Armitage is keeping an eye on him, and no doubt Sam Pearson will find some excuse to join her. I don't know how he runs his own farm nowadays.'

'When are they going to stop footling around and get married themselves?'

Maggie laughed. 'Soon, I think. I'll be sorry to lose Grace, but now Joe can do more on the farm and I've got Molly to help in the house, I'll manage.'

'Not much of a day for a summer wedding, is it?' said Janet Airey, coming up to join them, and holding grimly onto her hat against the stiff breeze. It was overcast and the grass in the graveyard was damp from rain earlier in the day. 'My rheumatism gives me gyp when it's damp like this.'

'I'm surprised Levi Dingle didn't pay for better weather,' said Dot. 'He's been throwing money around like there's no tomorrow. He asked me to do the wedding breakfast, and he didn't even blink when I gave him my shopping list. He came back from Bradford with great bags of flour and sugar and everything else I wanted. Must have cost him a fortune!'

And that was before her fee. When Levi asked her what she wanted to be paid, Dot had thought of a figure and quadrupled it, and he hadn't so much as quibbled!

'I heard Tom Skilbeck butchered two bullocks and six hoggets for him,' Betty Porter volunteered, joining them in time to pick up on the conversation.

'Well, and that's why we're here,' Janet pointed out with a wink. 'No point in turning down free food, eh? Or a chance to stick our noses in!' She looked over at the cluster of people by the church door. 'This is a bit of do, in't it? What do you reckon to them Ramages?'

'I haven't seen them yet,' said Maggie.

'That's them over there.' She pointed. 'Turned up in four motor cars and are carrying on like they own the place. I heard one of them pointing out manure on the road, like they'd never realised horses do their business like every other one of God's creatures.'

'Have you seen them furs the women are wearing?' Betty added enviously.

'I could do with a fur now,' said Dot with a shiver. 'It's parky, isn't it? I thought it was supposed to be summer?'

Janet leaned in conspiratorially. 'I heard that Cora's father is boss of some criminal gang in Bradford,' she said. 'Alf Ramage his name is. Did you ever come across him when you lived there, Dot?'

'No, I tried to avoid criminal gangs, Janet.' Dot couldn't keep the tartness from her voice. Janet

205

must think Bradford was the same size as Beckindale where everybody knew everybody else's business.

'He looks like a nasty piece of work,' Betty said, when Janet seemed about to take umbrage with Dot's tone. 'I saw him when they drove in earlier. I hope that Levi Dingle knows what he's getting himself into.'

'That one knows fine well what he's about,' Janet said with a sniff. 'He's no better than he should be, like all them Dingles. I wouldn't trust any of them further than I could throw them,' she added for good measure, which enraged Dot.

'Levi's a bad un, I'll give you that, but Mick's all right,' she said, 'and so's Jonah.'

Janet was unconvinced. 'Coming here and stirring everything up,' she grumbled. 'A garage, I ask you! Whatever next? As if Beckindale needs one of those.'

'You can't complain about Jonah buying the pub,' said Maggie pacifically. 'We've always had one of those.' She turned to Dot. 'I saw the Woolpack as we drove past. It looks so much better now it's got a roof on.'

'I know!' Dot brightened. 'We're getting the stairs put in next, and repairing the floors and plastering. Then we can start decorating.'

But Janet and Betty didn't approve of the pub either. Betty clicked her tongue. 'I can't believe Agnes is letting you get involved with a pub! Mary Ann thinks you're taking advantage of your ma when she's not well enough to object.'

A red haze of fury descended over Dot's eyes and she had to clamp her jaws together and blink it away before she said something she would regret. She needed the likes of Betty and Janet. If they came to the pub, all the other women would, so she could afford to alienate them completely, but oh, it was so hard not to lose her temper with them both!

'Ma *has* objected,' she said when she could ungrit her teeth. 'I know she's got reservations, but I hope she'll come to see that a restored Woolpack will benefit the whole village.'

'Nobody's got a problem with the Woolpack opening again,' Janet put in. 'We just don't hold with the idea of you running it. Decent women don't go into pubs, and that's that.'

'Ava Bainbridge was behind the bar at the Woolpack,' Maggie pointed out.

'That was different. Ava was married.'

'So it's the fact that I'm not married that's the problem, not that I'm a woman?' asked Dot.

'You're a young girl from a decent family,' said Betty firmly. 'You'll get quite the wrong reputation if you go ahead with this idea of running the Woolpack. It's bad enough that you've got that Jonah Dingle living with you and your ma the way she is. People will talk,' she told Dot, as if Dot was unaware of the fact that Beckindale ran on gossip.

Maggie's hand closed on Dot's arm as she opened her mouth to retort.

'It looks like everyone's going in,' she interrupted, and nodded to where the fashionably dressed Ramages were moving towards the church door. 'We'd better go in too. Cora will be arriving soon.'

Betty and Janet bustled off to get a good seat and Maggie beckoned to Joe. When he came up, she put her hand in the crook of his arm and urged him towards the church porch.

'Thanks for saving me from Betty,' Dot said, walking with them. 'I was about ready to clonk her!'

'I could tell.' Maggie sent Dot a sideways glance. *'People will talk*, eh?'

Dot made a sound somewhere between a snort and a laugh. 'Betty should know! She and Janet are the biggest gossips around. *And* Mary Ann Teale! She's got a nerve telling me I'm taking advantage of Ma. Ma's the reason I'm stuck here in the first place!'

'They just don't like change,' Maggie said sympathetically. 'I used to have a real problem with the busybodies, too, but I came to realise that they've got kind hearts underneath it all.'

'Oh, I know.' Dot sighed in frustration. 'I just wish they would try and imagine that things could be different. That you wouldn't have to be married to do what you want to do. It's like the war never happened. It would never occur to Betty and Janet that a woman could do just as good a job as a man.'

'Maybe things will start to change now that we've got the vote.'

'When we're thirty! I've got another eight years before I can vote,' Dot grumbled.

In deference to Joe's nervousness at the unfamiliar surroundings, they sat in a pew at the back of the church. Dot noticed that when Joe was restive, Maggie would pat his knee as she would soothe a child or a dog and her touch seemed to have a calming effect on him.

It must be hard not to understand who you were or where you were or what you were doing, Dot thought with a pang of sympathy for Joe. Not that he didn't deserve it, mean bugger that he had been, but as Maggie said, it was easier to think of him as a different man entirely now. Dot presumed there had been some way of identifying him after the explosion, otherwise how could you possibly tell that he was, in fact, Joe Sugden?

Levi Dingle was standing at the front of the church, wearing a natty checked suit the like of which Beckindale had probably never seen before. He looked inordinately pleased with himself and kept glancing over his shoulder at the crowded church. Dot saw his hot, hungry gaze resting on Rose Haywood, who was sitting next to her mother and looking deeply uncomfortable, and worried for her friend. She had assumed that his engagement to Cora would have marked an end to his obsession with Rose but seeing the predatory way he looked at her, Dot was afraid that it was far from over.

Mick stood next to his brother, carefully *not* looking at Rose. It was odd seeing him in his uniform rather than the oil-stained overalls he wore in the garage. Beside him was Jonah. Funny how he managed to look dangerous just standing there in a suit, Dot thought, firmly deciding to ignore the way her breathing had stumbled at the sight of him. It was just something in the way he held himself, the unconscious arrogance in his expression, the impression he gave of being about to leap into action.

Glancing around the packed church, Jonah caught Dot's eye and winked. She stuck out her tongue in return.

Maggie watched the by-play with interest. 'You seem to be getting on well with Jonah.'

'We're friends.'

It was true. Dot was glad that they had cleared the air when Jonah had taken her out to dinner. She was all too aware of how easy it would be to fall in love with him and that was the last thing she wanted to do. So she was keeping a careful guard on her feelings, and whenever her eyes drifted to the length of his thigh, the ugly scar that dragged down one cheek, the faint stubble along his jaw, a dangerous twist in her belly would remind her to wrench her gaze away.

But there was no denying it was good to have a friend to talk to and to argue with and laugh with, a friend who made her feel alive in a way she never had before.

Maggie's striking grey eyes flickered between Dot and Jonah. 'Just friends?' she asked.

'And business partners,' said Dot, and then wished she hadn't sounded so defensive. 'I know people are saying I'm after him because he's rich, but that's rubbish. I don't want a husband any more than Jonah wants a wife. Even if I had been his type, which I'm not, there's no way Jonah is going to settle down anywhere, with anyone. Least of all in Beckindale!'

Maggie thought about that while the church filled with the sound of conversation. It was as if everyone had forgotten why they were here and were all catching up with a good chat.

'Why aren't you Jonah's type?'

Dot stared at her. Wasn't it obvious? 'Because I'm a plain, mouthy Yorkshire lass. Jonah could take his pick of beauties, I reckon.'

'And yet, he's still here,' said Maggie, non-committally.

'I think he's enjoying working with Mick on the garage. He likes going out and getting customers, but he doesn't want to be tied down, so he'll do it until the garage is established and then he'll move on. That's what he says, anyway,' said Dot.

'I'm not sure he trusts me completely with the Woolpack either,' she added darkly. 'I want him to make me manager now, but he's insisting on waiting until he sees how the opening goes. If it's a success, he'll leave me to get on with it, but if not, he's going to put in a man. He says there's no point in alienating customers and losing money.'

Maggie's mouth turned down at the corners. 'I suppose if he's investing, he can do what he wants.'

'I'm putting my own money in, too,' Dot pointed out. 'And all the hard work. But we've made a deal. If the opening is a success, he'll move on and leave me in charge. If it isn't, he'll appoint a male manager. That is *not* going to happen,' she said, fixing Maggie with a steely gaze. 'I'll make a success of the pub if it kills me. This was *my* idea, and I'm not standing back so some man can take it on. We'll get it up and running, and then Jonah Dingle can swan off and do what he likes, as long as I'm in charge of the Woolpack.'

Chapter Twenty

'Goodness, look at all these people!' Edith Haywood glanced around the full church. 'I'd no idea Levi Dingle was so popular.'

'He isn't,' said Rose tersely. 'But he's laying on a wedding breakfast in the village hall, and nobody wants to miss out on that. Dot's been working on it all week. It sounds as if it will be quite a spread.'

She was horribly aware of Levi, who kept turning and staring at her while Mick, beside him, looked straight ahead.

Rose had tried to talk to Mick about Levi, as tactfully as she could. She'd told him that Levi made her uneasy at times and Mick had nodded as if he understood. 'I know he's a bit intense, Rose, and I can see that he comes over as a bit odd at times, but he's always been like that, even as a wee lad. He doesn't mean anything by it,' Mick said confidently. 'I think he's just trying to fit in. Now I can see that Nat and I did him no favours in crippling him. We thought we were saving his life, but maybe making him an outsider was worse for him in the end. I'm sure once he marries Cora he'll settle down.'

He'd paused and looked at her closely. 'Levi doesn't do anything to make you really uncomfortable, does he?'

What could she say to that? *Yes, he does? He's kissed me while you and Cora were sitting outside, only yards away?* Mick would be devastated if he knew what Levi was really like. He wasn't a fool, and he could see that his brother flirted with the law, but he had no idea of how much Levi despised him, and Rose couldn't bring herself to tell him, especially not since she had learnt the truth about Arthur. She couldn't repay him by destroying trust in his brother completely.

A rustle at the back of the church broke into Rose's thoughts and her mother nudged her as the organ struck up. 'Here comes the bride.'

They all turned for their first sight of Cora advancing down the aisle on her father's arm. She wore a white silk dress that barely reached her calves and had the older women exchanging scandalised glances. It had a narrow hem and flounces but most of the dress was hidden by an enormous bouquet of lilies and roses, while Cora herself couldn't be seen at all behind the veil that fell from a tight flowered headband to below her waist.

Rose exchanged a glance with her mother. It might be the latest fashion in Bradford but Beckindale had never seen such a dress before. She could see her father looking pained as he waited for the bride and groom in front of the chancel.

Determinedly putting Levi out of her mind, Rose concentrated on the lovely words of the marriage service. She watched back of Mick's head and wondered if she would ever be able to stand next to him and make the same vows.

When the service was over, Levi and Cora walked back down the aisle together, both looking triumphant. Cora's veil had been folded back and she looked from side to side of the church, smiling graciously. Levi caught Rose's eyes and ran his tongue around his teeth before smiling in a way that made her stomach churn.

Outside, it was still cool and damp and the wind snatched at the women's hats. Rose held onto hers with one hand as she and her mother waited for Charles to disrobe. Levi had been insistent that they all joined them for the wedding breakfast in the village hall. Oh, nothing had been said, no explicit threats had been made but Rose understood all the same that she was to go and bring her parents with her.

Charles Haywood had spent the morning grumbling at the prospect. 'It's bad enough I had to marry them. Levi Dingle's a Catholic and bounder,' he had fumed.

Levi's generous contribution to St Mary's Church had gone some way to mollifying him, although the vicar had been unimpressed by Cora Ramage, who he considered 'vulgar'.

'And now we have to go and socialise with these people,' he complained as he appeared beside them in the shelter of the porch. He looked glum at the prospect.

Rose tucked her free hand in his arm. 'You won't have to stay long,' she comforted him. 'And at least with Dot doing the cooking you'll be able to enjoy the food.'

When they got to the hall, Rose fixed a pleasant smile on her face and followed her parents as they stood in line to greet the newly married couple. Shuffling forward as far as the bride, Rose complimented Cora on her dress. Now that Cora had laid aside the grotesquely large bouquet, her dress was revealed in its glory of layers and ruffles and odd lengths.

Cora preened. 'Why, thank you,' she simpered. 'It's the dress of my dreams.' Her eyes flickered dismissively over Rose's old-fashioned outfit. 'I'd be happy to lend it to you if you ever get married,' she added with a sugary smile. 'You wouldn't find a dress like this in Beckindale and we *are* going to be sisters.'

Rose looked sharply to see if her parents had heard, but fortunately they had already moved past Levi.

'How kind of you,' she said with an equally in-sincere smile. She couldn't afford to fall out with Cora, who knew too much about her now, and Rose sensed that Levi's wife would have no compunction about spreading Rose's business around if she felt like it.

Rose was beginning to realise that too many people now knew about her love for Mick. She *had* to tell her parents the truth, especially now she knew about Arthur.

'Thank you for coming.' Levi pressed her hand too hard when Rose moved on to congratulate him. There was a speaking look in his eyes, and Cora looked at them sharply. Rose jerked her hand out of Levi's. She had hoped that his engagement and marriage would mean that he would lose interest in her, but if anything he seemed bolder, seizing chances to brush against her, or gazing soulfully into her eyes.

Rose didn't blame Cora for her jealousy. If Mick had behaved the way Levi did, she would have been hurt and humiliated.

With relief she turned to Mick, in his best man's role, looking tall and handsome in his uniform. Rose's heart warmed at the sight of him.

Mindful of her father nearby, who had contented himself with a brusque nod, she held out her hand demurely. 'Mr Dingle.'

'Miss Haywood,' he said, equally formally, but his eyes danced. 'Do help yourself to a drink. There's tea, beer or champagne.'

'Champagne!' Rose's eyes widened. Champagne was for Lord and Lady Miffield, not served in the village hall!

'Indeed. Brought by Mr Ramage for the occasion. I recommend that you try a glass.'

Rose was sure parents wouldn't approve of her drinking champagne, so she took a glass and slipped to the other end of the room before they could insist that she had tea instead. She sipped at the champagne gingerly, feeling the bubbles going up her nose.

Dot had outdone herself with the feast, which was laid out as a buffet on a long table. There was cold roast beef and pickled cucumber, mutton pies and a huge ham. Rose saw roast ducks, ready carved, sitting next to stuffed hard boiled eggs, cold potatoes and pickles. Dot had made good use of Levi's sugar, too, producing a mouthwatering array of cheesecakes and bilberry pies, jam tarts and brandy snaps ... none of them had seen such a spread since before the war, if then.

'Remember when we had to scrape together enough for the Christmas party in 1915?' Maggie said, joining Rose in contemplation of the table.

216

She had been sensible and was carrying a cup and saucer of tea. 'We could never have imagined eating like this again then.'

Rose was admiring the many-tiered and elaborately decorated wedding cake. 'Did Dot make that?'

'No, I think the Ramages brought that from Bradford this morning.'

'You'd never think butter was still being rationed!'

'I don't think rationing means much to the likes of the Ramages,' said Maggie in a dry voice.

Beside her, Joe Sugden was staring at the table as if he couldn't quite believe what he was seeing.

'Joe, you remember Miss Haywood,' Maggie prompted.

Joe darted a look at her and ducked his head in what might have been an acknowledgement although it was apparent that he didn't remember her at all.

Rose forced herself not to show her revulsion at the terrible injuries to his face. 'How are you, Joe?'

Joe sent a desperate glance at Maggie who smiled with remarkable composure. 'He's well, thank you,' she answered for him and touched his arm. 'Why don't you go and sit on those chairs over there until we're ready to eat?' she said to him and Joe nodded and made his way to the corner of the room. Several people drew away from him as he passed, repelled by his disfigurement, and some of the children stopped and stared, but Joe kept his head down and found a chair where he sat with his hands on his knees and his single eye lowered as he stared down into his beer.

Rose watched Maggie watching him with an odd expression on her face, and she wondered again what it was like for the other woman to live with a man who had beaten her so badly.

Children were squealing and running between legs. Most of the adults were ignoring them, but the Ramages were looking pained. Clearly they were not used to country weddings. Alf Ramage was a swarthy, barrel-chested man with small cold eyes. He gave off an air of menace, but there had been no denying the fact that he adored his daughter and he had been bursting with pride when he walked Cora down the aisle. Rose wished she could imagine her own beloved father being the same when she married Mick.

'That Grace Armitage not with you?' Beckindale's busiest busybodies, Mary Ann Teale, Janet Airey and Betty Porter had converged on Maggie. They nodded at Rose, but she was conscious of being the only one holding a glass of champagne while they all had tea.

'She's looking after Jacob.'

'And I daresay Sam Pearson is looking after *her*,' said Betty with an arch look.

Mary Ann sniffed her disapproval. 'Agnes allus hoped Sam might marry Dot, but seems like she's got her eye on another type of man altogether,' she said, and they all followed her gaze across the room to where Dot and Jonah Dingle seemed to be in the middle of a fierce argument. Slight as she was, Dot was drilling her finger into Jonah's chest and was obviously taking no nonsense

'He took her out to dinner in Ilkley, the Royal

no less.'

'*Did* he?'

'Bold as brass, the two of them.' Mary Ann leant in. 'Agnes reckons they're sweet on each other.'

Rose's gaze rested on Dot and Jonah. She wouldn't have said there was sweetness between them but there was no mistaking the spark snapping in the air. They weren't touching, but you could see it in the easy way they stood together, in the way their eyes met and Dot's anger was wiped out by a reluctant laugh. They were doing absolutely nothing improper but still it seemed as if they were sealed in a little bubble of their own, separated from the rest of the room.

Maggie was watching them too. 'Dot says she doesn't want to get married.'

'Oh, they all say that,' said Janet indulgently.

'They're making a good job of the Woolpack.' Rose thought it was time to support Dot and Jonah. 'Every time I go past, Dot's in there with her sleeves rolled up, and often as not, Jonah Dingle's there too.'

But that was apparently not the thing to say.

'I don't hold with young women smoking and drinking,' Betty Porter added looking pointedly at the glass in Rose's hand. 'Dot used to be a nice lass, but she's got very wild.'

Before Rose could retort in support of Dot, Levi was on his feet and tapping his knife against a glass to bring the chatter to a stop.

'Just before we eat, my wife, Cora, and I would like to thank you all for coming here to celebrate our wedding,' he said when they had all subsided into silence. 'We've had little enough to celebrate for the last few years, but we're turning a corner now.'

'No thanks to you,' Janet muttered.

'I'm delighted to have built a new house here in Beckindale which I hope will be as happy a home for Cora as it has been for me,' Levi went on. He was standing on the dais, very much at ease, with Cora simpering beside him. 'I'd like to thank Mr Ramage, of course, for allowing me to marry his daughter.' Here Levi tipped his glass to Alf Ramage, who summoned a sour smile. 'And I must thank my own family, too, especially my dear brother, Mick, who brought me to Beckindale. Without him, I would never have made my home here or met Cora.'

Rose caught a glimpse of Mick looking pleased and was glad that Levi had acknowledged him.

'I know you'll all agree that family is the most important thing,' Levi said, 'so I hope you will all join me in lifting a glass first to my dear wife, Cora, the new Mrs Dingle.'

There was a subdued murmur of 'Cora,' around the room.

But Levi hadn't finished. 'And now we can look forward to what I hope will be the next wedding in the family and in Beckindale, that of my brother Mick and Miss Rose Haywood. I can only hope they will be half as happy as Cora and I are.'

His words fell into a dead silence. Around Rose, people were glancing at each other wondering if they had heard right, until as if by common consent, they all turned to look at her. Rose stood as if rooted to the spot, still clutching her glass of champagne.

The silence was broken by her father, who had been sitting with her mother and now got to his feet, his expression one of disbelief and outrage.

'Nonsense!' he said.

Edith Haywood's eyes met Rose's across the hall. 'Rose?' she said, quite quietly, but her voice carried in the utter stillness. 'Is this true?'

Rose moistened her lips as she looked around for Mick. White-faced with rage, he looked ready to tear Levi down from the dais and beat him to a pulp, and only Jonah Dingle was restraining him.

'Yes,' she said clearly. 'It's true.'

'It most certainly is not true!' exploded Charles Haywood. He glowered at Levi. 'Damned insolence! How dare you suggest such a thing?'

'I'm sorry, Vicar. I was raised to speak the truth,' said Levi piously.

'Why, you–!'

'Charles!' said Edith sharply. She got to her feet and put her cup and saucer on a table nearby. 'We are taking attention away from the bride. I think we should discuss this at home.'

She took a firm hold of her apoplectic husband and drew him towards the door. 'Come, Rose,' she said in a voice that could not be disobeyed.

Rose felt Maggie touch her arm in sympathy as she forced herself to move at last. Very carefully, she set her barely touched glass of champagne on the edge of the table and followed her parents to the door.

'Rose, wait!' Mick had managed to shake off Jonah's restraining hand and was pushing through the crowds towards her.

On the dais, Levi wore an expression of mock dismay while Cora was looking furious at being upstaged.

As Mick reached Rose, he turned to look back at his brother with a murderous expression. 'You bastard!' he said and a sharp intake of breath ran around the hall.

'Mick,' Rose said in an undertone. 'Leave it. I should talk to Mama and Papa alone.'

'No, we'll do it together,' he said, taking her arm.

The last thing Rose heard before the door swung to behind them was Levi's gleeful voice. 'Oh, dear, I seem to have put my foot in it, don't I? But I thought *everyone* knew!'

Chapter Twenty-One

'I have never been so humiliated!' Charles Haywood swung round on Rose the moment she and Mick emerged from the village hall. 'Never! What on earth is going on, Rose? And as for you,' he added, turning furiously on Mick, 'you stay away from my daughter!'

'Papa...' Rose was on the verge of tears. 'I've been trying to find the right moment to tell you.'

'Do you mean to tell me that it's true?' Her father's voice rose 'That this ... this ... Irish *layabout* has had the temerity to put his hands on you?'

'Charles,' Edith checked him with a look before Rose could reply. 'Let us go inside and discuss this in a civilised manner.'

The vicar glared at Mick. 'I don't want him in my house!'

'This involves Mr Dingle too,' said Edith. 'And we're certainly not talking about it in the open street. Unless you want the whole of Beckindale to listen in?'

Muttering darkly, Rose's father strode up the lane to the vicarage.

'Mama,' Rose began but Edith held up a hand. 'Not until we're all sitting down, Rose.'

She set off after her husband and, exchanging a look, Rose and Mick followed in silence.

At the vicarage, the front door stood open. Charles could be heard bellowing at her mother in the drawing room. Rose felt sick, but she closed the door carefully and glanced at Mick as he took off his army cap.

He was looking tense but had himself well under control and he gave her a quick smile and a wink. 'Buck up,' he murmured, and she drew a steadying breath and even managed a smile in return. Pulling out her hat pins, she hung up her hat with his cap and led the way into the drawing room.

Her father had taken up position in front of the fireplace. His expression was thunderous. 'How could you do this to us?' he burst out at the sight of Rose. 'You've disgraced yourself and us!'

Edith, sitting in an armchair, ignored him as she indicated the sofa. 'Sit down, both of you,' she said and when they had perched on the edge, she sent Charles a warning look. 'Now, your father is right, Rose. I think we deserve an explanation, don't you?'

What could she say that would possibly make them understand? 'I love Mick,' Rose said.

'We thought you loved Ralph Verney,' said Edith. 'We thought you'd never got over his death.'

Rose sighed. 'I did love Ralph, but it wasn't really love. It was infatuation, and he never loved me.'

'What about all those letters he wrote to you?'

'They weren't to me, Papa. Ralph loved Maggie Sugden. He sent her letters to me so that Joe wouldn't find out and I passed them on to her.'

Charles Haywood's eyes bulged. 'You encouraged *adultery?*'

'Joe would have killed Maggie if he'd found out,' Edith put in quietly. 'He used to beat her.'

'Edith! Are you telling me you knew of this?'

'I didn't know about the letters, no. But I knew Joe made Maggie's life a misery.'

'What goes on between a man and his wife is none of our business,' Charles blustered.

'That's not a very Christian attitude,' Edith said. 'Maggie was deeply unhappy.'

Charles stared at his wife. They seemed to have temporarily forgotten Rose and Mick sitting nervously on the sofa. 'Are you telling me that you approve of Mrs Sugden's actions?' he demanded.

'I'm saying that I understand them. When you're beaten like that, it's hard to resist the possibility of love. I know what that feels like.'

The silence that fell over the room was deafening. Rose saw her father opening and closing his mouth in shock.

'I have never lifted a hand to you!' he spluttered at last.

'Why do you think I married you, Charles?' Edith sounded quite calm. 'I would have married anyone who got me away from my father. He would explode with fury at the slightest thing – the wrong spoon used for the marmalade, a strand of hair out of place. I dreaded playing the piano because if my fingers stumbled, my father's brow would darken and he would rant at me for clumsiness, for not practising hard enough. Sometimes he would drag me from the piano stool and lock me in a cupboard until I had learnt my lesson. At other times he'd pick me up in his big hands and throw me across the room. Once he broke my arm.' She rubbed it, as if the break still ached.'

'Oh, Mama...' Rose whispered. 'Didn't your mother protect you?'

'She would just whisper to me that my papa had a lot on his mind, that he didn't mean to hurt me. But he did. I think he probably treated her even worse.'

'Edith, this is hardly a suitable subject for the drawing room!' Charles blustered. He shot a venomous look at Mick. 'Especially with present company.'

'I'm telling you now because of Mr Dingle's presence,' said Edith. 'Brutality is not confined to the working class, Charles.'

'Be that as it may, it does not make Dingle a suitable husband for my daughter!'

'Why not?' cried Rose in frustration.

'He's Irish, for a start,' her father said with contempt. 'Look at all the trouble the Irish have caused over the last few years. Armed rebellion, demonstrations, outright war now ... they can't be trusted.'

A muscle was jumping in Mick's jaw. 'Look at this uniform I'm wearing,' he said tightly. 'I fought for Britain. I spent four years in the trenches to help protect this country and its empire, and precious little thanks I've had for it!'

'Nonetheless, a marriage between you and my daughter is out of the question,' said Charles. 'You have nothing whatsoever in common.'

Rose reached for Mick's hand. 'That's simply not true, Papa.'

'Indeed?' he replied in an arctic voice. 'What could you possibly have in common with a young man from the bogs of Ireland?'

'We're friends. He makes me laugh. He makes me happy.'

'Marriage isn't about laughing!' said Charles, ignoring his wife's wince.

'It should be,' said Rose with a defiant look.

'You can't live on happiness!' Her father glared at Mick. 'How would you propose to keep her?'

'I've started a garage, as you know.' Mick kept his voice even. 'We still have to establish ourselves but I hope to able to support a wife before too long.'

'A garage!' Charles snorted. 'Beckindale doesn't need a garage! It's fantasy!'

'Respectfully, sir, I disagree,' Mick said. 'I don't think it'll be long before you and people like you are coming to me and asking me to find you a motor car of your own.'

'I think that is highly unlikely!'

'Mick is right,' Rose put in. 'Motor cars are the future. I know the garage will be successful but even if it isn't, I'm going to marry Mick. I'm twenty-one now, and I don't need your permission. I'd like your blessing, of course, but if you don't give it, we'll get married anyway.'

'Oh, Rose, my dear!' Her father's voice cracked. 'How you've changed!'

Dropping Mick's hand, Rose got up and went over to her father. 'I'm sorry, Papa,' she said gently, 'but you're right: I have changed. At the start of the war, I was just a silly girl. All I thought about were dresses and parties and imagining myself as Lady Miffield – *that* was a fantasy! I'm glad to have changed. I've seen men die, or come to terms with a life without a limb or half a face, and all because they answered the call to go and fight for their country. That was a call you made too,' she reminded him.

Charles hung his head. 'I was wrong,' he admitted. 'I didn't think the war would turn out the way it did. But, Rose, this marriage you're proposing ... it goes against the natural order of things. Surely you can see that?'

'The war has changed things, Papa. All those social barriers have come down.'

'Not in a place like Beckindale. War or no war, people wouldn't like it if the vicar's daughter married a working class man.'

'I don't care what people think. All I care about is whether Mick and I would like it, and we would!'

Charles began to pace round the room. 'All this doesn't change the fact that you have lied to us,' he said, trying another tack.

'I'm truly sorry about that, Papa, but I knew you wouldn't like it and I wanted to spare you more distress. There never seemed to be a good moment to tell you when I knew that you were worried about John and lately you and Mama have been so full of grief for Arthur–'

'Don't you dare talk to me about Arthur!' Her father flung up a hand. 'Arthur died in the service of his country. He stood for everything that was good and strong and true while you, you were sneaking off with this Dingle fellow. How could you, Rose?' he demanded. 'The very least we expected of you was honesty. If nothing else, you should have thought about the honour of the Haywood name.'

'The *Haywood* honour?' echoed Rose with a short laugh. 'That's good!'

He frowned at her tone. 'What do you mean?'

'I'll tell you about the Haywood honour,' she began and Mick rose hastily to his feet and crossed over to her.

'Now, Rose–' he warned but she shook off his restraining hand.

'No, Papa wants honesty. Let him hear the truth.'

Her mother had been sitting quietly with her hands folded in her lap, but at that she lifted her head. 'What truth?' she asked

'Mick knows.'

'Rose.' Mick rubbed a hand over his face. 'Don't ask me to do this. I promised I wouldn't

228

say anything.'

'They need to know, Mick.' Rose turned to her parents. 'Mick was with Arthur in France.'

There was a charged silence. Charles and Edith stared at him. 'Were you with him when he died?' Edith asked in a threadlike voice.

Mick shifted uncomfortably. 'Yes. Yes, I was.'

'Go on, tell them the rest,' said Rose.

'I don't think I should...'

'Please,' said Edith, her eyes on Mick's face. 'Please, I need to know.'

Rose took the decision from Mick. 'Arthur was shot for desertion,' she said baldly.

She heard her parents' sharp intake of breath as the word seemed to reverberate around the room: *desertion ... desertion ... desertion*. Edith's hand had gone instinctively to her neck as if to hold in a heart that had leapt painfully into her throat, and the colour had drained from her father's face, leaving him grey.

The grandfather clock in the hall ticked relentlessly into the silence as it lengthened.

'Desertion...?' Charles echoed at last, barely above a whisper. His bombast and anger had drained out of him like a pricked balloon, and all at once he looked older and shrunken.

Mick sighed. 'He didn't want you to know. He was ashamed. I promised I wouldn't tell you. I wouldn't have said anything to Rose, except that she said that you kept pushing to know what had happened and I didn't want you to find out in a letter. I hoped she could persuade you that Arthur was just missing.'

'But he was so keen to go and do his bit!' said

Charles 'How...? Why...?'

'Listen, he was just a lad. It was easy to be keen when you were safe in England. I was exactly the same. I thought war would be exciting.' Mick gave a humourless laugh. 'I'll bet Arthur thought the same. But once you're out there... I can't explain what it was like. Shells screaming overhead. Machine guns and explosions and mud and blood. Filth everywhere. Arthur wasn't the only one who couldn't cope with the horror of it. He was scared. Any rational man was scared. I was, for four years.'

Charles moistened his lips. 'But you didn't run away.'

'I wasn't eighteen and I hadn't lived a privileged existence before I got to the trenches. It was different for me.'

'What happened to Arthur?' Her father asked after a moment, his voice harsh.

'He was attached to a brigade fighting near St Quentin,' said Mick. 'It was a regular mess-up by all accounts and they had a hard time of it, being pushed back by Jerry and counter-attacking when they could. They'd lose a wood, re-take it, lose it again until they were on the other side of the Somme. And then it turned into a rout. A lot of the young men who'd just come out and hadn't been hardened to battle lost their nerve then. It wasn't just Arthur.'

'So he just ... ran?'

'He said they were making their way along a sunken road between dugouts when they stumbled into some Jerries with a machine gun. He saw the men being mowed down and then the line broke, and the ones at the front turned and were running back towards Arthur and his men and then they were all running... He said he didn't remember what he was thinking. He was just running with the others and hoping not to get a bullet in the back.'

Edith made a small sound of distress in the back of her throat but when Mick paused, she gestured to him to go on.

'The Military Police found him hiding in a wood not far from Amiens and arrested him. I was driving trucks at that point and I recognised him. He didn't know me, but I'd seen him with Rose when I was home on leave, so I knew he was her brother. Prisoners were allowed one "Friend" to argue their case at the trial and keep them company, so I volunteered.'

'There wasn't any sympathy for deserters among the troops,' Rose said. 'Befriending Arthur made Mick very unpopular, but he stayed with him to the end. We owe Mick a great debt, Papa.'

'How ... how was he?' asked Edith.

'I'm not sure he really understood what was happening.' Mick spoke carefully. 'He was in shock, remember. We talked a bit about rugby and then I could see what a man he could have been if he hadn't had to face the horror of the trenches.'

He paused, remembering. 'He talked about his family too,' he went on, glancing between Edith and Charles. 'He kept saying that he was sorry, that all he'd wanted was to make you proud and that he'd failed you.'

Rose was watching her father. She saw his face

crumble with grief but he nodded at Mick. 'Go on.'

'There was a trial. I tried to persuade them that Arthur was just a boy and that he hadn't meant to run away, but they wanted to make an example of him because he was an officer.' Mick stopped and cleared his throat. 'He was executed by a firing squad.'

'Oh, dear God.' Edith covered her face with her hands. 'He must have been so frightened!'

'He was shot for desertion, but he died bravely,' said Mick. 'I was with him that morning.'

Rose took Mick's hand. 'This is the man who stayed with your son, Papa. This is the man who befriended him when he had no one and comforted him in his last moments. This is a man who spent four years at the front.' Her voice shook with emotion. 'So don't tell me this is a man who isn't worthy of me.'

'Gently now, *acushla*,' Mick said quietly. 'Your parents are grieving. Leave them be for now.'

Rose gave a jerky nod of agreement as he put his arm around her and urged her towards the door. At the last moment she turned in time to see her strong, vigorous father crumple into a chair, while Edith knelt beside him and held him while he wept.

Autumn 1919

Chapter Twenty-Two

'I think we should get the upstairs done now.'
Dot continued the argument they had started
inside as she poured Jonah a cup of cold tea and
handed it to him. They were sitting on the back
step at the Woolpack, where a patch of mellow
September sunshine warmed the stones.

'Let's just get started,' said Jonah impatiently.
'As long as the bars are painted and furnished,
we can leave the bedrooms until later. It's not as
if we've got anyone booked in to stay.'

'It'd be much better to do it all at once.' Although Dot was tempted, she had to admit. She
couldn't wait to throw open the doors of the
Woolpack once more.

She didn't tell Jonah, of course, but she was
secretly thrilled with how the ruined pub was
coming back to life. Now that the roof was on
and the carpenters had put in new windows and
replaced the doors, they could start repainting
and she was determined to do that herself. She
was tired of waiting for the workmen to finish;
her fingers itched to be doing. And Jonah, to be
fair, had agreed and had even volunteered to help
her. Whenever she wasn't cooking and he wasn't
demonstrating tractors to farmers or persuading
the local gentry to invest in a motor car, they
pulled on paint spattered overalls and whitewashed the walls of the downstairs bars.

That afternoon they had been painting what was to be the ladies' lounge. Dot had decided to keep the decor simple with whitewash and wooden tables. For a while she had hankered after the leather-buttoned settles, marble-topped tables and engraved mirrors that she had known in Bradford pubs but she knew the people of Beckindale would instinctively distrust anything 'fancy', so simple it was.

She offered Jonah a piece of fruitcake with his tea, and he took it with a grunt of thanks. 'I'm bored of painting,' he grumbled.

'You go and drive around the countryside on your motorcycle then,' said Dot. 'I'll do it.'

'If I hired some painters, you could come with me.'

Dot took a bite of cake. 'I want to do it myself,' she said indistinctly.

'You are the most stubborn woman I know,' Jonah sighed.

'If you got a team of men in here, they wouldn't listen to a word I said,' she pointed out. 'And that's always supposing you could get painters out here. At least if I do the painting myself I know it'll be done right. Besides, you spent enough money on getting a couple of bathrooms put in.'

'I couldn't stand you nagging me any longer about those.' Jonah finished his cake and brushed the crumbs from his fingers. 'I still don't see why we can't open the bars as soon as we've finished painting. I've been in touch with the brewery, and they can deliver the beer whenever we want. What more do we need?'

'Glasses, spirits, mats, tables, stools, settles...'

Dot counted them all off on her fingers until he waved at her to stop.

'All right, all right, but we still don't need to get the upstairs rooms ready just yet. I don't mind staying where I am. My landlady's an excellent cook.'

Dot bumped her shoulder against his. 'I wasn't thinking of you,' she told him. 'I'm the one who's going to be moving in.'

'You?' Jonah lowered his cup and stared at her. 'Since when?'

'Since we agreed that I would be manager.'

'I think the agreement was that we would wait and see whether I would appoint you manager or not,' he reminded her.

'Come on, Jonah, after all the work I've done, you don't seriously think you could put someone else in charge of me?'

He heaved an exasperated sigh. 'You probably wouldn't do what you were told anyway.'

'Exactly,' she said, pleased at his understanding. 'Besides, the deal was that you would leave me in charge if the opening was a success, and it will be. It's going to be great,' she went on confidently, 'and you'll be able to go off and leave the Woolpack safely in my hands. So I might as well move in sooner rather than later. I'll need to be here to cook breakfasts for the guests anyway.'

'We don't have any guests!'

'They'll come. If Mick's right about people starting to tour around t'country in their new cars, we could get all sorts of nobs wanting to stay.'

Jonah looked around the yard dubiously. 'To do what?'

'Well ... shooting?'

'Anyone in a shooting party would stay at Miffield Hall.'

'All right, mebbe they'd go fell walking,' Dot suggested after a moment's thought. 'There's folk that like that kind of thing. Ilkley has plenty of visitors to the spa, and now they've got motors they can explore a bit more and they're bound to break down every now and then. They can stay while Mick's fixing their cars.'

'I don't think we should rely on drivers breaking down conveniently in Beckindale.'

'I'm just saying that folk'll come,' she said. '*You* came.'

'True, and I think I should be able to stay in my own pub,' said Jonah. 'I can't live here if you're sleeping here too.'

'You're not going to hang around for much longer anyway,' Dot said, flicking cake crumbs off her overalls. 'You're already bored.'

'I'm bored of painting, not of Beckindale.'

The tetchy note in his voice made her raise her brows. 'What happened to Mr I-Never-Settle-Down? I thought you'd have moved on ages ago. Don't tell me you've given up on new challenges?'

'No.' He scowled. 'I'm waiting until I see whether I'm likely to get a return on my investment or not. I don't abandon challenges halfway through. Anyway,' he added, 'that's not the point.'

'What *is* the point?'

'The point is that it's not a good idea for you to live here on your own.'

'Why not?'

'It's not suitable. What if all these mythical

guests turn out to be men?'

'I expect they'll be able to keep their hands off me,' she said in an off-hand way. 'And don't worry, I'll definitely be able to keep my hands off them.'

'It's not funny. What about your reputation?'

'What reputation?' Dot scoffed.

'You know what the women in the village are saying about you,' Jonah said with a frown. 'They don't like idea of women in pubs at all, let alone running one. Imagine what they'd say if you were living here on your own. I know you don't like it, but you'll need them on your side if you want to succeed. Why don't you stay with your mother and I'll move in?'

'Because I want a place to live on my own,' she told him. 'Not at the beck and call of lodgers.'

'Hah! That's a joke,' said Jonah mirthlessly. 'It's the other way round if you ask me! I never met a bossier landlady.'

Dot only grinned and lifted the bottle of tea in silent invitation. He held out his cup as she topped it up. 'Seriously, Dot, you can't do this,' he said. 'I know you're independent but living on your own in a pub ... it won't do.'

'What, you think a husband would be some help?' she asked with an ironic look.

'At least he could look after you.'

She bristled. 'I can look after myself. What would a husband do for me? I'd be the one cooking and cleaning and putting his dinner on the table. What would *he* do?'

'Support you?'

'I'd rather bring in me own money, thanks.'

Jonah looked at her curiously over the rim of his cup. 'Have you really never wanted to be married, Dot?'

'I don't see the point of a husband,' she said. 'Women should be able to earn their own money and not be dependent on a man.'

'Husbands are good for more than financial support.'

'Oh, aye? Like what?'

'Well, there's ... how shall I put it? ... the pleasure of the marriage bed.'

Dot hooted with laughter. 'The pleasure of the marriage bed?' she echoed mockingly. 'It can't be that good.'

'You won't know until you try it.'

'I don't see *you* rushing to get married,' she pointed out as she got to her feet, brushing down the seat of her overalls. 'Come on, let's finish that lounge. I've still got supper to make.'

Jonah followed her into the room and picked up his paintbrush. 'Aren't you at all curious?' he asked after they had worked for a few minutes in silence.

Dot's tongue was caught between her teeth as she concentrated on the window frame. 'What about?' she asked absently.

'About what it would be like to have a husband. Have you ever even kissed a man?'

Outraged, she straightened and turned, paint-brush in her hand. 'That's none of your business!'

'Have you?'

'If you must know, yes, I have,' she said exasperated. 'I kissed George Kirby, who was farm hand at Emmerdale Farm before the war, and it

240

was nowt special, let me tell you. Thought he was God's gift to women, George did, but why I was supposed to like having a tongue rammed down me throat, I don't know.'

Jonah smiled. 'It doesn't sound to me like George knew what he was doing. You should give it another go.'

'Right,' she said sarcastically. 'And who is there to kiss me now?'

'Well...' Jonah made a big deal of looking around the empty room. 'There's me.'

Dot's pulse jumped alarmingly, but she kept her expression neutral. Ever since Jonah had taken her out to the restaurant she had been on her guard, although she was honest enough to realise that it was her own feelings she had to be careful of, not Jonah's. The truth was that he had made no attempt to seduce her – and naturally she was very happy about that.

It was just that she was always so *aware* of him. It was as if she lost a layer of skin when he was around, and her nerves skittered whenever she let her eyes rest on his mouth or wondered what it would be like to feel those strong hands on her.

But she was a practical lass, and she had no intention of making a fool of herself over Jonah Dingle. Dot had no illusions about herself. Rich, handsome men weren't in the habit of falling for plain, hard-headed girls, so she enjoyed his friendship and whenever that tingling warmth threatened to lure her into silly dreams, she pulled herself ruthlessly back.

Like now.

'You're offering to kiss me?' she asked, letting

amusement creep in to her voice.

'Why not?'

She tilted her head to one side and pretended to consider him. 'It's kind of you, but no. Thanks, anyway.'

Turning back to the window, she smothered a smile at Jonah's expression.

'Hold on,' he objected. 'You gave old George a chance! Why not me?'

'I'm old enough to know better now,' she explained. 'And I don't want to be rude, but I really don't fancy you that much.'

'Is that right?' Jonah sounded distinctly nettled. 'That sounds like a challenge.'

Dot dipped her brush into the pot of paint and caught the drips carefully on the rim. 'I'm sorry if you're offended.'

'I'm not offended,' he said huffily. 'I think you're scared that you might enjoy it too much.'

He was right, but Dot had no intention of letting him know that. 'Hah, not likely!' she scoffed instead.

But she had forgotten that if she always rose to a challenge, so did Jonah. She heard his footsteps crossing the new floorboards and then he was gently turning her to face him and taking the paintbrush out of her suddenly nerveless hand. He laid it across the top of the paint tin.

'Well, let's see shall we?'

'Come on, Jonah, you don't really want to kiss me,' she said, although it was an effort to keep her voice level.

'Don't I? Maybe I've been thinking about kissing you for a while now.'

'Right, me being the beauty that I am,' she said, trying for sarcasm even as she told her legs sternly not to tremble.

'You're not pretty,' Jonah agreed, his eyes moving over her face.

'Ta very much!'

'You're more interesting than that,' he said over her interjection. 'You're like a little sparrow, Dot. There's nothing obvious about you. You run around being small and busy and making no effort to attract anyone but I've been watching you and there's lots to see. I like how bright your eyes are. I like the way your mouth curves, the way you turn your head. I like the way you loosen your shoulders and stretch like a cat when you think no one's looking.'

'You're quite good at this, aren't you?' Dot managed. 'I like lots of things about you, too, but one thing I *don't* like, Jonah, is the idea that you expected me to fall at your feet the way every other woman you've met seems to have done. Are you sure you don't want to kiss me to teach me a lesson?'

The corner of his mouth kicked up. 'Maybe I just want to fluster you a little.'

Taking her gently by the waist, he drew her towards him. Dot's heart was hammering against her ribs and there was a booming in her ears far louder than anything she had ever heard in the munitions factory.

Jonah was pressing kisses along her jaw. 'Are you sure you wouldn't like to kiss? Just to see if I can do better than George?'

Her skin was burning where his lips had

243

touched and she could feel her will weakening.

'I thought we agreed no soppy business,' she said with difficulty.

'This isn't soppy,' said Jonah. 'This is an experiment. You can say no,' he added, no doubt sensing that she was weakening. 'I'll stop if you want.'

Why *not* let him kiss her? Dot asked herself. It was no use pretending that she didn't want him to, and at least then she could stop wondering. She might never get another chance to kiss a man. But she mustn't lose control.

'Will it take long?'

'That depends,' he murmured, his mouth skimming from her temple to below her ear and Dot sucked in a shivery breath of response. Who knew that skin could be so sensitive or that the slight scrape of stubble could unleash such a flood of feeling inside her. Desire was pooling in the pit of her belly, making it hard to think and it was a struggle to find the breath to speak.

'Because if ... if you want your supper, I'll ... er ... I'll need to go soon ... and I want to finish this window.'

She felt his lips curve against her cheek. 'Does that mean I can kiss you?'

'Oh, go on then,' she managed unsteadily. 'I may as well give it a go.'

Instinctively, she turned her head so that her mouth met his, and then, oh then it was a different thing entirely from George's kiss. Jonah's lips were warm and persuasive and he tasted so good that Dot wound her arms around his neck and pressed closer.

It was such a relief to give in to weeks of suppressed longing. Even if she never kissed him again, she would have this, she told herself hazily. She would make the most of it. She wanted to feel more, taste more. More of Jonah's mouth, more of his hard hands, more of that long, solid body against hers.

When Jonah gathered her tighter and deepened the kiss, she melted into him, meeting kiss with kiss while desire thudded through her and his hand curved possessively over her breast. When he broke the kiss, she couldn't prevent an instinctive murmur of protest.

'So,' he said raggedly, 'what do you think?'

Think? She was supposed to be thinking?

'About kissing,' he prompted her.

With an effort, Dot put her hands against his chest and levered herself away from him. She was hot and trembly, and her legs were as unsteady as a newborn lamb's but her mind was clearing. The important thing was not to let Jonah guess how much his kiss had affected her.

'Hmm, not bad.' Dot might be a little breathless still but she was rather pleased with her careless tone that gave no indication of the fact that her pulse was still pounding or that every part of her was screaming with frustration that he had let her go. 'You're better than George, I'll give you that.'

'I'm flattered,' said Jonah, with a smile. 'You're a pretty good kisser yourself. You were definitely getting the hang of it.' He cocked a brow at her. 'Want to try again?'

Dot moistened her lips. 'I'd love to,' she told

him, 'but I've got a rabbit pie to make and I want to finish this window first.'

'Rabbit pie?' Jonah shook his head and started to laugh. 'That's me put in my place!'

Dot couldn't decide if she was relieved or disappointed when he walked back to the whitewash he had abandoned and picked up his brush once more.

'Enough experimentation,' he said. 'Let's get back to painting, or we'll never be able to open.'

Chapter Twenty-Three

Mick twisted the spanner, tightening a wheel nut with excessive force. 'So now Levi's taking his Vauxhall to be mended in Ilkley, bypassing his own brother!' he grumbled.

Rose was sitting on a tyre in the workshop, fiddling with one of the strips of rubber that Mick used to mend punctures. She had slipped away from the vicarage earlier, hoping that he would take the opportunity to close the workshop so that they could go to bed, but she had found him in the middle of a rush repair job and complaining bitterly about Levi.

The two brothers had been estranged ever since Levi's announcement of their relationship at his wedding two months earlier. True, it had meant Rose's parents had learnt the truth about Arthur's death, and it was something not to have to keep her love for Mick a secret any more, but nothing

246

had really changed.

Charles Haywood was still not reconciled to the idea of their marriage. Rose had hoped that her father would change his opinion when he knew what Mick had done for Arthur, but grateful as he was, Charles refused to give her his blessing. He was unconvinced that Mick would make enough money from the garage to keep her and worried that the social gulf between them was too great.

'People won't like it,' he said.

Sometimes it seemed to Rose that she was trying to keep everyone happy and pleasing no one.

Mick had been furious at what Levi had done. The day Levi and Cora got back from their honeymoon, he had gone round to give his brother a piece of his mind, but Levi had turned around and made Mick feel that everything was his fault.

'I tried to tell you what he was like,' Rose had said when Mick told her about the confrontation.

'Levi knew it was a secret,' Mick fumed. 'He deliberately sabotaged us! He humiliated you in front of everyone, and you know what he said when I went to see him? That Nat and I had humiliated *him,* as if that excused it. He's never going to forgive me for shooting him in the leg,' he said wearily. 'I didn't realise that he hated me that much. What's happened to him, Rose? Ever since I came back, he's been making snide comments, and blaming me for Nat's death.'

Rose was outraged. She knew how much Mick grieved for his elder brother. 'How could it be *your* fault?'

'Oh, if I hadn't joined up, Nat wouldn't have done the same.'

'I thought he enlisted because Levi did?'

'So he did, but Levi only joined up because of me, so perhaps he's right. Perhaps it *was* my fault.'

'Once they brought in conscription, he would have had to fight anyway,' she pointed out but Mick refused to be comforted.

'He might not have been at the Somme when they sent us over the top. God, Rose,' he burst out, 'it was like a scene from hell. Wave after wave of men mowed down. I was next to Nat, waiting for the order to advance. "You be careful up there," he said to me. "Don't you be reckless now."'

Mick had smiled painfully. 'He always was a cautious bugger. Anyway, we climbed up together and off we went. I thought he was with me, but when I made it to a shell hole, I couldn't see him. I tried to go back for him but the officer made me go on. It wasn't until after the battle that I found him and by then it was much too late.' He rubbed his hands over his face, clearly forcing back the tears, and Rose put a hand on his back in silent comfort.

He leant back against her touch while she circled her hand soothingly. 'Nat's death is not your fault, Mick,' she said firmly. 'It's the fault of the men who started that war. Levi is wrong to blame you for that. He should be glad that you saved him from war, too, but I think he was warped by being made to feel that he was a shirker.'

'Maybe that's it,' Mick said. 'He's not the brother I remember, that's for sure. He was such a grand little lad, Rose. I wish you could have known him in Ballybeg. Our mammy used to spoil him but he was the youngest, and we didn't mind. He had a hard time of it being sick so often. When he was up and about, he'd follow us around and we'd let him tag along. Levi used to hero worship me once.' Mick looked sad at the memory. 'He was such a dreamer then. I don't understand how he could become so cynical and hard.'

'People change,' Rose had tried to console him.

Now Mick jammed on another wheel nut and wrenched it into place. 'You know, all the time I was in France, there were two things that kept me going: you and Levi. No matter how bad things got, I'd imagine being here again with you, and seeing Levi. He's *family*,' he went on, still unable to make sense of Levi. 'Family don't turn their backs on each other, or take their cars to someone else's garage to be repaired!'

Straightening from the car, Mick heaved a sigh. 'Ah, I'm sorry, Rose. I shouldn't be going on about it. The hell of it is, I miss Levi.'

'You miss your little brother,' said Rose, going over to him and taking the spanner from his hand to lay it aside, 'I know what that feels like, Mick. But that's not who Levi is any more, Mick. That Levi's gone, just like Arthur is gone, just like Nat is gone.'

Her heart ached at the distress in his face. 'You're asking me to accept that I don't have any brothers,' he said. 'That's a bitter feeling, Rose, and lonely.'

'You've got me,' she said as she took hold of his hands.

'Have I?' he asked bleakly. 'Not completely, Rose. Not until we're married, and your father's never going to accept me, is he?'

'Oh, Mick...' Rose drew a breath. It was easier to show him how much she loved him than to tell him. 'Let's go to bed,' she said, and after a moment's hesitation, he nodded.

'I'll close the workshop,' he said,

But as he was pulling the door to, a car came up the track, its cautious pace a contrast to the frantic parping of the horn.

'What the–?' Mick looked closer. 'That's Cora's car!'

Rose rolled her eyes. Cora was the last person she wanted to see right then and she lurked by the stairs, hoping that Mick would be able to get rid of Levi's wife soon.

'Rose! Rose, come quickly!'

The urgency in Mick's voice sent Rose running outside to see Cora, dressed in a houndstooth skirt with deep pockets and a pale pink blouse, its round neckline decorated with beads. Her fashionable hat had a low brim and in spite of the warmth of the day, an extravagantly plush fur stole was slung around her shoulders, but her expression was harried.

'Oh, thank goodness you're here!' Cora exclaimed at the sight of her.

Rose's gaze went to Mick, who was helping Maggie out of the car. 'What is it?' she asked sharply. 'What's happened? Is it the baby?'

Maggie nodded, her face twisted in pain.

'Her waters broke in the middle of the village shop,' said Cora, sounding torn between excite-

ment and disgust. 'I just went in to buy some bis-
cuits and suddenly there was water splashing
everywhere! Mrs Webster said I should drive
Maggie home, but she was asking for you, so I
came here to ask Mick to drive you to Emmerdale
Farm.'

'I think it's too late for that,' said Maggie, her
voice threadlike. She gripped Rose's arm in
panic. 'The baby's coming, Rose! You have to
help me.'

'Of course I'll help you.' Without thinking, Rose
reverted to a nurse's calm manner. 'But I don't
think you're going to make it back to Emmerdale
Farm. This baby's going to be born in a garage,
I'm afraid.'

'As long as it's all right,' Maggie managed between breaths. 'I should never have gone into the
village. I thought there would be lots of time.
And now I've made a terrible mess of Gladys
Webster's floor...'

'It'll give her something to talk about for years,'
said Rose. 'Mick, we'll never get her upstairs. Can
you find some bedding and we'll make up a bed
on the floor in the parlour? Bring some clean
towels, too,' she called after him, as he ran off, obviously grateful that she had taken charge. 'Come
on, Maggie, let's get you inside,' she went on.

'Well, er, I'll leave you to it,' said Cora, starting
to back away.

'Where are you going?' Rose snapped. 'I need
your help.'

'I don't know anything about babies!'

'You know how to put on a kettle, don't you?'

Looking incongruous in her pointed shoes and

251

smart hat, Cora was set to boiling water while a panicky Mick made up a bed in the dingy parlour and Rose made Maggie breathe through her contractions.

'This is Hugo's baby,' Maggie whispered to Rose between gasps. 'I don't want to lose it!'

'You won't lose it,' said Rose calmly. 'You'll be fine.'

She sent Mick to Emmerdale Farm to let them know what was happening. He was so clearly relieved to get away that she and Maggie couldn't help smiling, but that was Maggie's last smile before the pain took over. Cora hovered anxiously, grimacing at Maggie's groans and screams, while Rose did her best to keep them both calm.

'I can see the head,' she told Maggie. 'It won't be long now. Wipe her face, Cora,' she added to give Cora something to do.

For long minutes Rose was aware of nothing but Maggie's body as it pushed and stretched and she bore down at last with a ferocious yell. Tears stung Rose's eyes as the baby slithered into her waiting hands and a thin cry wavered through the musty-smelling parlour.

'It's a boy!' Tenderly, Rose wiped the baby's mouth and put him in Maggie's arms. 'A beautiful boy, Maggie.'

'Beautiful?' Cora peered over Rose's shoulder with such an expression of disgust that Maggie laughed weakly.

'He is to me,' she said.

Cora's face was white. 'I can't believe how *awful* that was,' she said, wonder at the miracle of new life evidently passing her by. 'I had no idea it hurt so much! I don't think I want a baby. All that screaming. And the ... eeuww, I think I might faint just thinking about it!'

Rose exchanged a glance with Maggie. 'We haven't got time for that,' she said in a brisk voice. 'Go and put the kettle on and we'll all have some tea.'

Muttering about bossiness, Cora trailed into the kitchen and Rose could hear her clattering cups and saucers around.

She turned back to Maggie who was stroking her tiny son's cheek with a marvelling finger. 'What will you call him? Hugo?'

Maggie shook her head. 'That wouldn't be fair to Joe,' she said. 'I'll call him Edward.'

By the time Mick came back from Emmerdale Farm, Maggie and baby Edward were clean and content, and Cora was beginning to look a little less revolted. The three women were drinking sweet tea as Mick came into the room, followed, to Rose's dismay, by Joe Sugden.

'Joe's come to take Maggie and the baby back to Emmerdale Farm when they're ready,' said Mick buoyantly, clearly mightily relieved that the birth was over. 'I'll drive them back in the four seater.'

Rose watched worriedly as Joe crossed the room to where Maggie lay with Edward cradled in her arms. He squatted down beside his wife and fixed her with his good eye.

'All ... right?' he asked her, struggling as always to sound the words clearly through his ruined mouth.

Cora's lips curled back in disgust at Joe's

distorted features but Maggie looked up at him quite calmly and smiled. 'I'm fine, Joe.'

'Baby?'

'He's fine too. His name is Edward.'

'Ed-ward.' Joe touched one rough knuckle to the baby's downy cheek, and all at once Rose's throat clotted with tears. 'Good,' he said.

Later, Mick took Maggie, Joe and Edward home to Emmerdale Farm. Cora, torn between elation and shock at the day's events, offered Rose a lift back to the vicarage, but Rose decided to walk. The evening was mellow with the September scent of fallen apples and damp leaves. Smoke curled up from chimneys into the crisp air. It was growing dark and Rose could see lamps lit in the cottages that she passed.

She kept thinking of the expression in Maggie's eyes as she looked down at Hugo's son, of how she had smiled at Joe. It seemed to Rose that Maggie had accepted that Edward's birth marked the point where she let go of her love for Hugo. Life kept moving on through heartbreak and joy, and it was time to look forward not back. The family that Maggie had was not the one she had dreamed of, but she would make the most of the one she had.

Rose smiled at the memory of Edward's small body. Her throat still ached with the wonder of his birth and she longed for a baby of her own. It was time for her to make a choice, too, she realised, and to look forward as Maggie had done. There was no point in wasting time waiting for everyone to be happy.

'I love Mick,' she told her father when she got into the vicarage. 'I don't want to wait any longer. I'd like you to give me your blessing, but with or without it, I'm marrying him. You can accept that, Papa, or you can lose me. I've made my choice, and now you can make yours.'

Chapter Twenty-Four

Before the war, Rose had spent many happy hours dreaming about her wedding. She had had it all planned out in her head. It was going to be a grand social occasion, as naturally she would be marrying Ralph Verney, heir to Lord Miffield. Bursting with pride, her father would marry them in St Mary's and she would walk up the aisle in a long white satin dress, embroidered with flowers and beads and covered in lace. She would have a wreath of orange blossom in her hair and a gauzy veil would shroud her face until Ralph lifted it lovingly at the altar after they were married.

After the ceremony, a carriage drawn by two white horses would have taken them to Miffield Hall where there would have been champagne and lobster patties for the breakfast. That night she and Ralph would have waltzed at a glittering ball and lived happily ever after. Oh, how gloriously happy they would have been.

But that was in 1914. Before the war that had killed Ralph and turned Miffield Hall into a hospital. Before she had met Mick Dingle. Before she had grown up and let go of silly dreams. They had all seen too much, suffered too much over the past few years. Too many assumptions about the way life should be had been turned on their heads.

So on her real wedding day Rose stood in her bedroom and smoothed down her simple dress. No lace, no frills, no beads. The war had done away with all of those – unless, like Cora Ramage, you had a wealthy and doting father who was happy to skirt around the edges of the black market – but Rose didn't mind. She was marrying Mick and nothing she had ever done felt as right as this. There would be no title, no grand house – though her father had given them some money to build a small house behind the garage. Rose was content with that.

Her father was not bursting with pride as she had once imagined he would be. He was disappointed in her, Rose knew, and nothing would change that, but at least he had accepted Mick rather than risk an estrangement. Between Arthur's desertion and death, his eldest son's insistence on living with Robert Carr, and his daughter's choice of a working class Irishman as a husband, Charles Haywood's certainties had crumbled. He was a subdued version of the man he had been.

'Ready, my dear?' Edith Haywood brought in a simple bouquet of flowers she had just picked in the vicarage garden. She offered it to Rose with a rueful smile. 'I couldn't find much, I'm afraid.'

Gently, Rose touched the petals of the chrysanthemums and Michaelmas daisies. 'They're perfect, Mama. Thank you.' She glanced up. 'Is Papa very unhappy that I am marrying Mick?'

'He'll survive, Rose.'

'And you?'

'I think you're lucky to be marrying a man that you love.'

The night before, Edith had come to her room and initiated an awkward conversation about what Rose might expect on her wedding night. Rose had stopped her, leaning forward to put a hand on her mother's knee. 'It's all right, Mama,' she had said. 'I know.'

Edith had looked at her, startled. 'You mean...?'

Rose smiled faintly. 'The war has made us all impatient,' she said.

'The war has changed a lot of things,' Edith sighed. 'Your papa is only just realising that now.'

'It has made me value you more than I did,' Rose confessed. She had always adored her charismatic father, but as the war had worn on, it had been her quiet mother who had shown the greater strength. And since learning how her mother had suffered from her own father's violence, Rose had looked at her in quite a different way.

Now she looked at her mother and hesitated. 'Did you love Papa?' she asked. 'When you married him?'

Edith shook her head. 'Not then,' she said honestly, 'but as the years have passed, I have learned affection, and since Arthur's death and learning the truth of that ... he needs me now in a way he never did before.' She looked at Rose with a smile tinged with sadness. 'Perhaps we are coming to love each other now.'

'I'm glad,' said Rose.

'We can be happy again, if we try to put the past behind us.' Edith said. 'But it's more important that you are happy, my dear. So, come, let's get you married.'

Outside, the mist was drifting over the beck and the air smelt of wet leaves. Rooks wheeled over the trees as Rose walked to the church with her mother and her brother, John, who was to give her away so that her father could perform the marriage ceremony.

Charles had been right about one thing. Her marriage was unpopular in the village, where it was generally felt that she was marrying beneath her. When the banns had been read the murmurs of disapproval had rustled around the church. Rose didn't care. The people she liked most would be there for her wedding. Maggie was still nursing baby Edward, but had promised to be at the service, and Polly and Robert Warcup would be there too. They hadn't forgotten how Rose and Maggie had helped at the birth of the twins nearly four years earlier.

Dot was waiting in the porch to act as bridesmaid. She was looking trim in a blue suit and a pretty hat that Rose had lent her. It framed her vivid face beautifully, and she winked as Rose arrived and fell in behind her as she set off up the aisle.

And there at last was Mick, waiting for her at the altar in his uniform, his cap tucked under his arm. Jonah stood beside him. Levi had refused to attend the wedding and had taken Cora to Bradford for a visit instead. Mick was hurt but Rose was privately relieved. She wouldn't have put it past Levi to stand up and claim that he knew of a just cause or impediment to her marriage. And while she had tried to make friends with Cora, she wasn't sorry to be spared that boastful presence on her wedding day.

The wedding ceremony passed in a blur, and it was only when her father pronounced them man and wife that Rose was able to relax and smile properly at Mick.

'Corporal Dingle,' she greeted him demurely as she had done when they had first met in secret during the war, and Mick grinned and kissed her.

'*Mrs* Dingle.'

They posed for a photograph outside the church, and then the bridal party had lunch in the vicarage which had been cooked earlier by Dot. It was a stiff occasion, with her father obviously uncomfortable sitting down with Dot, but Rose had insisted that she be there. 'Dot isn't a servant any longer,' she had said firmly. 'And she's my friend.'

Fortunately Jonah had the assurance to make conversation with the vicar while Mick set out to charm her mother. Still, it was a relief to Rose when it was time to go. They had planned two days in a boarding house in Scarborough for their honeymoon, and Jonah had offered to drive them to the station in Ilkley to catch a train that afternoon. After lunch he had slipped away to fetch the motor, but when Rose and Mick went outside, he cranked the engine but then stood back.

'I've decided you can drive yourself,' he said.

259

'What a beauty!' Mick walked round the car, running his hand admiringly over its bonnet and mudguards. 'This isn't one of ours, is it?'

'No, it's yours,' said Jonah. 'A wedding present,' he went on when Mick's jaw dropped. 'You can't run a garage and not have a motor of your own.'

For once, Mick was staggered into silence. 'I ... don't know what to say,' he stuttered at last.

Rose could see that he was too choked to speak properly so she tucked her hand into his arm. 'I'm *not* going to thank you, Jonah,' she said. 'It's quite clear that Mick is going to love this motor car more than me!'

She was already dressed in a warm coat and scarf with a motoring hat and veil ready for what she had thought would be a drive to the station. Jonah opened the passenger door and she settled herself into the leather seat while Mick put their cases in the back and wrung his cousin's hand.

'How can I thank you?'

'Take your wife on honeymoon,' said Jonah. 'Go on, I don't want to see your ugly face until the end of the week.'

He stood back with Dot and Rose's parents as Mick released the brake and Rose waved. They drove out of Beckindale with the wind in their faces, both smiling broadly as they headed for the sea and a new life together.

'Well, that's over.' Dot couldn't help feeling deflated as she and Jonah said a stilted farewell to the vicar and Mrs Haywood and walked away from the vicarage. Dot's hands were thrust into the pockets of her suit and for a while they walked in silence, their boots crunching through drifts of tawny gold leaves and fallen twigs.

'Where are we going?' asked Jonah eventually.

'Back to the Woolpack? It's not long until we open and there's still so much to do.' But even Dot could hear the lack of enthusiasm in her voice.

'Let's go for a drive instead.'

'Where?'

'Anywhere,' said Jonah. 'You've been working like a dog, Dot. You need a break, and we could both do with getting out of Beckindale for a couple of hours.'

'All right.' Now that he had mentioned it, Dot realised how restless she was feeling. It was something to do with watching the easy way Rose leant into Mick, with the look on Mick's face when Rose had stood beside him at the altar. With how happy they had seemed as they drove off together.

Dot treasured her independence, but she could still envy that kind of happiness. She loved the Woolpack, but it wasn't quite the same.

'We can take a picnic,' she said, warming to the idea.

'We've just had lunch!'

'I couldn't eat anything. I was too nervous of t'vicar.'

Jonah grinned and shook his head. 'I don't believe you. You're not nervous of anyone, Dot.'

'I didn't know what to say to him.'

Jonah had. He had kept the conversation going whenever it flagged, talking sensibly about flying in the war, and amusingly about his exploits in Australia. Dot could tell that the vicar had been agreeably impressed by him in the end.

'Just tea and a bit of cake,' she wheedled.

'All right,' said Jonah. 'You go and get that, and I'll fill up with petrol.'

They took Jonah's motorcycle, with Dot in the sidecar, a bottle of tea and some fruitcake wrapped in greaseproof paper on her lap. Jonah drove high up into the fells bumping along ever smaller farm tracks until at last they stopped with a spectacular view looking down over the dale. The earlier mist had evaporated to leave a pale autumnal sky. When Dot struggled out of the sidecar, she could see Beckindale huddled in the curve of the river that gleamed palely in the watery sunlight.

Jonah spread out a blanket on the springy heather and they stretched out side by side. For a while Dot was content to lie next to him in silence, looking up at a buzzard circling lazily above them and listening to its thin mewing call. His body was long and solid and she couldn't help wondering how it would feel to be able to roll onto her side and press close to him. The temptation was so strong that she could feel her skin twitching, and she sat up abruptly to pour out the tea.

'That was generous of you to give Mick a car,' she said handing him an enamel mug

Jonah propped himself up on one elbow to take the tea. 'He'll look after it. Besides, it's good for business if people see him driving around in a motor car.'

'Still, it's an expensive gift. You can't keep on handing out money. Look how much you've put

262

in to rebuilding the Woolpack. The lump of gold you found is going to run out some time.'

'It already has,' said Jonah.

Dot paused in the middle of unwrapping the cake. 'What?'

'Oh, I've got a bit left, but once the Woolpack and the garage are set up, I'll have to do something about my financial situation.'

'But ... why didn't you tell me you were running out of money?' she asked distressfully. She had lost her appetite. Handing Jonah a piece of cake, she put her own aside. 'I feel bad now. I wouldn't have suggested that you spend all that money on the Woolpack if I'd known. I thought you had lots of money.'

'I did, and now I don't.' Jonah took a big bite of the cake. 'Don't worry about it, Dot. Money's only ever been a way to do what interested me, and I'm interested in the garage and the Woolpack. It's been fun and I'm glad to have helped them get started. I don't mind not having any more money. It's exciting to start again.'

Dot picked at a sprig of heather. 'So, will you go back to Australia?'

'I haven't decided,' he said. 'There's South Africa too. I haven't been there.'

'You could always stay and earn money back on your investment in the garage and the pub,' she pointed out. 'That's what most sensible people would do rather than rush back to the wild and hope to find another lump of gold.'

Jonah grinned through the last mouthful of cake. Brushing the crumbs off him, he lay back down on the blanket with his hands under his head. 'I've never been sensible,' he agreed.

Not like her. Brisk, practical Dot, that was how everyone thought of her. Well, she'd had to be, hadn't she? But what would it be like to throw caution to the winds and do something not sensible for once?

She turned her mug between her hands. 'When do you think you'll go?'

'Not immediately,' said Jonah after a moment's hesitation. 'When the Woolpack is properly established ... I'll think about it then. In the meantime, I'll stay as long as my landlady doesn't start chasing me up for rent,' he added, obviously trying to coax a smile from her.

Dot didn't feel like smiling. She was thinking about the years stretching ahead without Jonah. She was going to miss him, there was no denying it. Thanks to him, she would have the Woolpack, but how much fun would it be without Jonah to talk and argue with? There would be no one to catch her eye or make her laugh. She had friends, of course, but no one who understood her the way Jonah did.

But she had always known that he would go. He had been honest about that from the start. She would be fine. She would send him off with a smile and her head held high – and she would make sure that she had some memories to comfort her when he had gone.

They hadn't kissed again since that day in the ladies' lounge, but Dot had relived it again and again in her mind, tossing and turning at night, burning with remembered heat and the dark, dangerous delight of it.

'Jonah?' she said now.

'Mmm?'

'Remember that time you kissed me?'

'How could I forget?'

'Could we do it again?'

Jonah's eyes flew open and he came up onto one elbow. 'Now?'

'There's no one else around,' she pointed out. Even the sheep were ignoring them.

'I'm happy to oblige, Dot, but what's brought this on?'

'I don't want to get married like Rose,' she said. 'I'm glad for her, but I don't want to be like that. Women kept this country going during the war and now we're supposed to go back to being good little wives, seen and not heard. We're supposed to look decorative and keep food on the table, but not to *think*... So I don't want that,' she went on. 'But at the same time I'd like to know what it's like. Not just kissing a man but ... more,' she said, blushing as she fumbled to explain. 'I think you'd be a good person to teach me, because you don't want to get married either and you'll be leaving Beckindale.'

Jonah sat up slowly, his eyes very green and intent. 'Do you know what "more" means, Dot?'

Her flush deepened. 'Well, not really,' she confessed. 'I mean, I know in general terms but not ... in detail.' She turned to look straight at him. 'I thought you could show me.'

Tenderly, Jonah brushed the hair away from her face, his fingers lingering on her cheek. 'Are you sure that's what you want, Dot?'

'Only if we both agree that what we do today

doesn't tie either of us down,' she said, her gaze direct. 'I don't want you thinking I'll have any expectations of you, Jonah, because I won't. And when you go, neither of us is to have any regrets.'

'A temporary affair? That's what you really want?'

'That's what I want,' said Dot, and smiled as he drew her down onto the blanket and showed her everything she wanted to know.

Chapter Twenty-Five

'I hope we'll see you at the opening of the Wool-pack, Mary Ann,' said Dot pleasantly as Mary Ann heaved herself up from her chair. She had been drinking tea with Agnes Colton and chatting away happily until Dot came in, at which point she had hurriedly remembered that she needed to make Tom his dinner.

'I've talked it over with Tom, and he doesn't think it would be fitting,' Mary Ann said. 'I'm sorry, Dot, but I've never set foot in a pub in my life, and I don't want to start now. I don't hold with women drinking and smoking and all that carry on.'

Dot bit her lip in frustration. She got the same story whoever she spoke to about the Woolpack. The men were delighted that it would be opening again, the women sucked in their breath and shook their heads and said they didn't know, they would ask their husbands or their fathers.

'You don't have to smoke, Mary Ann,' she said as lightly as she could. 'And you don't need to drink a lot. It's really meant to be a place you can meet up with your friends and have a chat.'

'We don't need to go to a pub for that,' Mary Ann pointed out. 'What d'you think your ma and I have been doing? A kitchen table does us fine, doesn't it, Agnes?'

'I wish you'd give up on this idea of a ladies' lounge, Dot,' Agnes agreed. 'Folk don't like the idea of women drinking.'

'It's not just about drinking, Ma. It's about women getting together and having a nice time. Why does that have to be in the home? Men are allowed to go out. Why not women?'

'Because that's the way it's always been,' said Mary Ann firmly. 'We're happy with the way things are. Why can't you be?' She shook her head. 'We've had too much change lately. Some of us want things to stay the same, young Dot.'

Dot turned to her mother in despair when Mary Ann had gone. 'You'll come, won't you, Ma?'

But Agnes shook her head. 'I don't want to be sitting there on my own. I wouldn't like that. If Mary Ann or Janet were going, it would be different.'

'Ma never used to worry about what anyone else thought,' Dot complained to Jonah that evening.

They were lying in her bed in the attic room at the Woolpack, Dot having won the battle of who would live there. She loved the independence of having a place of her own, even if it was just a plain little room tucked away at the top so that the rooms on the first floor could be let out to paying guests.

But Jonah had been right about one thing. The village didn't approve of Dot living on her own and the women muttered darkly about her reputation.

'Maybe she's worried about you,' said Jonah.

'Worried? About me?' Dot was astonished. 'Whatever for?'

'She's not a fool. She must know what we're doing here on our own, and so do all the old tabbies who think you're up to no good. And the fact is that you *are* up to no good. You're breaking all the rules, Dot. You're living alone, you want to run a pub, you smoke. You're sleeping with a man without being married. You're sleeping with a *Dingle,* for God's sake. You couldn't have made life more difficult for yourself if you had tried!'

Dot blew out an irritable breath. 'It's none of their business what I do!'

'This is a village. There's no such thing as minding your own business in a village as far as I can tell.'

Jonah sounded grim and Dot slid him a glance under her lashes. Lately he had been moodier than usual and withdrawn in a way she couldn't quite put her finger on. She was afraid that he was regretting the change in their relationship. Although he was enthusiastic about making love to her – and she definitely didn't want that to change – the rest of the time he was subtly distant. He was probably afraid that she was going to get all soppy, Dot thought, exasperated. She kept reminding him that their affair was only temporary, but that only seemed to make him crosser.

'Never mind, you'll be able to get away from Beckindale soon enough,' she said.

'What do you mean by that?'

'We're opening in a week. You said you'd leave after that.'

He scowled. 'Not immediately. It's not as if we'll know straight away if the pub will break even. A lot of people will come to have a look but I need to know how many will become regulars before I go anywhere.'

'All right,' said Dot equably. 'I only meant you didn't need to feel trapped here.'

'I suppose so.' Jonah was silent for a moment. 'What about you, Dot? Don't you feel trapped?'

'I did at first, but now I've got the Woolpack to run, I don't mind so much. And Beckindale's home. I belong here. I know I'm breaking the rules, but someone has to, and why should I have to leave my home to live life the way I want?'

'I just think you might find it ... lonely,' he said and she shrugged.

'Mebbe I will, but that's a price worth paying if it means independence and not just accepting that I have to do what women have always done.'

'Is independence really that important to you, Dot?'

She thought about it. 'It really is,' she said. She turned over to face him, nose to nose. 'So if you're feeling twitchy because you think I'm about to start hinting about wedding rings, Jonah, don't! All I want is a chance to run the Woolpack my way.'

'What about us?'

'What about us?' she countered. 'We're having

a lovely time and making the most of being to-gether, and when you go, we'll still be friends. Won't we?' she added when Jonah said nothing.

'Of course we will,' he said but his smile seemed forced as he drew her towards him.

Jonah pulled out his pocket watch. 'Almost eleven,' he said. 'Put on a coat, Dot. It's cold out there.'

Dot was glad of his advice when she stepped outside the Woolpack and was buffeted by the bitter wind. It was barrelling down the high street, tumbling leaves and twigs before it, and she pulled her hat more firmly on her head. Cold or not, everybody would be outside.

At church on Sunday the vicar had told them about the King's request for a two minute silence on the first anniversary of the Armistice which had ended the long and dreadful war. There would be no ceremony, the vicar said, but he read out a letter from the King explaining that on 'the eleventh hour of the eleventh day of the eleventh month' there should be 'a complete suspension of all our normal activities'. Those who could, the vicar suggested, should step outside and honour the fallen publicly.

The church bells were just starting to toll eleven. Dot saw the Websters and two of their cus-tomers leave the shop and stand with their heads bowed. Mr Bates stood on the step of the news-agents. Hannah Rigg was outside the Post Office with Peter Swales. Maggie was there, holding her new baby, Edward, with Grace Armitage by her side. Rose and Mick had walked up from the garage. One-legged Jim Airey was working at the butcher's now. He was wiping his hands on his blue-striped apron, his face sombre while Ernest Burrows stopped his cycle at the sound of the church bells and got off.

Dot peeped a glance under her lashes at Jonah. His face was set in grim lines and she wondered what he was remembering. At the last stroke of eleven, a silence fell over the village. It made Dot realise how many noises there usually were in the background, but now there was no hammering or humming or any sound at all. Just the sound of the wind, the rustling of golden leaves and, in the distance, the rush of the river after last night's rain.

Clutching the collar of her coat closer against the chill, Dot bowed her head. She thought of the people who had belonged in Beckindale and who would never walk down this street again, never lift their eyes to the fells or stand on the bridge to watch the water swirling below. They would never see how things had changed, or how much had stayed exactly the same. Her brother, Olly, who had punched her arm and grinned when he said goodbye. Bert Clark, with his abominable whistling, would never again cycle carelessly with his basket full of meat deliveries. George Kirby who had been so full of himself and too good looking to bestow more than a casual kiss on Dot herself once, would never kiss another girl. Poor Frank Pickles, with his vacant stare would never kiss a girl at all. There were so many who had died, too many, in Beckindale alone.

She remembered those years in Bradford, the

friends she had made who had lost husbands and fiancés, brothers and sons. The long, hard days in the factories. The feeling that she was doing something important.

The awful silence beat around her and her throat thickened with tears. Dot swallowed hard to force them down. Stupid to start crying now that it was all over.

The church bell tolled again and the two minutes were over, but everyone seemed stuck, as if their memories had bound them in place. Dot lifted her head and found Jonah watching her with compassion.

'I'm not crying,' she snapped before he could say anything.

'I can see that,' he said, and something in his smile steadied her. 'We need to remember, he says, but we need to look forward, too. This is a good day to open.' He raised his voice so that everyone nearby could hear him. 'Drinks on the house from five o'clock tonight: the Woolpack is reopening.'

Dot stood in the middle of the Woolpack and looked around her. It was hard to remember the terrible mess that she had seen when she first came back to Beckindale. Now the newly plastered walls were fresh and white, the beams picked out in black as before. There was a fire burning in the inglenook and old brass horseshoes she had retrieved from the rubble and polished were nailed above the mantelpiece. The beer taps had been installed and tested. The glasses were sparkling, the tables polished. Behind the bar, the spirits were lined up, every bottle fill.

Her heart swelled. It was all exactly as she had imagined it.

Together she and Jonah watched the clock tick round to five o'clock.

'Here we go then,' said Jonah, and Dot took her place behind the bar while he opened the door.

Mick and Rose were first in. 'I heard a rumour about free drinks,' said Mick with a grin.

Others had heard too and the Woolpack was soon crowded. In the main bar every table was taken and Dot and Jonah were flat out all evening, pulling beer and serving spirits. It felt good to hear the room filled with the sound of voices and laughter again, and several customers said how much they had missed the pub and how glad they were that it had re-opened.

But they were all men. The ladies' lounge remained stubbornly empty except for Maggie and Rose who had come loyally to support her.

By the time they closed at eleven, Dot was exhausted. Jonah bolted the door behind the last customers and turned to her as she gathered up empty glasses.

'You did it!' he said.

'*We* did it,' she corrected him. 'I couldn't have done it without you.'

She wanted to go over to him and thank him properly for everything he had done. She should be able to put her arms around him and kiss him and tell him how grateful she was, but since they had made love, things had changed. She was very careful now not to give him any reason to fear that she was going to get clingy.

So she set the glasses on the bar. 'I'm going to need more help when you go,' she said briskly. 'It won't always be as busy as tonight with no free drinks on offer, but it's made me realise that I can't manage on my own.'

There was a tiny silence. 'We talked about this. I'm not going yet.'

Was that outrage in his voice? Was she not supposed to remind him that he would be moving on as soon as it suited him? Anyone would think that he wanted her to beg him to stay.

'No,' she agreed casually, 'but I'll have to think about it at some point.'

Another pause. 'You don't sound as excited as I thought you would be,' said Jonah after a moment. 'I thought it went really well.'

'I'm disappointed there weren't more women here,' Dot confessed. Putting down the glasses in her hand, she dropped abruptly onto one of the settles. 'I talked to everyone and tried to make them understand what I was trying to do, but not one of those women came along to support me. Not even my own ma!'

Jonah came over and sat beside her. 'Dot, you've done something incredible here,' he said. 'You've taken a ruined building and brought it to life again. People came and enjoyed themselves tonight. It takes time to overcome prejudices but it'll happen, I promise you.' He took her hand. 'You're just tired,' he said. 'Leave all this now. Let's go upstairs.'

Dot let him draw her to her feet. 'Well, why not?' she said wearily. 'My reputation obviously can't get any worse. You might as well sleep here.'

274

'Certainly not,' said Jonah. 'I'll go back to your mother's later and keep the gossips quiet, but for now, we should celebrate, just the two of us.' His smile set Dot's heart tumbling in her chest. 'And I wasn't thinking about sleeping,' he said.

Spring 1920

Chapter Twenty-Six

Rose ducked under the porch and shook out her umbrella. She straightened her hat and tightened the belt of her coat, and then told herself sternly to stop fussing and just knock on the door.

How hard could it be to talk to Cora? There had been a moment when Rose had even thought she might grow to like Cora, that day when Edward Sugden had been born, but she had barely seen her since. She should have come before, perhaps, but her stomach still churned whenever she remembered how close Levi had come to trapping her in the house.

But she wouldn't let that happen again. Lifting a hand, Rose rapped firmly at the door.

It was opened by a sour-faced maid. 'Yes?'

'Is Mrs Cora Dingle in?'

'She en't here.'

'Oh...' It had taken all of Rose's courage to decide to tackle Cora that morning. She didn't want to have to go through it all again. 'Will she be back later?'

'I couldn't say I'm sure. Mrs Dingle is in Bradford.'

'Well, well, look who it is!'

About to turn away, Rose was dismayed to hear Levi's voice. It had never occurred to her that he would be at home at this time of day. But there he was, coming out of the room he had called his study.

Glad of the maid's presence, Rose forced a smile. 'Hello, Levi.'

'I wasn't expecting to see *you*,' he said, his eyes crawling over her face. 'Come in.'

'Well, I–' Rose fumbled for an excuse, only to catch herself up. Perhaps it would be better to try and talk to Levi himself. It was past time to face her fear of him. Besides, he had already taken her umbrella off her and shoved it towards the maid. 'Bring tea to the drawing room, Ida.'

Ida jammed the umbrella in the stand with a resentful look and stomped off towards the kitchen.

Rose cleared her throat. 'I was hoping to see Cora.'

'Cora?' Levi's gaze sharpened suspiciously. 'Why?'

'I wanted to talk to her.'

'She's in Bradford. She hasn't adjusted well to village life,' he said with an indifferent shrug. 'Talk to me instead, Rose.'

Choosing an armchair so that he couldn't sit beside her, Rose perched on the edge. 'I hoped that between us, Cora and I could bring you and Mick together,' she began and Levi raised his brows.

'Is that what this little visit's about?'

Rose took a breath and ploughed on. 'There's been a rift between you since you told everyone our secret. I won't pretend we weren't both angry with you for what you did, but that's in the past now, and it's time to move on. Mick was so hurt that you didn't come to our wedding, Levi. I know he'd always hoped you would be his best man.'

'I'm sure he was quite happy with Jonah Dingle as a substitute,' said Levi waspishly.

'He's very fond of Jonah, but you're Mick's brother,' Rose pointed out. 'I know how important his family is to him. Losing Nat was a terrible blow, but it was comfort to know that you were still here in Beckindale.'

Levi was looking sulky but he was listening, so she tried a coaxing smile. 'Mick's told me so many stories of your family in Ireland. He said you were always your mother's favourite.'

'They treated me like a child,' Levi said resentfully.

'Because they loved you.'

'Shooting someone is a funny way to go about showing that you love them!'

Rose took a breath and carefully curbed her impatience. 'You know why they did that, Levi. They saved your life.' She waved a hand around the ugly room. 'Look at this house, think of the money you've made. You wouldn't have any of that if you had gone to war with Mick and Nat.'

'They made me a laughing stock.' Levi hunched a petulant shoulder. 'Nobody in Beckindale respects me! And that Jonah just swans in and everybody falls over themselves to be friends with him.'

Rose wanted to be brave enough to say that was because Jonah hadn't taken full advantage of the black market, but she didn't want to provoke Levi.

'But why are we talking about that,' said Levi

281

with one of those disconcerting changes of mood. 'Tell me what you want.'

'I just want you and Mick to be friends again,' she said slowly. 'It would mean such a lot to Mick, Levi. He misses you.'

Levi put his head on one side and looked at her, his expression calculating. 'But what would it mean to *you*, Rose?'

'What do you mean?' she asked, taken aback.

'Is Mick's happiness so important to you?'

'Of course it is. He's my husband.'

'And I'm wondering just what you'd do to make him happy,' said Levi, and his voice clogged unpleasantly.

'I'd do anything for him,' Rose said. 'I was hoping Cora could help.'

'Why would Cora be able to do anything?' He sounded genuinely mystified, and she stared at him.

'She's your wife.'

'Our marriage is very much a business arrangement between Alf Ramage and myself,' said Levi. 'Cora doesn't have any influence on me.'

Poor Cora, thought Rose. No wonder she spent so much time in Bradford.

She ploughed on. 'I was going to suggest that you two came to dinner at the garage. It would be nice to meet Cora properly and it would give you and Mick a chance to talk again the way you used to.'

Levi put his head on one side. 'The trouble is, that I've definitely had the impression that you're the one who doesn't want to talk to me, Rose.'

'I'm talking to you now.'

'That's true.' He nodded as if struck. 'So, you really want me to come to dinner?'

Rose kept her smile even with an effort. 'You and Cora, yes, of course.' She took a breath. 'Levi, it's 1920. Isn't it time we drew a line under the past and started afresh? Mick is my husband, and I love him. The war is over. Whatever you did or didn't do for me before is *over*. You're married to a nice woman. Let's be a family. Mick needs you, Levi, and I think you need your brother as much as he does. I would really like you to come.'

Levi's expression was unreadable as he stared at her in silence. Rose began to wonder if he had even heard her, but after a moment he let out a long sigh and got to his feet. 'If that's what you want, Rose,' he said grandly, 'then of course we will come.'

'Thank you, Levi.' Trying to conceal her relief, Rose got up too. 'I'll arrange a day with Cora when she comes home.'

Why hadn't she tried talking to Levi before? Rose asked herself as she walked back into Beckindale. She had built him up into a monster in her mind when all she needed to do was to face him down.

Elated, she called in at the Woolpack to tell Dot what she had agreed with Levi and to ask if she and Jonah would come too.

'I dunno,' said Dot doubtfully. 'It sounds like a family occasion to me.'

'Jonah is family.'

'I'm not.'

'You come with Jonah.'

Dot had been sweeping the floor of the main

bar but she stopped at that and looked at Rose. 'We're not a couple, Rose,' she said firmly.

'Are you really going to try and tell me you're not in love with him or him with you?' Rose rolled her eyes. 'It's obvious!'

'We're enjoying each other's company,' Dot said with a shrug that seemed a little too carefully careless to Rose, 'but that's as far as it goes. Jonah will be leaving soon.'

'He hasn't said anything to Mick about leaving. Mick and I think he doesn't really want to go.'

Dot went back to her sweeping. 'He's told me that he'll be heading off, and that's fine.'

Rose studied Dot's back, sure that her friend must be feeling more than she let on. 'Well, if he's not going before Levi and Cora come to dinner, will you come with Jonah? I'll need some moral support to cope with Cora!'

'It'll have to be a Sunday when the Woolpack's closed.'

'That's fine,' said Rose quickly. 'And will you help me with the menu?' she cajoled until Dot grinned.

'Want me to do the cooking for you?'

She shook her head. 'Thanks, Dot, but I need to learn to do it for myself. I just need help deciding what to cook.'

Rose's mother had given her a recipe book at the wedding and Dot had given her the occasional lesson when she had a free moment. Rose had had a few disasters but the day before she had managed to roast some beef for lunch without burning it and cook potatoes that at least weren't like bullets. It was true that the Yorkshire pudding had slumped but it hadn't tasted *too* bad and Mick had had second helpings.

Agreeing a Sunday with Cora, Rose extracted a firm promise from Jonah and Dot to come along and threw herself into preparations. The builders had promised to start work on the new house they planned for the old field behind the garage at any day, but in the meantime she and Mick were still living in the cramped conditions of the old smithy.

Rose was doing her best to brighten it up. She had done plenty of cleaning as a VAD nurse and the experience had come in handy as she scrubbed tables and floors, beat rugs and swept out piles of accumulated dust. Matron would have been proud of her, Rose told herself.

The kitchen was too cramped to sit six at a table, so she cleared out the parlour and made Mick manoeuvre in a table. Rose laid it carefully with a tablecloth and cutlery, and placed a vase of daffodils in the centre as she waited for her guests.

Dot had vetoed her first ideas for a menu as too ambitious. Instead, Rose had cooked a ham and made a rather lumpy parsley sauce to have with it. Pastry was still a challenge so she had allowed Dot to bring a rhubarb pie for pudding.

Jonah and Dot arrived first, and much to Rose's relief, Dot immediately took over in the kitchen, where she stood at the stove, beating out lumps in the sauce and insisting that she was more comfortable there than poncing around as a guest.

She was still stirring when Levi and Cora made a grand entrance. They were both overdressed as usual, Levi in a striped suit and Cora in a finely pleated silk dress with a beaded neckline and embroidery on the skirt. Graciously, Cora let Mick take her fur coat, unaware of the expressive grimace he made behind her back.

When Dot came out of the kitchen with a wooden spoon in her hand, she could hardly have made a greater contrast to Cora. Plainly dressed as she was in a long skirt and pale yellow blouse, Rose thought Dot looked sweet with her brown hair in a bob but it was obvious that Cora was not impressed.

Cora, in fact, was not impressed by much. Having made it clear that she disapproved utterly of Dot's involvement in the Woolpack, she largely ignored her after that, and talked condescendingly to Rose. She commented on how cramped the smithy was and pitied Rose for how inconvenient it must be. She talked at length about how difficult it was to find decent servants and marvelled that Rose managed without any help at all. There were many references to the size of the house where she had grown up in Bradford, to her father's importance, to the superiority of the shops in the city and to the time it had taken her to find the perfect shoes to go with her frock.

Mouthing a silent apology to Dot behind her hand, Rose murmured dutifully in response every now and then. It was worth being patronised by Cora to see Mick so pleased to have his brother back at the table. Levi, too, was behaving better than Rose had dared hope. It seemed that he had, at last, got the message. He didn't try to touch her or stare intensely into her eyes. Instead he seemed almost bashful, and took Mick's joshing in remarkably good part.

Gradually they all relaxed. Even Cora stopped boasting and let Mick tease her. Delighted with how things were going, Rose offered Levi an un-shadowed smile and he beamed back at her.

'That's a grand motorcar I've seen you driving around in, Cora,' Mick was saying. 'A Bentley, isn't she? How does she go?'

Cora simpered. 'Oh, I'm very pleased with it.'

Jonah leant over the table. 'I hope you didn't let Mick teach you to drive. I have it on good authority that he's the worst teacher ever. Am I right, Rose?'

She laughed. 'Completely right!' She turned to Cora. 'I asked Mick to teach me to drive but we fell out so badly in the first lesson that we nearly got a divorce!'

Cora looked shocked. 'A *divorce?*'

'Well, maybe it wasn't quite that bad,' Rose allowed. 'We can laugh about it now, but I put my foot down. I said I wasn't getting in a car with him again.'

'So I've been teaching her instead,' said Jonah. 'I've been driven all around the dales by Mick's beautiful wife and she's my star pupil.' He winked at Rose. 'I can't think why Mick found it so difficult to teach her!'

Rose fluttered her eyelashes at him. 'I had a wonderful teacher,' she said demurely.

'All teaching requires is a little patience,' Jonah said to Mick, who pretended to scowl but couldn't help laughing.

'Wait till you try teaching your own wife to

drive, Jonah Dingle!' he said.

There was a tiny, awkward pause when no one wanted to look at Dot or comment on the fact that on several occasions Jonah had declared that he would never marry.

They were all grateful when Levi broke the silence. 'Why didn't you ask *me* to teach you to drive, Rose?' he demanded and Mick roared with laughter.

'Levi, you're my brother and I love you but I wouldn't let you teach my dog to drive!' he said, oblivious to the flush of furious humiliation that stained Levi's cheeks. 'One of these days you're going to have to learn how to change gear properly.'

Jonah clapped Levi on the shoulder. 'Don't listen to Mick,' he said. 'He couldn't teach his own wife how to change gear! He may be a genius with an engine, but he can't teach for toffee. If you need help with the gears, come to cousin Jonah,' he said with mock grandeur. 'I'll put you right. Rose will vouch for me as a teacher, won't you, Rose me darlin'?'

Rose was laughing and about to answer in kind when she caught Levi's eye and saw such a blaze of expression there that her smile faltered. Pushing back her chair, she started to gather up the plates. 'What about some rhubarb pie?' she said brightly.

Chapter Twenty-Seven

There were days when Dot thought spring would never come to Beckindale. Days when the wind blew raw and rain swept down from the fells and sleet stung her cheeks like needles. And then, just when she least expected it, the temperature rose and the air softened.

The Sunday after that uncomfortable dinner at the garage, Dot woke to sunlight striping her bed and she stretched luxuriously. Her feet had been aching when she went to bed but it had been a busy night in the Woolpack and she had been pleased to see that takings were up. The bar had been full and the banter good-humoured.

The ladies' lounge stood empty still. Jonah told Dot to give it time and not to worry but she couldn't help fretting. Every time she went in there, she looked around and saw how inviting and comfortable it looked. She couldn't understand why the women wouldn't come and enjoy the special place she had made for them.

Still, the pub was drawing a good crowd of men, and Dot had taken on Fred Airey to help behind the bar. Jonah would change casks if they were busy, but otherwise left the running of things to her, spending most of his time on the other side of the bar talking up the benefits of tractors to dubious farmers.

Dot watched the dust motes drifting in the sunlight as she contemplated a whole day to herself. It would be good to open the windows and air the whole pub, and there were still the final touches to be put to the bedrooms on the first floor before she could open for guests. There was lots to be done and absolutely no reason to be lying here feeling lonely. Jonah never stayed the night and she told herself she was glad of it. It would make things too cosy between them. They were having a temporary affair, just as she had told Rose. It would never do to get used to waking up with him or to wish that he could always be there.

Pushing the thought aside, Dot dressed and went downstairs. She loved the Woolpack when it was busy, but there was something appealing about having it to herself like this, too. It was still a thrill to remember the charred ruin and to see what she had created in its place. She wouldn't have been able to do it without Jonah, but the Woolpack was Dot's vision made real.

She opened the windows to let in the sunshine, smiling as she looked around her. Everything was as she had imagined it: the polished brass rail where the men rested their boots; the tankards hanging in a neat row; the inviting mixture of settles and tables with chairs and stools at the bar. The lingering smell of ale and the echoes of laughter and conversation. It was all perfect.

Dot always tidied up before she went to bed, no matter how tired she was. So the ashtrays had been cleared and the table tops polished. The chairs were still stacked on the tables so that she could sweep the flagstone floor. But the brasses on the wooden beam over the fireplace could do with a clean, she noticed and went to get a cloth.

She was buffing the brasses to a high shine when Jonah banged on the door.

He frowned at the cloth in her hand when she went to answer it. 'Don't you ever stop working?' he demanded.

'I'm not working. I'm just giving the brasses a polish.'

'It looks like work to me. Have you even seen what a beautiful day it is? Come on, leave that.' He took the cloth and the brass from her hand and put them on the bar. 'Let's get out of here.'

'Where are we going?' asked Dot, puzzled by the sense of urgency.

'Anywhere that's not Beckindale.'

'Why, what's happened?'

'Nothing,' he said. 'It's just that sometimes I feel I can't breathe here.'

He would be going soon, Dot could feel it. Her heart twisted. Well, she couldn't say that she hadn't known that right from the start. Through the door she could see the sunshine warming the grey stone houses opposite. Intent on polishing, she hadn't realised that people had come out of their cottages and had turned their faces up to the sun. They were sitting at their doors or chatting over their walls or digging their gardens, while the children played in the street. They were all making the most of the unexpected warmth and the fact that spring had come at last.

She would make the most of it too.

'All right,' she said. 'Let's go.'

She climbed into the sidecar of Jonah's motorcycle and refused to think about the future as they sped through the countryside, cow parsley nodding along the verges in their wake. It was enough just to be with him on this beautiful day. The dales were hazed with a fresh, zingy green and overnight, it seemed, the hawthorn had burst into blossom.

At Malham, Jonah parked the motorcycle and they walked out to the pool below Janet's Foss. Dot remembered being taken to the waterfall years earlier and watching the sheep being dipped but today they had the dappled water to themselves and could splash around the edges like children. They wedged the bottles of beer they had brought with them between the stones to keep cool, and ate bacon and egg pie.

Afterwards, Dot sat on a rock with her knees drawn up and watched Jonah as he stretched out beside her and closed his eyes. A gentle breeze stirred the leaves above them and sent shifting shadows over his face. Dot let her gaze linger on the angles of his face, realising with almost a shock how achingly familiar he was to her. She could have drawn the line of his mouth in her sleep, knew exactly how the hair grew at his temples, how his thick, dark brows arched over his eyes.

She was in love with him, Dot admitted to herself. He had been more relaxed today and she was sure it was because he had decided to go. So she wouldn't tell him how she felt. That wouldn't be fair. She had promised that she wouldn't ask anything of him. She'd make it easy for him to go, Dot vowed, even though it would break her heart.

Fickle as ever, the weather closed in that afternoon. Dark clouds rolled over the fells as they made their way back to Malham and they sought shelter from the rain in a tea room for a while. In the end it was dark by the time they drove back into Beckindale. Dot sat in the sidecar while her eyes kept straying to Jonah's profile. She could make out the hard line of his cheek and jaw, and every time her gaze rested there, desire clutched savagely at her. He would go, but she wouldn't regret a moment of the time they had spent together. Perhaps she did break the rules, Dot thought, but it was worth it.

The street was deserted when they got back to the Woolpack. Gripped by lust, Dot could barely wait while Jonah unlocked the door to the Woolpack and she laughed as he pulled her inside and swung her round to press her against the back of the door and kiss her.

'Take me to bed,' she said when they broke for breath.

'With pleasure,' said Jonah and took her hand but as they turned for the stairs the realisation that something was very wrong struck them both at the same time. 'What the–?'

How had they not noticed the smell straight away? The air reeked of spilt beer and destruction.

'Stay here,' Jonah said grimly and went to fetch a paraffin lamp.

In its hissing light they surveyed the devastation. The main bar was in ruins. Tables had been overturned, chairs and stools broken. The walls they had whitewashed were now daubed with obscenities in red paint. Every single one of the bottles behind the bar had been swept from the shelves and emptied while glasses lay smashed and the floor was covered in sticky pools of beer.

The shock was so great that Dot couldn't take it in. She felt as if she had taken a great blow to her stomach, and her breath hitched despairingly in her throat as Jonah swore quietly beside her.

'Who would do this?'

Dot didn't answer. Dully, she walked over into the middle of the bar, her shoes crunching over broken glass, and looked around. Everything she had dreamed of, everything she had worked for, everything that would keep her going when Jonah had gone: ruined. Her heart crumpled.

'Oh, Jonah.' Covering her face with her hands, she began to weep. She, who never cried and had carried stoically on through all the griefs of the past few years.

Jonah picked her up in his arms and carried her to bed. 'We can't do anything about this tonight,' he told her. 'Try and get some sleep.'

But having started crying, Dot couldn't stop. She sat, sobbing helplessly, while Jonah took off her shoes and undressed her like a child, and then held her until she cried herself to sleep.

They woke at first light and went downstairs. Any hope that things would not seem as bad in the morning was soon dashed. They looked worse.

Dot bent to pick up a chair, realised that it was missing a leg and dropped it back onto the floor. Defeated, she looked at Jonah.

'How could this happen?'

His face was set. 'I'm guessing that whoever it was waited until everybody had gone indoors when it started raining and then got in the back.'

'I left all the windows open to air the house,'

Dot said tonelessly.

'It's not your fault, Dot. They were going to get in, whatever it took.'

She let out a long sigh. 'What are we going to do?' she asked.

'You make some tea,' he said. 'I'll go and tell your mother where I am.'

'Mary Ann will notice. The whole village will know you spent the night here.'

'We'll worry about that later,' said Jonah firmly. He gave her a gentle push towards the kitchen. 'Get the range going and put on the kettle. I'll be back in a minute.'

Dot was pouring water onto the tea leaves when Jonah came back. He had changed into the faded shirt and worn trousers he had once used to paint in, and she remembered how he had told her that all his money had been spent on the Woolpack and Mick's garage. He wouldn't be able to go out and buy new furniture as he had done before.

She felt utterly defeated. 'I don't know if I can do this all over again,' she said bleakly.

She was still trying to summon the energy to put down her tea and get started when her mother put her head round the door. 'That's a right old mess in there,' Agnes said with an angry jerk of her head back to the bar behind her. 'Mary Ann's coming to give me a hand clearing up.'

Dot started to get up. 'Thanks, Ma. I'll come and–' she began but Agnes motioned her to sit down.

'You stay where you are, love. You've had a shock.'

Ignoring her mother, Dot followed her out to the bar in time to see Mary Ann Teale and Betty Porter come in carrying mops and brooms. A moment later Janet Airey appeared with Nancy Pickles and Polly Warcup close behind her.

After they had all exclaimed at the mess, Janet took charge, and divided up the tasks. Rose and Mick had come running as soon as they heard the news, and as the word spread around the village, more and more people came to see what they could do. Maggie heard on her way to see Grace Pearson, who was expecting a baby any day, and immediately came to help Dot. The Woolpack was soon full of women with their sleeves rolled up, cleaning and sweeping and mopping.

Jonah and Mick set about whitewashing over the red paint while Tom Teale repaired as much of the furniture as he could. Dot's throat was tight with emotion as she watched how unquestioningly the village chipped in to help. Even the Reverend Haywood came down and offered to chop up the irretrievably broken chairs for firewood.

With so many hands, it was not long before order was restored. Contemplating the pile of broken stools, Betty Porter remembered that she had a spare one in her parlour that she never used and Hannah Rigg thought there were a couple more in her shed too. They went off to fetch them while everyone else entered into a spirited discussion about how to replace the other items until the door opened once more and one by one they fell silent.

Cora Dingle was standing there, looking wary. 'I heard your glasses had been broken,' she said to

Jonah who moved first to greet her. 'I've brought you two boxes of new ones. They're in the car.'

'They lost more than glasses, Cora.' Rose's voice was hard. She waited until Mick and Jonah had gone out to bring in the glasses. 'It's taken all of us all morning to clear up the mess. Where was Levi yesterday afternoon?'

The colour drained from Cora's face. 'He was with me,' she said. Her eyes met Dot's. 'He was, I swear it.'

Dot, too, had been wondering if Levi was behind the vandalism, but Cora seemed to be telling the truth. With a warning glance at Rose, she went to take Cora's arm. 'It was kind of you to think of bringing the glasses,' she said.

'Well,' said Maggie after a momentary pause, 'now that we've got some glasses, why don't we see if we can find something to put in them?'

Polly Warcup said that she had some cordial in her larder and sent Robert back to fetch it and some of their home-brewed beer. Janet Airey confessed to having some elderflower wine, and the vicar went home to find a bottle of whisky.

Before Dot realised what was happening, the women had made themselves comfortable in the ladies' lounge, and were all talking at once. Cora was wedged on a settle between Hannah Rigg and Polly and looking happier than Dot had ever seen her. Her mother was chatting to Edith Haywood while Maggie, Rose and Janet were laughing uproariously about something.

In the main bar, the vicar had poured Mick and Robert Warcup a glass of his whisky as they stood at the bar together, each with a foot propped on the brass rail, while the rest of the pub had gradually filled with regulars who had got wind of what was happening. They must all be drinking home-brew, Dot realised, as all the casks had been emptied. People kept disappearing off and returning with jars and bottles. It was the best party Beckindale had had in a long time.

Dot was too emotional to join in. Her chest was tight as she looked at the ladies' lounge, full of women having a good time just as she had imagined it. When Jonah put his arm around her shoulders, she glanced up at him with tears in her eyes.

'How can I thank everyone for today?'

'You don't need to,' said Jonah. 'They're just realising what a special place the Woolpack is.'

She leant against him. 'It's funny, I thought it was perfect before. The right furniture, the right glasses, the right bottles. But now it's all battered and the glasses don't match and there are odd stools and chairs, I think it looks better. The Woolpack was mine before, but now everybody's a part of it. It belongs to all of us now.'

Chapter Twenty-Eight

From the workshop Rose could hear the sound of banging and clanging as Mick worked on an engine. It mingled with the distant rumbling of thunder. The unsettled weather had continued, lurching from a soft spring day to sudden downpours and a storm had been building all morning behind the fells. Rose wished that it would hurry up and break, and shatter the electric tension in the air.

Restlessly, she stepped out into the garden, as unsettled as the weather. She didn't know why she felt so scratchy. Yesterday had been a good day. It had warmed her heart to see how the village had rallied around Dot, but best of all had been the moment she had seen her father and Mick leaning on the bar together, deep in conversation.

Levi had done them all a favour, did he but know it. Rose took a certain grim pleasure in thinking how angry Levi would be if he knew just how his actions had brought people together. Cora might have seen him that afternoon, but Rose was certain that Levi was responsible for what had happened. He had burned down the Woolpack and killed a woman. He wouldn't hesitate at vandalism.

How could she have let herself believe that Levi had changed? She had been so happy to see him sitting at the table with Mick, so relieved to think that the awful business at the Woolpack was over and done with, so certain that the Dingles would be able to move on as one happy family. What a fool she was!

Levi was a better actor than she had given him credit for. There had been no boasting from him that day, no snide remarks or sly looks. Instead he had been quiet and almost humble. There had just been that one flash in his eyes when Mick and Jonah had been teasing him about driving. For most people, that wouldn't have been enough reason to vandalise a pub, but Levi wasn't most people.

Rose shivered at the thought of the malevolence Levi must carry within him.

'Rose!'

The sound of her name being called startled her out of her reverie and she turned to see Jonah and Dot making their way around the back of the smithy, supporting Cora between them. As they came closer Rose was horrified to see that Cora's face was swollen and bruised. She had a nasty cut along her cheekbone and her puffy mouth was bleeding where her lip had split.

She hurried towards them. 'What's happened?'

'Levi,' said Dot briefly, her lips folded in a tight line of distress. 'Can you help? We thought as you used to be a nurse...'

'Of course,' said Rose instantly. 'Bring her inside.'

They helped Cora lie down on the old horsehair sofa in the parlour. Sending Jonah out to explain to Mick what was happening, Rose examined Cora as gently as she could.

'I don't think any bones are broken, but you may have a cracked rib or two,' she told Cora. 'I'm sorry, it'll be painful for a while. Let's clean up your face,' she added when Dot had brought in a bowl of water from the kettle and a clean cloth.

It felt good to be nursing again, as if she had put on a familiar cloak. Carefully, she cleaned Cora's face and put iodine on her cuts.

Tears were leaking from Cora's eyes by the time

she had finished. 'It hurts like buggery,' she admitted. 'I'm such a fool,' she said bitterly as Rose helped her to sit up. 'I should have left him months ago.'

'Why would Levi hurt you like this?'

'It was my own fault.' Cora took a sip of the sweet tea Dot had made for her. 'I took those new glasses to the Woolpack.'

'We were grateful,' said Jonah, 'but what made you do that?'

'I overheard Levi talking to someone a few days ago. I couldn't hear it all but they were saying something about the Woolpack. When I heard that you'd had a break in, I felt bad.'

She looked at Dot. 'I really thought you might just have had a few broken glasses, and so I thought I'd replace them, but when I was there, I realised the damage had been much worse than that and I didn't know what to do. It's true that Levi was with me that afternoon, but I think he paid someone to vandalise the place. I confronted him when I got home and ... well, let's say he didn't take it that well.'

Cora put down her cup and winced as she touched her cut lip. 'It's not the first time he's taken his fists to me, but he's never lost control like that before. I blacked out in the end and when I came round, Levi had gone and Jonah and Dot were at the door.'

'We'd gone to have it out with Levi,' Dot told Rose. 'I was sure he was responsible and Jonah was angry enough to beat the truth out of him if necessary. We found Cora like this and we couldn't leave her there in case Levi came back.'

'Of course not.' Rose studied Cora with concern. 'How are feeling now?'

'Better. Thanks,' Cora muttered as Rose urged her to finish her tea. 'You've been really nice to me and I always hated you.'

'It doesn't matter.'

'It does matter.' Cora's eyes slid away and the colour rose in her cheeks. 'Levi was obsessed with you. I could never decide if he loved you or hated you. He'd talk about you all the time, even when we were ... you know ... in bed ... sometimes he'd shout out your name.'

Rose's heart twisted with pity. 'I'm so sorry, Cora.'

'I thought for a while you must be leading him on. I imagined you meeting him secretly and I was jealous. I wanted him for myself.' Cora's laugh was harsh. 'Can you believe that? What a dolt!'

'It's not your fault,' said Dot stoutly, 'and it's not Rose's neither. Levi's not right in the head.'

'Well, I've had enough,' Cora said. 'I'm going back to Bradford, and when my pa hears what he's done to me, I don't fancy much for Levi's chances,' she added with satisfaction. 'Pa's had some business dealings with him but Levi's made too many mistakes lately. Someone saw him talking to Len Arkwright, and he's not someone you want to mess with. If Levi's got any sense, he'll leave Yorkshire.'

'And good riddance to him,' said Dot.

Mick was devastated when heard Cora's story. 'But why would Levi want to do that to the Woolpack?'

'I don't know,' said Rose, 'but my guess is that it's because Jonah has been teaching me to drive.'

Mick looked uncomprehendingly at her. 'What?'

She went over to sit next to him and take his hand. 'I should have told you before, Mick,' she said. 'The truth is that Levi has been obsessed with me since he first came to Beckindale.'

'But...' Mick shook his head. 'Why didn't you tell me?'

'I knew you loved him. I didn't want to make you choose between us, and I hoped that once you were home, he would accept that it was you that I loved. Levi was all the family you had left here after Nat died. How could I spoil that for you?'

She told him how Levi had set fire to the Woolpack and claimed he had done it for her. 'Ava Bainbridge had one of your letters and was threatening to show it to my father,' she said. 'Levi said he would make sure it wasn't a problem but I didn't realise how far he'd go.

'Ava died in that fire,' she told Mick, who was listening, aghast. 'I should have told someone my suspicions but suspicion was all I had. If I'd said something, I would have had to tell you that I'd been responsible for sending your brother to prison, and I didn't want you to hold that against me. But I've felt guilty ever since.'

Mick put his head in his hands. 'I can't believe this. I know Levi's changed but I never thought he'd be violent. He was such a gentle lad! I thought we'd agreed to draw a line under the past.'

'I thought that too,' said Rose. 'I blame myself.

I should have realised that Levi will always expect the world to revolve around him. He isn't interested in anyone else. He says he loves me but he doesn't really know me or care about me. The only person Levi cares about is Levi.'

Cora nodded with a sour expression. 'That's true enough.'

'The point is, where is he now?' asked Dot in her practical way.

'He's not at the house,' Jonah said. 'I had a look round but he seems to have taken his motor. My guess is that he's realised he has gone too far but I don't think we should take any chances. Cora wants to go back to Bradford and I can't say I blame her. Can I borrow your car, Mick?'

'Of course.' Mick rubbed his face. 'I'm sorry, Cora,' he said as he helped her to her feet. 'You've had a raw deal.'

'Aye, well, Levi's the one who'll have the raw deal if he comes near me in Bradford,' said Cora. She glanced at Rose. 'But you look after your wife. I don't think Levi's done yet. He's got nothing left to lose.'

When Jonah had driven off with Cora, Dot announced that she had to get back to the Woolpack. 'We persuaded the brewery to send us some new casks so we're opening again tonight. I'd better get on.'

Rose and Mick were left looking at each other. 'Should I have told you?' she asked.

'Maybe I wouldn't have believed it,' said Mick. He shook his head. 'I've been blind. Why couldn't I see what he was capable of?'

'Because you love him.' Rose went over to kiss

him. 'There's nothing we can do about Levi now, Mick. Go and fix that engine and I'll find something for lunch.'

Above them the sky was darkening dramatically as black, boiling clouds loomed over the fells. It reminded Rose of the days before the war, when the air had seemed to thrum with tension. The day was not as hot but it held the same sense of disaster lurking behind the hills, the same strange mixture of anticipation and fear.

Standing in the kitchen doorway, she clutched her arms and watched the first jagged flashes of lightning in the distance. It had grown so dark it might almost have been night time. There was a moment of utter stillness before a deafening crack overhead as the sky split and the thunder boomed and rumbled and the first few drops of rain splattered in the dust. Then the clouds emptied and the rain poured down in a torrent, drumming on the ground and the rooftops.

Rose stood for a minute, marvelling at the sheer noise and power of the storm before turning and going inside to the pantry to find something for lunch. There was some cold beef under the fly guard. She could boil some potatoes to have with it.

Picking up the enamel plate with the beef, she backed out of the pantry door and turned to find herself face to face with Levi.

'Hello, Rose,' he said.

With a gasp of shock, she dropped the beef and the enamel plate clanged on the flagstones. Jarring as the noise was, it was still almost drowned out by the thunderous rain on the roof.

'L-Levi!' she stammered. 'You gave me such a fright!' She bent to pick up the beef and the plate, her mind running furiously. 'What are you doing here?'

'I've come for you.'

Rose put the beef on the table, her hands shaking. 'Does Mick know you're here?'

Levi tilted his head to one side, considering the question. 'Well, he *did* but I'm afraid he can't hear you now if you were thinking of calling for him.'

She stiffened, her blood turning to ice. 'What have you done to him?'

'Just a little tap on the head,' said Levi dismissively. 'I drove right up to the workshop, tooted my horn and he opened the doors for me so that I could drive inside. He didn't even realise it was me,' he smirked.

'I didn't hear anything...' Rose trailed off, realising the storm had cancelled out any other noises.

'Yes, the weather has been fortunate, hasn't it? Mick was quite taken by surprise.'

'We know what you did to Cora,' said Rose but Levi waved that aside.

'I know that. I've been watching until that interfering fool Jonah drove her off to Bradford. Her precious pa is welcome to her!'

Rose's voice trembled with a mixture of fear and fury. 'You're a brute! I want you to leave now, Levi.'

'Oh, I'm leaving,' he agreed. 'I'm sick of Beckindale.'

'And Beckindale is sick of you!'

'Well, I hope you aren't, Rose, because you're coming with me.'

She shook her head. 'I'm not going anywhere with you,' she said, wishing that the rain would stop and that someone would come round, but outside it was still pouring in relentless sheets. Nobody would be stirring from their houses for a while yet.

Her refusal had no effect on Levi. He simply reached into his pocket and brought out a revolver. He pointed it straight at her stomach. 'Oh, yes you are,' he said pleasantly.

Rose swallowed hard. She had seen guns during the war, and she knew what they could do. She had helped dress the wounds of soldiers who had been shot.

Levi held the revolver in a steady hand. 'That's better,' he said approvingly. 'I like it when you're quiet and you don't argue with me.'

'I ... I thought you loved me,' said Rose, her mouth dry. 'Why would you threaten to shoot someone you love?'

'Because, Rose, it seems to be the only way I can get your attention. I really thought you had come to care for me. You said you wanted to be close to me, you smiled at me so sweetly and I let myself believe that when you invited me to dinner, it would be the start of something special between us. But then you *laughed* at me,' he said furiously.

'We were teasing you, Levi. We weren't laughing at you.'

'Oh yes, you were! Do you think I don't know the difference? Mick and Jonah and Cora and *you*, all laughing at me. And *Jonah*,' he said, his face twisting with hatred, 'boasting about driving around the country with you. You spent all that time with him, when you could hardly bear to *talk* to me. You lied to me, Rose. You didn't want to care for me at all.'

Rose couldn't take her eyes off the gun. 'I'm sorry, I didn't mean to hurt you,' she said carefully. 'But I never pretended to love you, Levi. You don't want me to go with you knowing that I don't love you, do you?'

'I'm not waiting for you any longer,' he said. His voice had taken on a fretful note that frightened Rose. 'I'm sick of waiting, sick of never getting what I want and watching Mick with you instead. This time, you're coming with me. If you know what's good for you, you'll forget Mick and be nice to me. I'll treat you better than he does, that's for sure.' Levi looked around the kitchen in disgust. 'You won't have to live in this squalor any longer.

'Now, come along,' he added briskly, jerking his gun in the direction of the door. 'It's time we were going.'

'Could ... could I take a coat?' Rose said. Clearly she wasn't going to be able to reason with Levi, but perhaps she could try and pick up a weapon of some kind? 'I think it might get cold.'

'If you're quick about it.' Levi followed her into the narrow passage and watched narrowly as Rose took down her coat and put it on.

Mick was sprawled unconscious on the floor of the workshop. Forgetting the gun, Rose rushed over and dropped to her knees beside him.

'Mick! Oh, God, what have you done?' She felt

desperately for a pulse. It was thready, but there.

'He's lucky I didn't shoot him the way he shot me,' said Levi viciously. He was pulling open the big doors, careful to keep one eye on her. 'Now, leave him and get in the car.'

Scrabbling under Mick, Rose's fingers closed over a spanner and she managed to slip it into the deep pocket of her coat. She had no plan but it felt better having a weapon. 'In the car, Rose.' Levi's voice was implacable.

Slowly she stood up, lifting her hands in surrender. Without taking her eyes off the gun, she walked towards the passenger side of the car, only for Levi to order her to the other door.

'All those lessons with Jonah are going to pay off,' he said. 'You're driving.'

Chapter Twenty-Nine

Rose's hands trembled on the wheel. Levi's car had electric wipers hanging down from the top of the windscreen but they were useless against the torrential rain and she could barely see the lane as she inched down it and onto the road.

'Go faster,' Levi ordered, prodding her with the revolver.

'I can't! We'll drive off the road.' Her mind was spinning frantically. What was she going to do? She should be planning how get back to the smithy and help Mick, but all she could think about was the gun in Levi's hand, black and brutal and unwavering.

Would he really shoot her? Rose couldn't believe how quickly things had changed. One minute she had been happily thinking about Mick's lunch, and the next she was driving through a downpour with a madman pointing a gun at her.

And Levi must be truly mad, she thought in terror. He had tipped over the edge into insanity and how could she reason with a madman. Did he really think she would meekly pretend to be his wife and settle down with him? I'd rather *die*, thought Rose wildly, and then she glanced at the gun and realised that she might indeed die, and she didn't want to do that. She wanted to spend her life with Mick and that meant she had to be strong now.

Blinking away tears, she made herself draw a steadying breath and took a firmer grip of the steering wheel.

'Where are we going?' She had to shout over the noise of the rain pounding on the leather roof of the car.

'Just drive.'

'Drive where?'

'I don't care!' Levi shouted. 'As long as we get out of this bloody village. I never want to see it again!' His face was twitching and he gnawed at his lip, but the hand holding the gun was rock steady.

So he didn't have a plan. That gave Rose hope. *Think!* she told herself as she drove cautiously towards the bridge. Could she drive up to Miffield Hall? Someone there would help her surely? But Levi would realise as soon as she turned into the avenue and she didn't dare provoke him. Somehow she needed to leave a trail so that Mick could follow her.

The Warcups' cottage was coming up. Unsurprisingly, there was no one out in the rain, but Polly or Robert might be looking out of the window and at least notice a car behaving erratically.

Without giving herself time to think about it, Rose jerked the wheel and the car skidded over the road outside the cottage.

'Careful!' Levi shrieked.

'Sorry.' Rose's voice wobbled. She had frightened herself. 'I'm not a good driver yet.'

'Don't try anything clever,' he warned. Just past the turning to Emmerdale Farm, the road forked. 'We'll go that way,' he said, pointing.

Rose slowed down, horrified. The track was famous for its views, but it was notoriously steep, and once over the top of the hill, it wound its way down into the next valley past precipitous drops and narrow gulleys.

'Levi, it's too dangerous.'

'Not as dangerous as being shot at close range,' said Levi coldly. 'Now, drive.'

The conditions were appalling. Rose drove as slowly as she dared, hunched over the steering wheel as she peered through the windscreen in a futile attempt to see where she was going. The wipers moved backwards and forwards but they weren't fast enough to deal with the rain that was still thundering down. In the heart of the storm, it was as dark as night, and she had switched the headlights on but their feeble beams barely reached beyond the bonnet.

Once past the fork, the track was unsurfaced. It climbed steeply up the fellside while the water gushed down it in torrents, swirling stones out of potholes and ruts. It was like driving up a muddy river and the effort of keeping the car on the track was so great that Rose even forgot about the gun.

The leather roof was designed to be taken down in fine weather and it was no proof against the storm roiling around them. Water was soon leaking into the car and dripping onto Rose's head, trickling into her eyes. Not daring to take her hands off the wheel, she had to blink it away. She was rigid with tension, her teeth clamped hard on her bottom lip as she fought to keep the car under control. The back wheels skidded in the wet and the engine screamed with strain as they inched up the hill. Surely Levi had to be as terrified as she was?

'This is madness!' she shouted. 'We have to stop!'

'No!' His eyes darted from side to side and he dug the revolver into her side. 'Keep going!'

On and up the car crept through the storm until at last the track seemed to level out slightly. They must be near the top of the hill, Rose decided, blenching at the thought of the hair-raising drop on the other side.

'Please,' she said, raising her wobbling voice over the sound of the drumming rain. 'Levi, we'll never make it on this road. It's bad enough in good weather, but in this rain, we'll crash. We'll die if we carry on like this, Levi! *Please* let me stop.'

'No!' he spat at her. 'I don't care if I die! What have I got to live for? At least this way we'll be together for ever.'

'Levi!' she begged, horrified, but he jammed the gun into her again. 'Drive on, Rose,' he told her. 'You can die by the gun or take a chance on the road with me. You choose.'

A bang out of nowhere sent the car swerving and skidding wildly across the track. Icy with terror, grappling with the wheel, Rose managed to turn it at the last minute so they didn't drive head on into the drystone wall. The side of the car hit the wall instead with a terrible noise and lurched to a halt.

The impact smacked Rose's head against the side of the door and she slumped, stunned, over the steering wheel. Levi had dropped the gun and he was scrabbling frantically for it in the footwell as she lifted her head blearily.

'What have you done?' he screamed at her.

Rose put an unsteady hand to her temple. 'I didn't do anything!'

'You've stopped! I told you to go on.'

'I'm sorry.' Frantically, she tried to clear her head. 'I didn't mean to. I think we might have a puncture.'

Levi stared at her, breathing heavily. He had found the gun and levelled it at her once more. 'You'll have to change the wheel.'

Shaking with tension, Rose could barely think beyond the relief of not clinging to the steering wheel. She had no idea how to mend a puncture, but she could buy a little time and surely, surely, somebody would be looking for her soon...

'I'll try,' she said, 'but I can't do it in this rain.' She pointed into the field where a stone building could just be made out through the sheeting rain. 'Look, there's a field barn. Why don't we shelter in there, just until the rain stops?'

'You'll try and run away,' he said, his face screwed up with suspicion.

'Where would I go?' said Rose, trying to sound reasonable. 'We're miles away from Beckindale, Levi. Nobody knows where we are, and nobody else would come up this road anyway, even if it wasn't too dangerous to set out in the rain. We both need to get dry and have a rest, and then I'll mend the puncture.'

Levi thought about it then gave a grudging nod. The driver's door was wedged against the wall, so Rose had to struggle over and get out the passenger side. No longer caring about the gun, she clambered over the wall and over to the field barn. It was packed with sweet smelling hay and it was such a relief to stumble into shelter from the rain that Rose could have wept.

'Don't get comfortable,' Levi warned. 'It's just till it's stopped raining.'

Rose subsided into the hay, pulling her sodden coat closer around her, shaking with reaction. She was cold and wet and hungry and her head was aching like the devil where she had banged it, but far worse was the terror slamming her heart savagely against her ribs that was making it hard to breathe.

Levi was completely insane. He would think nothing of lifting that gun and shooting her like a dog. Or he would make her drive down that hill and laugh as the car tumbled down the slope and smashed into the ground below.

She was going to die.

She would never see Mick again, never hold him or lie close to him at night and listen to him breathe.

Rose squeezed her eyes shut, unable to think past the suffocating fear.

The storm rumbled on while Levi watched her like a hawk, the gun he held in his hand twitching at her slightest move. The sound of the rain was so mesmerising that it was some time before Rose realised that it had stopped. The black clouds rolled away to leave patches of pale evening sky and a dripping world.

Levi got to his feet and stretched. 'Time to get going,' he said.

'I need to go outside.'

'Why?'

'Why do you think?' she snapped. 'Unless you want a mess in your motor, I need to relieve myself, and I'd like some privacy.'

He hesitated. 'Very well. But no trying anything! I'll see you if you run and I've still got the gun, remember.'

'I'll just go around the back of the barn.'

Her legs trembled as she squatted in front of the interested gazes of a herd of sheep, but when she straightened and adjusted her skirt, she caught a glint of sunlight on glass far below. Another car! And it was following the track.

Her heart leapt. The hope that rescue might be on its way gave her the courage to trudge back across the field before Levi's gun.

At the car, he told her to get out the spare wheel. Rose dragged it out obediently and bent to take the wheel off the car. The bolts were wet and stiff, and her fingers kept slipping.

'Use a spanner!' snapped Levi. 'Hurry!'

Rose thought of the spanner in her pocket. 'There isn't one,' she started, trying to distract Levi from the sound of a gear being changed further down the hill, but his ears had pricked up.

'Someone's coming. Leave that,' he said, grabbing Rose by the arm and dragging her behind the bonnet just as Mick's car came sweeping round the bend and squealed to a halt at the sight of them.

Rose whimpered in relief. Jonah was driving, but Mick was sitting beside him, wearing a rough bandage around his head.

Jonah shut off the engine and a strange silence fell. For Rose, it felt as if time had stopped and she could only drink in the sight of Mick. His expression eased as his eyes met hers and she would have run to him if Levi hadn't jerked her back.

Easily and with no sudden movements, Jonah got out of one side of the car, Mick out of the other. 'What are you and Rose doing up here, Levi?' Jonah asked pleasantly.

'Stay back!' Levi's voice was shrill.

'Well, now, why would I want to stay back from my own cousin?'

'I've got a gun!'

'I'm thinking you should put that down, Levi,' said Jonah in the same steady voice. 'There's no call for shooting anyone. We're all family here.'

'Let Rose go, Levi,' Mick added in a voice from which all warmth and humour had drained.

'No, she's mine!'

'She's not yours, Levi. Rose is *my* wife. You go on if you want, but let her come home with me.'

Rose could hear Levi's quick, panicked breath. His finger was jittering on the trigger and she watched, mesmerised, as the gun wavered between her and Mick.

'Don't come any nearer!' he cried. 'I'll shoot.'

'Shoot who? I'm your brother,' said Mick. 'Shoot Rose? I thought you loved her.'

A new voice broke in. 'I've got a better idea.' Cora popped up beside Jonah and regarded her husband with hostile eyes. 'Why don't you shoot yourself and put yourself out of your misery?'

Cora's appearance took Levi by surprise and as she felt him start, Rose pulled the spanner from her pocket and swiped at him. She missed, but it was enough to make him stagger off balance, and Mick lunged for him.

Levi fired a deafening shot, but his aim was wildly off and the next moment Mick had him pinned to the ground and was driving his fists at his face. 'If you've hurt a hair on Rose's head, you bastard, by God ... I'll kill you!'

'Mick, stop!' cried Rose.

Having calmly retrieved the revolver, Jonah expertly disarmed it and put it in his pocket. He let Mick get in a few more blows then dragged him off Levi. 'You'll be no good to Rose if you're locked up for murder,' he pointed out.

Mick shook off Jonah's hand but made no attempt to attack Levi again. Instead, breathing hard, he looked at Rose. '*Did* he hurt you?'

'No.' She managed a wavering smile. 'He didn't. I was terrified, but he didn't hurt me.' Her eyes filled with tears as she stumbled past Levi who was sprawled on the ground and into Mick's arms. 'I thought I'd never see you again!' she said as he caught her against his wonderfully warm, solid body. 'How did you find me?'

'We can thank Cora for that,' said Jonah. 'I was driving her to Bradford when the rain hit us and she said we should turn back.'

'I decided I'd rather wait a while than drown on the road,' said Cora. She fingered her bruised face as she looked at her husband with disgust. 'Besides, why should I be the one to run away? It was my pa gave you the money to build that house in the first place.'

'So we turned round and went back, and that's when we found Mick out cold on the floor,' Jonah took up the story. 'You'd gone and there was no sign of Levi, so we feared the worst.'

They told Rose how they had to restrain Mick from driving frantically around in the rain but had used the time to find out if anyone had seen anything. 'Dot organised that,' said Jonah. 'The weather was terrible, of course, so the only people who'd seen anything were the Warcups. They said a car had swerved outside their cottage and who else would have been out in that rain?'

A scrabbling sound made them jerk round. Levi was on his feet and jumping into Mick's car that Jonah had left open. Mick started towards him but Jonah pulled him back as Levi swung the wheel, forcing them to jump out of the way. The tyres span and skidded across the track, squeal-ing in protest and spraying gravel before Levi managed to regain control and the car screeched off over the brow of the hill and out of sight.

'Why did you let him go?' Mick demanded of Jonah who stuck his hands in his pockets.

'Did you really want to hand your own brother over to the police?'

'No, but–'

'That road ... it's terribly dangerous.' Rose was staring after the car, white-faced. 'Levi won't be able to control the car at that speed going round those bends.'

The words were barely out of her mouth when the air was rent by a huge, splintering crash, fol-lowed by a screeching sound and another, more distant, explosion.

Mick began to run.

Panting with exertion at the crest of the hill, Rose stared down at the hairpin bends. She could see where the car had spun out of control, hitting the wall and somersaulting over the edge to catch first on a thorn tree before the weight of the car sent it falling remorselessly down to bottom of the gully.

'Levi!' Mick cried and seemed as if he were about to climb down to the wreckage but Rose gripped his hand.

'There's nothing you can do for Levi now,' she said.

The words were barely out of her mouth before the car below burst into flames with a great whoosh, scattering metal across the gully. Hold-ing onto Mick, Rose watched it burn until silence fell over the valley once more, broken only by a skylark calling for its mate as it darted over the heather.

Chapter Thirty

From behind the bar, Dot could see into the ladies' lounge, where her mother, Mary Ann and Betty Porter had decided they might as well stay and have a drink and now had their heads happily together. They had drifted in soon after opening, ostensibly to see how Dot was coping after the vandalism but really to find out more about the shocking events of the previous day.

Dot had disappointed them. 'I wasn't there,' she said. 'I don't know what happened.'

In fact, Jonah had told her about the awful crash that had killed Levi Dingle but it felt wrong to gossip about it. Dot had been there when they brought Rose back, shaken and exhausted but very relieved to be home. Watching the tenderness with which Mick helped his wife out of the car and into the house, Dot's throat had tightened at the obvious love between them.

She didn't have that with Jonah. They had friendship, they had healthy lust, but they didn't have love. They didn't need each other or trust each other or feel that they were two halves of a whole.

And that was what she wanted now, Dot admitted to herself. She didn't want just a bit of

Jonah, she wanted all of him.

She couldn't complain, Dot knew. Jonah had been clear from the start that he wouldn't stay in Beckindale for ever. She had always known that friendship was all that he had to offer.

So it wasn't his fault that friendship wasn't enough for her any longer.

It wasn't Jonah's fault that she wanted what Rose had with Mick.

It wasn't his fault that she had fallen in love with him.

Dot finished pulling a pint and slid the tankard across the bar with a cheerful smile that she knew didn't reach her eyes.

She had to stop being such a wet blanket. Look at all the reasons she had to be happy! She was independent. Her mother was almost her old self. The Woolpack was thriving, and the ladies' lounge at last was full. Ernest Burrows was in there, flirting with one of Cora Dingle's maids from Bradford, and some guests from Miffield Hall, up for the shooting, had gathered in there too, in deference to the young ladies among them, who had been daring enough to come along to try the village pub.

They seemed to be enjoying themselves. Jonah was leaning on the bar talking to them. It was what he did best. He could chat just as easily with a grizzled farmer or an ex-soldier like Jim Airey or a pretty girl like the one fluttering her eyelashes at him right then. He could get on with anybody and make them feel welcome. Dot envied him that ability but she often thought about what he had told her about his family and that sense that while he might fit in anywhere, he belonged nowhere.

They were doing brisk business in the main bar that night too, Dot thought, continuing to serve drinks in the main bar while keeping a surreptitious eye on Jonah, who seemed to be enjoying flirting with the young lady. Her eyes were sparkling, her face powdered, her mouth painted a bright red, and in her fashionable dress she looked like an exotic bird against the plain backdrop of the Woolpack. She was waving her cigarette around as she talked and gesticulated with what Dot considered an incredibly irritating laugh, although Jonah didn't seem to find it annoying at all. He was positively encouraging her, smiling down at her with that lazy smile that Dot knew all too well.

'Dot,' Jonah called from the ladies' lounge. 'Can we have another round here, please?'

'Coming up!' Dot forced a smile. This was her business. She didn't have to like someone to serve them a drink. But there was something galling about the way the young lady took her drink without looking at Dot at all. She laid her slender hand on Jonah's arm and smiled up at him.

Dot couldn't help looking down at her own square, work-roughened hands. Earlier that day she had looked in the mirror and had been appalled at her own reflection. She had never been pretty but the liveliness that had once given character to her face had drained away, leaving her wan and with shadows beneath the eyes that seemed too big for her thin face. Why would Jonah want to stay with someone who looked so plain and worn out? He deserved to be with someone bright and glamorous and fun.

It was time to let him go, Dot realised dully. The longer he stayed, the harder it would be to say goodbye.

'You're quiet tonight,' Jonah said when he had closed the door behind the last customers and was gathering up the glasses that Dot was washing in the kitchen. 'Is everything all right?'

'I'm fine,' she said. 'Just tired.'

'It's been a difficult few days. Perhaps we should have closed for the week?'

'This is exactly the time people need somewhere to gather,' Dot said.

'I suppose so.' Jonah went back to the bar and brought back more glasses. 'It was good to see the ladies' lounge being used. I'd say your mother and her friends are converted, anyway.' He paused. 'They don't miss much those women, do they?'

'Why?' she asked, looking up sharply. 'What have they been saying to you?'

'Oh, you know, how much time we're spending together, how late I stay here. Mary Ann didn't miss my early arrival the other day. There were lots of nods and winks.'

Dot rolled her eyes as she turned back to the sink. 'Don't pay any attention to them.'

'The thing is...' Jonah trailed off, unusually hesitant, and she frowned.

'What?'

'What if they're right? Maybe we *should* get married.'

'*What?*' Dot swung round to stare at him.

'We could get married,' he said. 'Run the pub

together and–'

'Stop right there!' Dot interrupted him, flinging up a hand still covered in soap suds. 'You're out of your mind, Jonah! We agreed right from the start that neither of us wanted to get married and I've got no intention of changing my mind because you're suddenly worried about what some busybodies think! That wasn't the deal. We were going to have a temporary affair and then you were going to move on. In fact, why are you are even here?' she demanded.

Jonah looked taken aback. 'What do you mean?'

'We agreed you'd wait until you saw how the Woolpack was doing, but I think it's obvious now it's going even better than I hoped, so with any luck we'll start making a profit soon.' She set the washed glasses on the draining board and reached for another two, swirling the dish mop briskly around each. 'I was just thinking that now the pub is up and running I could open up those rooms and start taking guests. It would be a new source of income.'

'Haven't you got enough to do, Dot?'

'The sooner I can make a profit, the sooner I can pay you back.'

There was a taut silence behind her. 'I don't need to be paid back,' said Jonah. 'That wasn't part of the deal you keep going on about.'

'You put all your money into this place,' Dot pointed out, not looking at him. 'Have you even got enough to move on?'

'It doesn't cost money to move on.' His voice held a definite edge. 'I've done it before with nothing in my pocket, and I can do it again.'

Dot turned from the sink, wiping her soapy hands on her apron. 'Then what are you waiting for, Jonah?'

'You want me to move on?' he said after a disbelieving pause.

'It's what you said you would do. I'm grateful for all you've done, Jonah, but I don't need you any more. I'm betting that Mick will feel the same. And now that bugger Levi is dead, I reckon we'll all be a lot better off. So if you're ready to move on, as I think you are, then there's nothing stopping you.'

'I see.' Jonah set the last lot of glasses very carefully on the table. 'You're right, Dot. I'm not needed here. Perhaps I should have gone before.'

Not, *I want to stay.* Not, *I need you.*

Well, what had she expected? Dot schooled her face to give no sign of the way her heart had plummeted.

She went over and put a hand on his shoulder. 'We've had a good time, Jonah, but we always knew it wouldn't last. I think it's time to call it a day, don't you?'

'In that case I'll go tomorrow. No point in hanging around.' Was that relief shading his voice or something else? 'We'll stay friends, though, won't we, Dot?'

'Of course we will,' she said, her voice thickening and she picked up the glasses and turned back to the sink before he could see the tears in her eyes. 'All I want is for you to be happy.'

He drove up to the Woolpack on his motorcycle early the next morning. Dot was in the bar, mopping the floor, but when she heard the engine, she propped the mop against the wall and went outside to say goodbye. Jonah was straddling the motorcycle in his flying jacket, helmet on his head and goggles pushed up, and the sidecar was as empty as the day he arrived.

'I see you're travelling light,' she said. She was *not* going to make this difficult. She was *not* going to cry. She was *not*. But her chest was so tight that she could hardly breathe.

'It's always the best way,' said Jonah with a half-smile.

'So...' Dot swallowed. What could she say? 'Thank you, Jonah,' was all she could come up with in a gruff voice. 'Thank you for everything.'

'It's been fun,' he said. There was a yearning silence as they looked at each other, and then Jonah reached out to tug her towards him for one fierce kiss. 'Goodbye, Dot,' he said as he let her go. Settling the goggles over his eyes, he kicked the engine into gear and drove off before she had a chance to recover.

One hand pressed to her mouth where he had kissed her, Dot stood outside the Woolpack and watched him out of sight. She stood on, listening to the sound of the engine as it receded into the distance, imagining him driving over the bridge and out along the dale, into the world beyond. When all she could hear was the low burbling of a wood pigeon, Dot turned and went inside to finish mopping the floor.

'What were you thinking, letting him go?' Agnes demanded when she heard that Jonah had gone.

'I didn't "let him go", Ma. It was my idea that he went.'

'But why?'

'Jonah didn't want to stay. I didn't want him to feel that he was tied to me.'

Agnes sighed, exasperated. 'You're a fool, Dorothy Colton. That lad was the best thing that ever happened to you and you've just thrown him away.'

Days passed, a week, a month. The misery Dot had felt when she watched Jonah ride away slowly intensified until it was a raw, constant ache inside her. She kept telling herself that she had done the right thing, but she was unprepared for how much she would miss him, how she would look up every time the door opened in the hope that it would be Jonah.

She was desperately lonely. Running the Wool-pack kept her busy but in the long, dark hours of the night, Dot admitted to herself that now she had everything she had worked for so long, it was not enough. She wanted Jonah to talk to, to celebrate a good day with and commiserate on the days that went less well.

She had friends, but it wasn't the same. 'I'm worried about you,' Rose said.

'I'm fine,' Dot insisted, not meeting her eyes.

'I miss Jonah. So does Mick.'

Everybody missed Jonah, but nobody missed him the way Dot did. She threw herself into work and opened up the bedrooms on the first floor. The first party of six arrived like a flock of exotic birds some three weeks after Jonah had left. They had sent a telegram to book and turned up in three cars, exclaiming loudly at the charm of the pub and the beauty of the landscape. They drank and smoked and ate all of the meals Dot prepared for them all without ever properly registering her existence. They danced to records on the gramophone they had brought with them while the rest of the village eyed them askance from the bar.

'Jonah was right,' Dot heard one languid young man say in the pub, and her heart jolted at the sound of his name. 'It's the perfect place to get away from it all.'

So she owed this booking to Jonah. Dot told herself she was grateful to him, but she hated the idea that these people were his friends too, just as the people of Beckindale had thought of him as their friend. That Jonah had taken off his life in Beckindale like an old coat, and put on a new one. Had he changed women too? Dot tortured herself by imagining him with one of those fast young women with their long white throats and sophisticated gestures.

She missed him all the time, with a longing that was bone-deep. Wherever she looked, she bumped into memories of him and she would catch her breath as the pain of absence bloomed like a fresh bruise on her heart.

She had done the right thing, Dot told herself. Better that Jonah had gone when he did, rather than linger and grow bored and resentful.

But she wondered constantly where he was, what he was doing, how he was. Did he think of her, the way she thought of him? Was his life as empty as hers? Did it stretch bleakly into the future, dull and joyless without the one person who could make him laugh however bad things seemed?

Six weeks after Jonah had left, Dot woke to another sunny Sunday. The countryside trembled on the verge of summer and the sunshine poured in through her attic window. This time there would be no Jonah to take her away for the day, no Jonah to knock on the door and make her forget everything but the warmth of his hands, the dark, dangerous pleasure of his touch.

Despising herself for the misery that gripped her, Dot dragged herself downstairs to the bar. There had to be some job to take her mind off Jonah. But everything was swept, everything polished to a high shine. The casks were full, the bottles topped up, the glasses perfectly aligned.

She slumped onto a stool at the bar and realised that she had everything she had ever wanted, and none of it meant anything without Jonah.

The knock at the door made her start but she couldn't face talking to anyone. 'We're closed,' she shouted.

But the knocking persisted and in the end she sighed and slid off the stool and trailed over to the door. 'We're clos–,' she began as she opened only to stop as she saw who was standing there.

Jonah.

'Hello, Dot,' he said. He looked unaccountably nervous and his scar stood out on his tense cheek.

'What are you doing here?' she said when she could speak.

'There's something I need to tell you,' said Jonah. 'Something I forgot to say before I left.'

'You'd better come in then.' Dot stood back, pulling the door fully open and he stepped past her.

'How are you, Dot?'

'Fine,' she lied. 'And you?'

'I'm fine,' he started, then caught himself up. 'No, what am I saying? I'm not fine,' he told her. 'I haven't been fine since I left.'

Dot's heart was thumping, slow and heavy in her chest. 'You'd better sit down,' she said.

They took a round table with two chairs facing each other. Jonah seemed to have forgotten that he wanted to talk to her. He was studying her face as if memorising it.

'So, what was it you forgot to say to me?' she asked at last.

Jonah nodded as if reminded. 'I forgot to tell you that I love you,' he said. 'I didn't want it to be true. I'd been trying so hard to pretend that I wasn't really in love with you, but when Mary Ann Teale started hinting that marriage should be on the cards, I leapt on the idea. And so I made a mess of it,' he said. 'And you turned me down, and that was the worst night of my life.'

The booming in Dot's chest was making it hard to hear. 'Why didn't you tell me?'

'Because I'm an idiot. Because I'd spent so many years being afraid of getting close to anyone in case I hurt them the way my parents hurt me. Because I knew you didn't love me and I thought, I don't know, that you might consider it if I didn't spook you by telling you how much I wanted you.'

'You *are* an idiot,' Dot agreed shakily.

'I know. I went about it all wrong. I'd always

been so certain that I didn't want to be tied down to anyone or anywhere,' he said. 'I was sure that I didn't want a family, that I didn't want to be needed. You didn't want me to interfere with the Woolpack. Mick can manage the garage fine on his own. He doesn't need me either.

'But the truth is that I wanted you to need me. I'd been so restless, trying to pretend that I didn't love you. You were so definite that you didn't love me and I realised that I'd put myself in an impossible position. I was afraid of telling you the truth. When you told me to go...'

He shook his head as if to rid himself of a painful memory. 'Instead of trying to convince you to let me stay, I told myself that you were right. And I did try, Dot. I did everything I could to enjoy myself. I took stupid risks and pushed myself to the limit, but nothing was as much fun as being here with you.'

He looked across the table at her. 'I thought I didn't belong anywhere, but I do. I belong with you. I belong in Beckindale. I came back to ask if you'd give me another chance. Will you marry me, Dot, not because of gossip, but because I love you and I want to spend my life here, with you. I know you don't want a husband who tells you what to do, but what would you think about a partner?'

'Like a business partner?' she said, putting her head on one side and pretending to consider.

'Exactly, but with other benefits, like living together and waking up together every morning.'

A smile was uncurling inside Dot but she pressed her lips together to stop it escaping too soon.

'You wouldn't want to tell me what to do?'

'I know better than that, Dot.'

'And I suppose I wouldn't have to repay your loan either, if we were married.'

'Of course not.' He reached across the table and took her hands in a warm clasp. 'You could look on it as a sound business decision. I know how practical you are, my Dot.'

'Hmm. Well, those are all good points,' she said.

'So you'll marry me?'

Her fingers curled around his. 'I will, but not for those reasons, Jonah.'

'Then why?' he asked, suddenly wary.

'Because I love you with all my heart.' At last Dot released the smile that was fizzing through her. 'Because I've have missed you so badly, Jonah. Because life is no fun without you, and independence will mean so much more if I can share it with you.'

An answering smile spread across Jonah's face. 'Those, darling Dot, are the best reasons of all.'

Spring 1921

Epilogue

One soft spring day, one of the smaller Pickles came running to the garage with a message from Maggie. As soon as she heard it, Rose pulled off her apron and rushed into the garage where Mick was, as usual, under a car.

'Mick! Dot's had her baby! Hurry up!'

'The baby's not going anywhere in five minutes,' grumbled Mick, but he wriggled out from under the car. Rose was already halfway down the track by the time he caught up with her and they hurried to the Woolpack together.

Beneath a pale blue sky dotted with delicate puffs of cloud, the dale was flushed with a fresh, hopeful green. In the fields newborn lambs staggered after ewes and daffodils thrust jauntily up in clumps along the verge. The air was sweet with the smell of blossom and new growth while a gentle breeze carried the distant bleating of sheep down from the fells to mingle with the twittering and cheeping of the birds that hopped from branch to branch as they built their nests, but Rose barely noticed, so anxious was she to see Dot and the new baby.

A dazed-looking Jonah met them at the door of the Woolpack, his smile a mile wide. 'I have a son!' he cried.

'Congratulations!' Mick slapped him on the back and wrung his hand. 'And just in time for opening too!'

'Can I run up and see Dot?' Rose asked.

'Yes, she'll want to see you,' Jonah said. 'Maggie's with her. I sent for her to beat some sense into Dot. Left to herself, my wife would have given birth in the bar! She insisted on working until Maggie arrived,' he sighed and clapped a hand on Mick's shoulder as he led him into the bar. 'I hope the boy's not going to be as stubborn as his mother!'

Putting her head round the bedroom door, Rose saw Dot, sitting up in bed and cradling her new-born son. She looked exhausted but the smile she gave Rose was ecstatic. 'Come and meet my little lad,' she said.

'What are you going to call him?' Gently, Rose pushed aside the soft blanket the baby was wrapped in so that she could see his face properly.

'Jonah wants to call him Jedidiah.' Dot stroked the baby's cheek with her finger. 'It's a mouthful, in't it? I think he'll be Jed to me.'

'He's beautiful.'

Rose swallowed a lump in her throat. A miscarriage at Christmas had left her bereft. She longed for a child, not just for herself, but for Mick, who she knew still mourned quietly for Levi. She'd hoped that a baby would fill that void, and they had both been sad when she lost it. But now she thought she might be pregnant again. It was too early to tell for sure but she pressed a hand surreptitiously against her belly. She hoped so.

'Can I hold him?'

Dot put the sleeping baby in her arms, and

Rose's eyes filled with tears at the soft, warm weight of him. When she touched one of the tiny hands groping at the air, it closed instinctively around her finger with surprising strength.

Something about the baby's grip made Rose's heart swell with hope. The years since the war had been dreary ones but it felt as if things were changing at last. On Armistice Day the previous year, the same day that the Cenotaph had been unveiled in London and the Unknown Warrior buried in Westminster Abbey, in Beckindale they had dedicated a memorial to their dead and missing. It had been an emotional occasion but at the same time it seemed to Rose that by giving them a focus for their grief the memorial had allowed them to let go of some of the lingering despair of those terrible years.

The economy was picking up at last, too, and there were noticeably more cars on the road. The garage was doing even better than expected and Mick had replaced the motorcar that Levi had crashed. His main business was with farm vehicles, though, and he had finally managed to sell Maggie a tractor for Emmerdale Farm. In the old smithy, he had installed a pump to supply petrol instead of cans, and drivers were coming from all round the area to fill up their motors.

From the pub below came a buzz of conversation. Clearly word of Jed's birth had spread and Jonah had thrown open the doors. Maggie tutted. 'How's Dot going to get any rest with that racket going on?'

'I don't mind,' said Dot, snuggling into the bed. 'It's good for business.'

When Jonah came in, he went straight to his wife. 'How are you doing, my Dot?' He brushed the hair tenderly from her face. 'Can I get you anything?'

'No, I'm fine. Is everything all right downstairs?'

'Stop worrying, and don't even *think* about coming downstairs!' said Jonah. 'Fred's here and Mick's helping him behind the bar. For tonight, the Woolpack can run without you!'

When Rose put the baby in his arms, Jonah looked down at him in wonder. 'Can I take Jedediah downstairs?'

Dot smiled sleepily. 'As long as you bring him back.'

Jonah's expression as he bore Jed off made Rose's throat tighten.

'It's lovely to see how proud he is!'

'Anyone would think nobody had ever been a father before.' But Dot's face softened. 'He was always afraid he'd be a lousy father like his own but I'll make sure he's a good da to Jed.'

'Come on,' Maggie said to Rose. 'We should let Dot get some rest.'

At the bottom of the stairs, Jonah lifted his baby son high so that all could see him. 'Drinks are on the house!' he said.

A great cheer went up at that, and Rose slipped behind the bar to help Mick and Fred while Maggie took the baby from Jonah and carried him to the ladies' lounge. The women of the village had brought cakes and pies and knitted baby clothes for the baby and put them on the end of the bar before settling down for a chat. Rose could see Grace Pearson, rocking her baby, Annie, and

Polly Warcup, who was obviously pregnant again, half-heartedly trying to control her naughty twins as they ran around with Jacob Sugden. Dot's mother, Agnes, was talking to Janet Airey and Mary Ann Teale while Betty Porter and Hannah Rigg had their heads together. A tasty morsel of gossip was evidently doing the rounds. Agnes took charge of her small grandson, who was passed round to be cooed over and took it all in remarkably good part.

Less interested in the baby, the men had come in from work, stamping their boots at the door, and were leaning against the main bar or had found a table. Rose was surprised to see Joe Sugden, sitting in the corner and sharing a quiet pint with Robert Warcup and Sam Pearson. Joe rarely went out, even though everyone in Beckindale was used to his disfigured face now, just as they were used to the fact that Jim Airey only had one leg and Robert Carr still twitched with the effects of poison gas when he was upset – although tonight he seemed calm enough sitting next to Rose's brother, John.

Ernest Burrows hid his face in his beer and blushed every time he glanced at Molly Pickles who had evidently come down with Maggie and Joe to look after the children and was holding a sleeping Edward against her shoulder.

Tom Skilbeck looked as if he had come in for a quiet drink and wasn't too happy about finding himself in the middle of a celebration.

The door opened and conversation broke off as Cora Dingle came in, swathed in furs as usual with her hair tightly waved under her hat. To everyone's surprise, Cora had opted to stay in Beckindale. Rose and Mick had assumed that she would go back to her much-vaunted pa in Bradford, but Cora, it seemed, had acquired a taste for independence and liked being a widow, especially since her father had, somehow, managed to sort out Levi's debts and leave her with a handsome settlement. Rose thought privately that Cora enjoyed being able to flaunt her smart clothes out here where there was little competition as far as fashion went. Her airs and graces didn't go down well with everybody, but Rose had grown fond of her in spite of everything.

Now Cora, who liked to make an entrance, paused so that everyone could appreciate her latest fashionable outfit. 'I hear there's a new Dingle in town,' she said.

Slipping out from behind the bar, Rose took Jed from his grandmother and carried him over so that Cora could inspect him critically.

'Small, in't he?'

Rose smiled. 'He'll grow.'

It was hard to imagine that this tiny baby would one day grow into a boy and then a man. What would Beckindale be like when Jed was grown and had a son of his own, Rose wondered.

Mick was knocking a spoon against a glass to break through the hubbub of laughter and conversation. 'Quiet now!' he bellowed, pulling forward a chair so that he could climb onto it. 'Thank you,' he added as the noise subsided and everyone crowded into the bar to listen. 'I want to make a toast.'

He cleared his throat. 'We've been through

some bad times together over the last few years,' he started soberly. 'The war, the flu, the economy ... there isn't one of us that hasn't been affected. There isn't one of us that hasn't known grief and loss.

'But we've come through it as a community and things *are* getting better. Take the Woolpack here. It's not long since this was a charred ruin, and look at it today!' he said. 'It's thanks to Dot and Jonah that we've got this pub, this place where we can all meet and share what it means to live here. So it's fitting that today they've had a fine son to carry things forward.'

He gestured to the baby Rose was rocking in her arms. 'Jed here's a symbol of what's to come. He won't remember the war, and God willing he won't know what the flu is either. He'll be looking forward, not back, but he'll grow up here, part of this community, part of us all. So I ask you to raise a glass with me and drink to his health and happiness,' Mick finished, lifting his own beer high. 'To Jed, to Beckindale and to the future!'

EMMERDALE 1918:
FACTUAL OVERVIEW FOR THE BOOK

Many of the stories in this book have been inspired by real accounts, diaries and letters of men and women from Yorkshire who lived through the Great War, including stories from Esholt – the real Yorkshire village – on which the Emmerdale set is now based. Whilst Emmerdale is a fictional village, it embodies the community life of villages across the whole of the country; villages that hold the stories of ordinary men and women whose lives were transformed entirely in 1914.

The country had never mobilised in such a way; as sons, husbands and brothers marched out of villages across Yorkshire, women were thrust into jobs typically done by men, and with that work came a new era of female liberation. Maggie Sugden's story is inspired by a real farmer's wife, Annie Marriot. In 1914 Annie's husband George enlisted and left his milk dairy the sole responsibility of his wife. For the next four years Annie successfully kept the dairy running, as well as bringing up her young children. George returned in 1918 with a shrapnel wound to his leg and sadly died in 1920 of septicemia. For the first time in history, women just like Annie proved they could take on any role a man had done and played an enormous part in winning the war.

The story of Rose Haywood working as a nurse at Miffield Hall is based upon real accounts from Temple Newsam, a country house outside Leeds. The house became a fifty-bed hospital for injured soldiers run by Lady Dorothy Wood, wife of the owner. First used for Belgian officers in 1914, it gave comfort and care to thousands of men who had been wounded, gassed or suffered the devastating psychological effects of shell shock.

But not all soldiers were lucky enough to make it to hospitals in England; just over 700,000 British soldiers would never return. Across Britain mothers, sisters and wives were robbed of their men. In Esholt, the village the Emmerdale set is modelled on, Joshua Booth – the son of the real Woolpack landlord – was killed in 1917 by a stray shell in the trenches of Ypres, leaving behind his young sweetheart Winnie. Winnie would never fully get over the loss of her first love and kept all the precious letters Joshua had sent to her from the trenches until her death in 1992.

The Dingle brothers appearing at a training camp on the edge of the village was inspired by real accounts of Raikeswood Camp in Skipton, which opened in 1915 to house the newly formed Bradford Pals. The opening of the camp resulted in young recruits flooding the area; going on route marches through the local countryside; seeking their own entertainment in the evenings and forming new relationships with local women. It is easy to imagine the three Dingle brothers amongst the fresh-faced trainee soldiers fraternising with local villagers.

The war transformed the country; for all the loss and pain endured there were also huge advancements in technology, class and gender roles. Suddenly the heir to an estate like Miffield was fighting alongside the penniless Dingle; the old order fell away and with it came the vote for women in 1918 and new opportunities for a modern Britain. There is not a village, house or street in England that was not touched by war, and its legacy is still felt today. We must never forget the great sacrifice made by so many; the gallant acts of bravery and the quiet stories of transformation of these ordinary men and women.

The publishers hope that this book has given you enjoyable reading. Large Print Books are especially designed to be as easy to see and hold as possible. If you wish a catalogue please ask at your local library or write directly to:

Magna Large Print Books
Cawood House,
Asquith Industrial Estate,
Gargrave,
Nr Skipton, North Yorkshire.
BD23 3SE

This Large Print Book for the partially sighted, who cannot read normal print, is published under the auspices of

THE ULVERSCROFT FOUNDATION